The Baron's Cufflinks

P. J. MacLayne

Acknowledgments

My thanks to Cornelia Amiri, who stuck with me through the entire process of getting this story ready for you, the readers.

To my cover artist, K.M. Guth,
for the time and energy you put
into making my characters come to life.

Chapter 1

A burst of raucous laughter from the cluster of men near the bar reminded me once again this wasn't our usual haunt, the Pink Flamingo. The dim lighting did nothing to cover the layers of grime that coated the walls and ceiling. The other customers weren't much better—most of them looked as if they'd lived a rough life. As I pretended to study the meager selection offered by the stained menu, I surreptitiously checked the reactions of my companions.

Although they had smiles plastered on their faces, Sarah and Janine didn't look happy. Only Merrilee didn't seem bothered by the atmosphere and clientele of the Dog House. Aptly named, because if the men here were married, that's where they'd be once their wives found out where they spent their evenings.

It wasn't the female staff's skimpy costumes that bothered me. Well, not much. But the way they shoved their 'assets' in the faces of the male customers made me uncomfortable. Add in the loud music that gave me a throbbing headache the instant I walked in the door, along with the stench of stale alcohol, and I knew we'd made a mistake. I couldn't figure out a graceful way to leave without offending my friends and ruining Girls' Night Out.

Naturally, the one time I wished we had our men along, none were. Freddie was working, Janine had broken up with her short-term boyfriend, and Eli was in Florida, as always. Even Jake, who occasionally got invited to join us, had other plans.

I gave the waitress a vague smile before placing my order for the house special—a hamburger. The Pink Flamingo closed after the fire in the storage area and Big Daddy Al, the owner, took the opportunity to do major—and overdue—remodeling. With the anticipated date for its reopening several months away, it wouldn't take long for us to cycle through the available restaurants and bars in Oak Grove for our weekly get-together. I was already tired of the "trying out new places" routine.

After taking a swallow of the too-warm generic American beer, I glanced around, trying to figure out my path of escape. Janine leaned over during a break in the music and said, "Whose idea was this, Harmony?"

"Merrilee's."

Merrilee seemed to be enjoying the scenery as the waitresses moved among the tables, delivering booze and food. The all-too-familiar prickle at the back of my neck alerted me we were being watched, and I swiveled to identify the culprit.

Or culprits. Several of the men at the bar were eying us. I assumed they'd focused their attention on Merrilee, as her blond hair and good looks always attracted men, until one of them grinned at me and lifted his bottle of beer in a salute. Not wanting to encourage him, I pretended not to notice and turned back to my friends.

I should have known that wouldn't be the end of it.

"The older patrons will hate it," Janine said, running her fingers through her short brown hair. "But the kids are going to love it."

"You're right," Sarah agreed. "Will it decrease staff costs?"

We were talking about Janine's plan for installing self-serve check-out kiosks for the library. In my humble opinion, a long-overdue move for improving customer service. I'd kept my mouth shut because I wanted Janine to be able to take credit for its success, even if I'd suggested it to her.

"Not at first," Janine started. She was interrupted by our waitress. Her nametag read "Brandy" but I doubted that was her real name. Not when I'd noticed another of the ladies was "Ginny" and a third "Sherry." I suspected the nametags were interchangeable depending on the mood of the bar's owner.

"The guys at the bar sent these over," she said, setting four drinks on the table, harder than necessary.

In unison, the four of us frowned. "You might as well take them back," Merrilee said. "And tell them we're not interested."

"Now that wouldn't be nice," said a male voice from behind me.

"And don't go saying you're taken," another man said. "We checked—none of you are wearing a ring."

A third man pulled an empty chair from a nearby table and planted it between Sarah and Janine. He wasn't a typical patron of the Dog House, younger than most, and his khakis were out of place in the jeans-and-T's atmosphere. "Don't pay any attention to those jokers," he said. "I'm Brent. You ladies looked like you needed company, so we decided to be heroes and rescue you." He nodded toward his companions. "That's Paul and Tadd. And you girls are?"

"Underwhelmed, annoyed, and irritated," Merilee said. "If we wanted your company, we would have asked for it."

Wow, that was a good line. I'd have to remember it. But first I needed to back Merrillee up. "We're fine on our own. If we change our minds, we'll let you know." No chance of that happening.

Neither approach worked. Paul or Tadd—I didn't know which was which—put his hand on my shoulder. "You have the drinks. You owe us a dance at least."

The Dog House didn't have a dance floor. I didn't bother pointing it out.

"Perhaps you didn't hear what we said. Not interested." I pushed his hand away.

The man leaned close. The stench of booze on his breath turned my stomach. "You don't want to make me look like a fool in front of my friends," he said. "Do you?"

From the corner of my eye, I saw Sarah pulling her cell phone from her purse, and assumed she was calling Freddie—Detective Thomason of the Oak Grove Police Force. I didn't think we had time to wait for him. Besides, I could handle a drunk.

I pushed my chair back and stood, almost knocking over Paul-Tadd. A second later, Merrilee and Janine were on their feet as well. "You're doing a fine job of looking like a fool without my help," I said. "So why don't you slink back to where you came from? You're not welcome here."

A switch tripped and he moved into angry-drunk mode. "You think you're too good for me and my buds, bitch?"

"Did I say that?"

"That's what you meant." He swayed and bumped into my shoulder. "Let's dance, girlie."

I took a step backward. "I said no."

Brandy stopped on her way back to the bar and laid her hand on his arm. "Come on, let's get you another drink. On the house."

That should have worked, and I appreciated her

effort. But Paul-Tadd was in a class by himself. With a hard push, he shoved her away. Luckily, one of the other customers caught her before she fell, but the tray of empty glasses she carried clattered on the floor. Broken glass scattered everywhere. I widened my stance and prepared for action. He lurched forward, reaching for my arm.

And missed. I didn't even need to use any of my self-defense moves. All I did was step to one side and his aim was so bad he didn't even come close to touching me. I hoped he'd fall flat on his face but was disappointed when he kept an unsteady but upright stance.

Everyone in the bar seemed to be enjoying the free entertainment we provided. The bartender, a large man that reminded me of a heavyweight boxer, must have decided enough was enough. He hustled out from behind the bar and strode our direction. I wasn't about to let my guard down until Paul-Tadd got thrown out, so I kept my eyes focused on him.

"Time to call it a night, buddy," the bartender said, stepping between us. "You know the rules. No one messes with the staff."

"I just wanted one dance," Paul-Tadd grumbled.

"Do you see anyone else dancing? I don't think I've ever seen anyone dance in here."

"Except that one time we got Emma and Bert to dance," someone said.

The bartender grinned. "Yeah, I forgot about that. But there's no dancing tonight. Now, you got a ride home?"

"I'll take him. I have to head out anyway," Brent said. That only seemed fair. He was somewhat responsible for the fiasco. "You said you had to get up early tomorrow, remember?"

Well, at least Brent partially redeemed himself. The combined peer pressure made the difference. "Yeah, I guess so," Paul-Tadd mumbled.

The third man left with them. I didn't relax until the trio made it out the door. "Thanks," I said to the bartender who had returned to his place of glory behind the bar. The jukebox was unnaturally quiet.

"Sorry about all that. Tadd can get a little crazy, but he's normally not like this. Strange thing is, I only served him two drinks. He shouldn't have been that out of control." He paused. "You girls going to stick around?"

A quick glance over my shoulder towards our table and I knew we had a consensus. "No, no offense, but this isn't our kind of place. We'll settle our tab and get out of your hair."

He nodded. "I'll cash you out and get Harley to walk you to your cars, just to be on the safe side."

"We'd appreciate it."

Sarah had stayed on the phone with Freddie during the whole episode, so it was no surprise to see his red Mustang pulling into the parking lot as Harley walked us out the door into the warm August night. The Dog House was outside of Oak Grove's city limits, so even though Freddie was a detective on Oak Grove's police force, he had no authority there. Still, he had the pull to get county sheriff department to show up *en force* if needed. Thank heavens it didn't come to that.

When Sarah spotted Freddie, she abandoned our little group and hurried over to where he'd parked. He got out of the car and gave her a swift hug before turning on his cop face. "Everyone all right?"

They made a good looking couple. Sarah had pulled her long brown hair into a simple ponytail instead of the fancy updo she wore when she showed houses. With her help, Freddie had updated his wardrobe, and the suits he wore on duty were no longer ill-fitting. Janine and I had a bet on how soon Freddie would pop the question.

"We're fine," Sarah told him. "Thanks to Harmony and the bartender."

"Mostly the bartender," I insisted.

"Yeah, but I was just waiting for one of your self-defense moves. You could've taken him."

Privately, I agreed with her. But the last thing I needed was another crazy story circulating about my supposed heroics. "I'm glad I didn't have to try. You can never be sure what a drunk will do. Sorry you got pulled away from work for nothing, Freddie."

"I needed the break. The Chief asked me to go through old reports and pull some statistics, and my eyes were going cross-eyed. But why the heck did you guys pick this joint for your night out? Its reputation sucks."

Merrilee grinned sheepishly. "My idea. I thought it would be fun to take a walk on the wild side."

"Next week it's my turn to pick locations, so I'm sure we'll end up someplace tamer." Sarah glared at Merrilee. "And you better not complain."

"Miss Harmony Duprie?"

Startled, I dropped the book I was taking notes from, a historical perspective of the role of women in the Roman Empire. I blinked my eyes to adjust my range of vision and focus on the man standing in front of me. "Yes?" I asked hesitantly.

"I'm Deputy Theo Nelson. I'd like to ask you a few questions." The impossibly young man's starched uniform crinkled as he moved.

Instinct had me reaching for my purse then I remembered the lessons Freddie had drilled into me about dealing with officers of the law. "I'm going to get my phone out of my purse to make a call," I told him. "If that's okay with you."

"Can it wait? I need to ask you a few questions concerning the incident last night. May I?" With a wave of his hand, he indicated the chair.

Instinct and experience told me to tell him no, but I found myself nodding.

He adjusted his duty belt, took a seat, and pulled out a small notebook. "For the record, I understand that you and some of your friends were at The Dog House last night?"

"Yes," I said curtly, planning on keeping my answers short and to the point. I wasn't comfortable with the situation, but couldn't deny the truth.

Hos monotone delivery of the rest of the night's event made it seem boring. I answered each statement with either a curt "yes" or "No." Mostly.

"One witness said Mr. Foard hit you."

"The witness is wrong. He pushed the waitress but was so drunk that when he tried to grab me, I avoided him with no problem. The bartender put an end to it and one of his buddies offered to take him home."

He scribbled a few notes then looked up at me. I recognized the technique—he hoped the silence would make me uncomfortable and I would say more. It didn't work. I waited. He sighed.

"How long did you stay after they left?" he asked.

"Only long enough to pay the bill."

"Can anyone corroborate your story?"

"Besides the staff and other customers? Talk to Detective Thomason. He met us there."

"Fred Thomason?"

"Yes, do you know him?"

"By reputation. Can Detective Thomason vouch for your whereabouts the rest of the night?"

"No. He was on duty. Once we were safe, he took off and the four of us headed home."

The deputy closed his notebook, pulled a card out of his pocket and dropped it on the table. "Thank you, Miss Duprie. If we need anything we'll be in touch." He tapped the card. "That's my number if you remember something else."

"Deputy," I said. "What's this about?"

He paused as if considering what he could reveal. "Mr. Foard was shot last night."

"Is he going to be okay?" Even if I didn't like the man, I wished no ill on him.

"He's dead, Miss Duprie."

My instincts were right. I should have called my lawyer.

Chapter 2

I stood, groaned, brushed the dirt from my knees, took several steps back and admired my work. I'd been working at the Aldridge house the last few days instead of going to the library, avoiding the stares from library patrons. Until the sheriff made some progress in the investigation of Tadd Foard's murder, I was still under suspicion.

The bright orange and yellow zinnias lining the base of the front porch made for a cheerful, welcoming touch. I'd wanted to see the house surrounded by flowers since the first time I drove up the driveway. With the outside painting finally finished, I didn't have to worry about the flowers getting trampled.

The Aldridge house, the old Victorian that Luke, Joe and I had been fixing up, was almost complete. Oh, and Jake, of course. He'd been helping out between jobs. A company hired him to fill in as a bouncer for three clubs, but his schedule changed constantly. Until he found steady work, I'd 'hired' him to stay at the house and act as a watchman. I'd borrowed a small travel trailer from a friend so he'd have all the comforts of home. His presence had stopped the occasional disappearance of building materials.

Jake bounced down the front stairs and put his hand on my shoulder. "It looks good, Angel."

"It does, doesn't it?" I reached up and tried with no success to clean a spot of blue paint off his cheek. The contrast of the paint against his tanned skin added to his charm. He and the boys had been painting the dining room. "I'd like to tackle the rose garden next."

He grinned. "Are you going to leave anything for the new homeowners to do?"

All along, the plan had been to sell the house after the renovations, but in the process of fixing it, I'd grown attached to it. I'd even toyed with the idea of living in it myself, but it really needed a happy family to bring it to life. I couldn't provide that. And Eli, my boyfriend, and I hadn't gotten to the stage of discussing long-term prospects for our relationship let alone children.

"I should get Sarah over here so she can tell me the best way to get it ready to show." With Sarah being a real-estate agent, she was the obvious choice to handle the sale. I trusted her to do a good job. Still, it would be hard to let the house go.

"When you sell it, I've spotted another one that deserves help."

There were lots of houses in Oak Grove that needed a little help, and more than a few that needed a lot of help. I wasn't sure I wanted to tackle another major house project right away. Or ever, honestly. Although it was interesting, it also had been a major distraction from my real job with little promise of making back more than what I'd put into it. I didn't think Luke and Joe felt the same way. Since they were retired, they liked having a project to fill their free time.

"We'll see." Jake still talked about renovating houses for a living, and I didn't want to dash his hopes. Until the Aldridge house sold, and I got at least *part* of my investment back, I wasn't going to commit to anything. I needed to change the subject.

"I talked to Eli this morning. He said to tell you hi."

Jake and Eli were cousins. Once I made it clear that I no longer had a romantic interest in Jake, they settled back into a close relationship. It still bothered Eli that I spent more time with Jake than with him, but he tried to hide it from me.

I'd made it to Florida to visit him in July. It was fun spending time with him, but it was too hot, too muggy, and too busy to suit me. Eli claimed it was better in the winter. I'd have to wait and see for myself.

"What's he up to?" Jake asked.

"Same as always. Working too hard."

Eli had mentioned he'd been working on a project having to do with the government, but didn't give me any details. Knowing his need for secrecy, I didn't ask but it could have been federal or state.

Jake shook his head. "He needs to slow down and enjoy life a little. Spend more time with you."

Privately, I agreed with him.

"So you had a little excitement the other night," Jake said, oh-too-casually.

The Oak Grove rumor mill even picked up on things that happened out of town.

"You could say that."

"Has the sheriff figured out who murdered the guy yet?"

I didn't have a direct line to the Sheriff's Department like I did to the Oak Grove Police. "I haven't heard anything." That worried me. The least Deputy Nelson could do was call me and tell me I wasn't a person of interest anymore.

"Foard's been involved in some shady deals."

"Like what?" I didn't ask Jake where he'd gotten his information. I didn't want to know.

"I'm not sure. But the word is that he's been arrested more than once. He's banned from one of the clubs. You might want to talk to Freddie."

I might. Or I might want to hit the internet.

A couple of DUI's and one arrest for marijuana possession do not a villain make. I was almost disappointed. Other than a few waitresses he'd manhandled, Tadd didn't seem to have any enemies. He wasn't necessarily popular, but no one hated him. Not on record, at least. So who had the motive to kill him?

A talk with my favorite FBI agent seemed to be in order.

Not that I particularly liked Agent Felton. But I only knew two FBI agents and couldn't tolerate the other one. Although Felton didn't count as a friend, he wasn't an enemy either. Still, it surprised me when he agreed to meet for lunch, no questions asked.

I spotted him right away when I entered the small Chinese buffet place, his suggestion, near his office. He stuck out like a sore thumb amid the crowd of secretaries having lunch. It had been a few months since I'd seen him, and gray hairs were now scattered in with the brown. Meeting him on his home turf meant I'd need to be on my best behavior, but I was good with that.

The restaurant's Shanghai soup dumplings were a treat and I was on my second serving when Felton wearied of our sporadic chit-chat. "You didn't call me to talk about the weather. Or to tell me you've realized that you're deeply in love with me. What is it you want, Miss Duprie?"

I could play it for kicks or play it straight. The choice seemed obvious if I didn't want to tick him off. I swallowed and looked him square in the eye. "Information. Do you know anything about a guy by the name of Tadd Foard?"

The agent leaned back in his chair, crossed his arms, and thought for a moment. "Can't say that I do. Why?"

"He was murdered a few days ago."

"And you care why? Are you sticking your nose where it doesn't belong again?" He grinned as he raised a spoonful of the egg drop soup towards his mouth.

"I may be a suspect."

We spent the next few minutes cleaning up the soup that had sprayed everywhere.

"Did you kill him?" Felton asked after we'd settled back into our seats.

It was my turn to sputter. "Of course not!"

"You realize that from here on out I'm acting in an official capacity. How are you connected to him?"

Funny how I felt comfortable talking to Felton even though he was a federal agent. I guess the fact that he'd come to my rescue the previous spring and that I'd helped him capture a wanted criminal had soothed over our mutual dislike. "My friends and I were out at a bar. We were chatting amongst ourselves when he and his buddies decided we needed company. He asked me to dance, I turned him down, he swung at me, got thrown out, my friends and I went home."

"And this makes you a person of interest in his murder how?"

I was glad Felton didn't call me a suspect. "Someone shot him that same night. I haven't been able to find any motive for anyone to kill him. I figured the FBI's records would provide information that the internet didn't."

Both of his eyebrows arched. "You expect me to share confidential FBI files with you?"

"No, but I hoped you would tell me if the FBI had been keeping an eye on him." Heat rose in my cheeks.

He leaned back in his chair, took a deep breath and blew it out loudly. "Who's in charge of the investigation?"

"The county sheriff's department. The murder happened outside city limits." I dug into my purse and pulled out a business card. "This is the deputy who questioned me."

"Don't think I know him," Felton said, taking the card and studying it. "But I haven't had much interaction with the sheriff's department up there."

"From the way he looked, he was a newbie. Too young, too starched, too eager for anyone who's been around for a while."

"Which makes him more dangerous to your case. If he's out to prove himself, he might jump to an easy conclusion and not dig deep enough to find the truth."

Not what I wanted to hear. My face must have reflected my feelings of dismay, because Felton quickly added, "I tell you what. I'll see what I can find on this guy and pass the information along to the sheriff."

Every bit would help. "Thank you." I wouldn't get the inside information, but if it got me out of the radar, I didn't care.

Silence prevailed as we both resumed eating.

"How's Hennessey doing?" Felton asked after finishing his second plate of food.

"Fine. We talk online almost every day." At

Felton's quizzical look, I realized my mistake. "Oh. You meant Jake, not Eli. Jake's doing okay, but he's getting antsy. There's not enough in Oak Grove to keep him occupied."

"So why is he sticking around?"

I sighed. "My theory is that he thinks he's protecting me. He makes a point of dropping by the library almost every day just to say hi. But the way I get involved in my work, I never know how long he's been there watching me. It's almost like having a friendly stalker. I should tell him to knock it off, but it gives him something to do when he's not working. It's not like there are many opportunities in Oak Grove for a man with his record."

"I'm beginning to think we were wrong about him." The Feds had been convinced that Jake was a jewel thief, but were never able to come up with the evidence needed to arrest him for any crimes.

It's a trap, Harmony. Don't react. I shrugged my shoulders. "I understand why you were suspicious based on what the police showed me, but I'm glad I gave him a second chance. He's proven himself to be a good friend." *And the evidence I have against him will remain locked away until it's absolutely needed. I hope that time will never come.*

Chapter 3

The dust in the warehouse of Gary's pawn shop wreaked havoc on my sinuses, but I was having too much fun to stop what I was doing. I sneezed, twice, and sniffed. The piles of books scattered around me threatened to topple from their unsteady stacks.

My plans for yard work at the house had been rained out as Oak Grove got drenched by a late afternoon thunderstorm. I was avoiding the library because I couldn't concentrate on my research, still hoping for a call from Agent Felton.

Gary had bought an abandoned storage locker, and these books were part of his haul. Although most of them were mass-produced paperbacks, there were enough old hard covered books to make things interesting. We'd made a deal—I'd dig through them and check if any of them were valuable, and he'd give me a bargain price on any I wanted for my collection.

The old oil painting leaning against the wall was keeping me company. It came from the same locker, but didn't fit in with rest of the artwork Gary had acquired. The man in the picture was dressed in clothing from a gone-by era. I'd never studied fashion, so I didn't know which one.

So far, the hunt for treasure hadn't turned up any gold. No first editions, nothing signed by a famous author, no rarities. I'd located several books I wanted for their subject matter, but they weren't worth more than a few dollars. I hoped Gary got paid for his investment in the furniture he'd gotten from the unit because these books wouldn't fund his retirement. Still, the search distracted me from my worries about the murder. Since my meeting with Felton a few days earlier, no new information had been released to the press.

Near the bottom of the seventh box, I yawned. Didn't even bother covering my mouth. As I glanced down, I noticed what appeared to be a leather-bound book half-buried under some old college textbooks. I set them aside, picked it up, and with my other hand, and rubbed my forehead in puzzlement. As thick as the volume was, it should have weighed more.

I ran one finger across the gold-embossed title. *Wolf's Knight, Tasha's Tale.* Another unknown. I gingerly lifted the cover, half-afraid the book would fall apart.

The book was hollowed out to create a hiding place. Inside the empty space was a small, purple velvet covered box. I hesitated for the briefest of moments before taking the box out and setting it on top of the nearest stack of books.

My mind raced as I imagined what the box contained. A diamond ring? A pair of fancy earrings? Or just some child's plastic beads? With unsteady hands, I lifted the lid.

I studied the contents, then closed the lid and put the box back inside the book, and closed the cover. "Gary?" I hoped he wasn't with a customer.

"Give me a sec," he yelled back.

The way Gary liked to chat, the second would turn into several minutes or longer. Instead of twiddling my thumbs, I dug into the pile of textbooks to fill my time. They all were out of date and would end up in the dumpster out back. An inglorious ending that I hated for any book, but I didn't have a good excuse to save them.

"What's up?" The old floorboards creaked as Gary strolled into the room. He was a massive man, but there were muscles hiding under the outer bulk.

I handed him the book in question. "Look what I found."

Puzzled, he bounced the book in his hands. "Is this special? I've never heard of it."

"Open it." I worked to keep my expression stoic and not give away my excitement.

"All righty then."

I cringed as he flipped the cover without the care I'd shown. I almost died when he tossed the book aside after pulling out the box. But when he opened it, I could no longer contain myself.

"Are they real?" I blurted.

The box contained a pair of cufflinks. To my untrained eyes, they appeared to be gold in the shape of a fleur-de-lis. Each had what I assumed to be a diamond adorning the bar at the base of the stylized flower. The diamonds sparkled in the harsh yellowish light of the bare sixty-watt bulb overhead.

Gary didn't answer right away. He held one close to his eyes, twisting it to examine it from different angles. "They look real," he answered. "I don't see any manufacturer markings, so I can't be sure."

He put the cufflinks back in the box. I trailed behind him to his office. Never having been there before, it surprised me to see how clean and organized it was compared to the rest of the store. He sat in his chair, set the jewelry box on his desk, and turned on his desk lamp. He opened a drawer and took out a strange-looking contraption that reminded me of a pair of glasses I'd seen at a steampunk convention. I almost giggled as he slipped them on his face because they were so weird. He opened the jewelry box and, reverently, picked up a cufflink.

Holding it close to the lens, he repeated the twisting and turning motion he'd used earlier. I sat in silence waiting for his decision like a little kid waiting for a promised piece of candy. He took a piece of porcelain tile out of another drawer and rubbed the cufflink against it. With a sigh, he put the cufflink back in the box. He repeated the process for the second cufflink.

"The diamond is real," he said. "The gold is too. And to think I was planning on just throwing all those books out. I would have, if I hadn't known you would want to go through them."

I smiled broadly and picked up the box. "Any idea how much they're worth?"

Gary shook his head. "A couple hundred dollars at a minimum. But I'd like to determine if they're old."

I didn't know anything about the age of the cufflinks, but the box itself seemed ancient. The velvet covering was worn at the corners and edges, and the once-white lining on the inside of the box was yellowed, tattered, and slit down the middle. I reached in to pull the edges together and realized that there was a piece of paper tucked under the lining.

"I wonder if this will tell us anything." I worked the piece of paper out. Yellowed with age, it crackled as it moved. I held my breath, praying it wouldn't crumble in my hand as I slid it onto the desktop. "Do you want to do the honors?"

"Naw. You're doing a fine job."

I grinned, nodded, and wiped my hands on my already dusty jeans. With the greatest of care, I opened the several layers of parchment.

The faded writing wasn't in English. I took Spanish in high school and a couple of semesters of Latin in college, but it wasn't either of those languages. But it looked like a Romance language, French maybe?

I slid it across the desk to Gary. "Can you read it?"

He shook his head. "Sorry, no. My second language is sign."

Gary often volunteered at community meetings

to provide translation for the small group of deaf citizens. When the speakers got excited and started talking rapidly, it amazed me how fast his hands would fly. At other times, when the pace slowed down, his movements were more like a dance.

The unreadable words in front of my eyes taunted me. Who did I know who spoke French and could translate for me? Or at least tell me it wasn't French? Or tell me what language it was? The date, however, I could interpret even with all the fancy scrollwork—1847.

As I stepped out of Gary's shop, the all-too-familiar prickle at the back of my neck alerted me I was being watched. Although the rain had stopped, the dark clouds overhead blocked enough of the fading sun that the streetlights were struggling to turn on. From the relative safety of the pawnshop's entrance, I scanned the parking lot and nearby street, trying to determine who or what had set off my internal sensors. A light touch of the purse dangling by my side assured me Betsy, my Beretta, was right where she belonged. Nothing out of the ordinary caught my eye.

Just in case, I pulled out my cell phone, wondering if the pictures I'd taken of the note had already uploaded to the cloud. The original, now encased in a plastic sleeve, was stored in Gary's safe along with the cufflinks. Merrilee agreed to set up a meeting with the high school French teacher for me, and I planned to make use of several translation sites on the internet. The problem would be interpreting the faded ink and fanciful lettering. It was possible that the spelling or meaning of some of the words had changed, creating an additional challenge.

Even though there'd been an empty parking space in front of the store when I'd arrived several hours earlier, I'd parked my salsa-red Jag, Dolores, across the street in front of an empty lot. Saved the good slots for actual customers. She chirped happily at me as I pressed the button to unlock her and hurried across the otherwise deserted pavement. I guessed everyone was home eating supper and relaxing after a hard day's work. Leftover stew waited for me at my apartment, and another couple of hours searching the internet for hidden bits of information.

The sweet purr of the engine chased my gloomy mood away until I detected the undertone of a miss. Unless Nikos, the mechanic I took her to for service had overlooked something, she shouldn't be having any problems. And Nikos took care of Dolores like his own prized possession, so it didn't make sense. I leaned forward to listen harder and realized the faint sound was not emitting from the front of the car. A glance in the rearview mirror and I saw that someone was in the car behind me. The miss must have been from that car.

I would have been relieved, but the prickly feeling at the base of my neck grew stronger. Something about the man looked familiar although I couldn't see his face clearly. I pulled out my cell phone and pretended to make a call, wanting to see how he'd react. If he pulled away, I'd chalk it up to coincidence, but if he stayed put I'd be trying to figure out his motives.

When he didn't take off, I took the next step. I got backup. Gary was a phone call and a few feet away.

"It's Harmony," I said when he answered. "Look out your front window."

"Did you forget something?"

"No. I'm still parked across the street. Do you recognize the car behind me?"

"Can't say I do," he said.

"I'll pull out. Keep your eye on him and see if he follows me."

"Better idea. Wait a minute."

I heard fumbling noises in the background, then the door to the shop opened and Gary strolled out with a bag in his hand. Puzzled, I rolled down the window.

"You forgot this," he said. He handed me the package and winked. "And no, I don't recognize the car. Chances are it's not one of my regulars. Did you call the cops?"

"I don't have a reason." But I didn't want to risk being followed home by a stranger.

"Tell you what. You take off, I'll stand here, and that should discourage any whacko. Plus, I can get a picture of his tag." Gary grinned. "I'll make it obvious. That should scare him off."

There was only one flaw in his plan. "What if he tries to run you down or something?"

With a snort, Gary tapped the holster at his side. I'd seen it so often, I'd forgotten he always carried. Running a pawn shop could be a hazardous occupation.

I smiled. "Right. I'll call you when I get home. And send me the picture of the tag. Maybe I can find out who our mystery man is."

Chapter 4

I made it home without any signs of being followed. After a quick call to Gary, I put my stew on to heat, opened my laptop, and got to work. I had a couple of options to track down the license plate. Pay a couple of bucks to a website who had access to the DMV database, or see if Freddie could trace it. I debated my choices and decided to go with the website. I'd feel silly asking Freddie to pull the information if the car belonged to a little old man who was waiting until no one would see him heading into the pawn shop. Although, according to Gary, he'd left three or four minutes after me.

I decided on the website. The site's information said it could take as little as fifteen minutes or as much as a day to get the preliminary results. They wouldn't come any faster if I sat and stared at the screen, so I wandered back to the kitchen to stir the stew.

As I ate, I played with the possibilities of who the mystery man was. A drug addict looking for a quiet place to get his fix. Or a homeless vet living out of his car trying to scout out a place to park for the night and sleep. A real estate agent trying to find a location to put a big-box store. An undercover sheriff's deputy checking up on me. Which reminded me, it was time to scan my apartment again.

After six or seven months, I'd given up the professional service out of Pittsburgh I'd been using to check my apartment for unauthorized electronic equipment. I still used my portable scanner once in a while to ease my mind. I hadn't found any new bugs since last fall but I was a bit paranoid. At one time, someone had put listening devices in my little slice of heaven—someone besides Eli—so checking for them became a habit. I had Eli's word of honor—sealed with a kiss or two—that he wouldn't plant any more.

With his kisses on my mind, I fired up my video chat program and pinged him.

"Hey, good looking," I said when his face appeared on my screen. His eyes, so pale blue they were almost gray, twinkled. A tailored white long-sleeved shirt only partially hid the muscles in his arms and chest. Judging from the stack of paperwork piled in front of him, he was still at his office. "Isn't it time for you to go home?"

"Past time." With a wry grin, he tapped the pile of papers. "But I'm not done here yet. How was your day, Buttercup?"

His term of endearment made me smile. "I went treasure hunting today."

"Arr. Spy any pirates, matey? Dig up their hidden gold?"

I had a sudden vision of Eli in a loose shirt with big sleeves, open to his waist. In my imagination, I wore a flowing skirt with a tight blouse and corset. I hoped the dim lighting in my front room would hide the sudden rush of blood to my cheeks. "Nope. But I did find something interesting. Check your email, I sent you a picture." I'd sent him an image of the cufflinks taken with my cell phone.

"They're nice, I suppose. Where did you get them?"

"I found them stashed inside a hollowed-out book at Gary's pawn shop."

Eli whistled. "So they aren't costume jewelry?"

"Not according to the tests Gary ran. By the way, do you speak French?"

"No, I took Spanish. It's more useful in Florida. Why?"

"There was a note in the box with the cufflinks. I can't figure out what language it's in, but it's old. I'm trying to find someone to tell me what it says."

"I'll ask around and see if anyone here can help. Can you send me a picture of it?"

It took next to no time to forward it on from my phone. "Parts of it are hard to make out, but it's the best I could do with the phone's camera. If you can help me with this, you'll get to name your reward." I grinned and batted my eyelashes at him—well, at the computer screen with his image.

Even through the crummy built-in speakers of my laptop, I heard his sharp intake of air. "No fair.

I'm working on a new contract and I'm stuck here."

"Yeah, and I'm stuck in Oak Grove too. At least until the sheriff decides I'm no longer a person of interest in the murder."

"You haven't heard anything more about it?"

I'd made Eli promise not to try and hack into the sheriff's computer system when I'd told him about the murder. "No, and I don't know if that's a good thing or a bad thing."

"No news is good news, according to my mother."

I could easily imagine his mother saying just that. She and I had spent some quality time together during my trip to Florida, and she'd treated me like a member of the family. We chatted every so often, but I wouldn't tell her about the current situation until things cleared up. No need to worry her unnecessarily.

But the lack of news made me nervous. I made a mental note to do what I do best and dig into Mr. Tadd Foard's background. Not the criminal stuff because that was a dead end. Everything else was fair game. Where he was born, where he grew up, what high school he attended. Anything and everything that might give me a clue as to why someone wanted him dead.

A sudden burst of light lit up my apartment, followed by a loud clap of thunder. "I guess that's my cue to go," I said.

"Aren't you on your laptop?" Eli asked.

"It's not my laptop I'm worried about, it's my modem. The battery backup died, and I haven't replaced it." Most of the wiring in Luke and Joe's house, and my apartment, was old and not up to handling a major surge. They'd lost a TV earlier in the summer when lightning scored a direct hit on a nearby utility pole.

Sometimes our goodbyes took a long time, but another nearby lightning strike cut them short that night. After unplugging the modem and lighting a candle in case the electricity went out, I settled onto my loveseat with one of the many books I'd bought and hadn't ever found time to read. It would be nice to pretend for one night that there was nothing more urgent in my life than reading a good book.

The morning sky sparkled as I bounced downstairs to retrieve my newspaper and pat Piper, Luke and Joe's dog. The rain had washed the dirt out of the air, and the world smelled fresh and clean. I'd brought my coffee with me, and I sat on the second-to-bottom step and opened the paper.

From the day's headline, it looked to be another laid-back day in the quiet town of Oak Grove. 'City Council Approves Funds for New Playground Equipment.' A robin landed on the fence, cocked his head and warbled a few notes as I turned the page. 'Football Coach Predicts a Winning Year.' That one made me smile because Coach Henderson had predicted the same thing for the last fifteen years, and it hadn't happened yet. The school was too small to field a team that matched its rivals. But there was always hope.

Having received my daily dose of uplifting news, I turned to the financial section. Although Keith, my financial adviser, made most of my investing decisions, I still followed the stock market to see how my portfolio was doing. With the nation's economy on an upswing, there was nothing but good news.

Piper's low growl warned me that not all was right in my little bubble. I instinctively reached behind me to where I wore Betsy and found nothing. Shit. I'd only planned on getting the paper when I'd gotten dressed, and left her upstairs in the apartment. But I had another weapon at hand.

I grabbed Piper's collar with one hand and opened the gate with the other. He wouldn't stop a bullet, but he made an excellent ally in combat. His growl turned into loud, aggressive barking when a familiar-looking man came around the corner of the house. I tightened my grip on his collar as he tried to pull away. The back door of the house squeaked as it opened, but I didn't turn when two sets of footsteps came up behind me.

"Can we help you?" Joe asked as he placed a hand on my shoulder.

The man took several steps closer but stopped when Piper nearly escaped my grasp. "I'm with the Sheriff's Department. I need to speak to Miss Duprie. Get the dog under control."

"Do you have a warrant, Deputy Nelson?" I asked between Piper's growls.

He held up his hands. "I just want to talk."

"What do you want to do, Harmony?" Luke asked softly.

"One of you take Piper inside. Then call my lawyer. I've got my cell phone in my pocket and he's in my contacts. The other one stays here with me as a witness."

I sensed rather than saw their nods of agreement. Joe bent over and picked up Piper. "You want to stick your phone in my shirt?" he asked.

I didn't want to make the deputy any more nervous than he already was. "I'm reaching for my cell phone. Okay?"

At his nod, I pulled it out of my pocket and stuck it in Joe's. "Dan Albright," I told him. "Call the emergency number, not the office."

"Got it." Carrying the struggling Piper, he returned to the house.

Most of the tension drained out of the deputy's stance. "Can we go upstairs and talk?" he asked. "Someplace where we can sit?"

"Not without that warrant."

"I'll grab the lawn chairs off the porch and we can sit out here," Luke suggested.

"Works for me. How about you, Deputy?"

He didn't have much of a choice. He waited for Luke to haul the chairs to the sidewalk, shifting uncomfortably from foot to foot. I suppose me standing with my arms crossed glaring at him didn't help make the situation easy for him. I wondered how long he'd been with the department—he had a lot to learn about controlling a scene.

"Your lawyer will be here in a couple of

minutes," Joe said, bringing a chair of his own as he rejoined us. Piper didn't like being left in the house, and his barking carried through the walls.

The hospitable thing to do would have been to offer the deputy something to drink, but I wasn't feeling very neighborly. I sipped my coffee while Luke arranged the chairs so four faced one direction and the fifth faced them. Then Joe and Luke took their seats leaving an empty chair between them. It was glaringly obvious where they wanted me to sit, and where my unwelcome visitor was exiled to.

I turned my back to the deputy and winked at the boys before I settled between them. "Think we'll get some more rain today?" I asked casually.

"Hope so," Luke answered. "The grass is looking a little brown."

"Time to mow it again," Joe grunted. "That weed-n-feed we used sure makes it grow fast."

"I'm still thinking about laying down some sod at the house," I said. "Or at least reseeding the front. It will boost curb appeal, according to Sarah."

We'd had this discussion before, but I was enjoying seeing Deputy Nelson get increasingly uneasy. My fun ended with the arrival of Dan.

Dan was another asset I'd 'inherited' from my father, like Keith, my financial adviser. I'd worked with him on several occasions, mostly on contracts and other financial matters. But when I was arrested for drug trafficking, he jumped on the opportunity to represent me. Said it would keep him from getting stale.

He certainly didn't look stale as he strode up the

sidewalk. The only sign of his age—he was in his late sixties—was his silver hair. A few wrinkles graced his face but he still had the energy of a much younger man.

Joe shuffled to the empty chair at the end of the line so Dan could sit by me. He smiled at me and put his hand on the arm of the chair so it touched mine. It looked like a gesture of comfort, but it was a scenario we'd used before. If I was asked a question he didn't want me to answer, he'd push ever-so-slightly. To the unobservant bystander, my refusal to answer would seem to be totally my own idea.

"I'm Dan Albright, Miss Duprie's attorney," he said, "I understand you have some questions for her. May I ask what this is in reference to?"

I almost felt sorry for Deputy Nelson. Why was the Sheriff allowing him to handle the investigation without the assistance of a more experienced officer? He was outclassed and about to be outdone.

The deputy swallowed, hard. "I just have a few questions for your client. May I?"

Dan nodded.

"Miss Duprie, what is your relationship to a Miss Annabelle Susannah Leroix?"

Dan's hand remained relaxed. With a name like that, I would have remembered her if I'd ever met her. I wondered if she was originally a Southern girl. "Annabelle LeRoix? Sorry, Deputy, the name doesn't ring a bell," I said. Luke groaned at my very bad pun. "Should I know her?"

The deputy reached into his shirt pocket and pulled out a piece of paper. He leaned forward and handed it to me. "Here's her picture. Does she look familiar?"

I didn't need to study the image, but handed it to Dan so he could look at it. "That's Brandy. At least, that's what her nametag read. She was our waitress that night at The Dog House. In fact, she was the one who stepped in and tried to calm things down when Mr. Foard got out of line. But you already knew that."

"You haven't talked to her or seen her since that night?"

"No, although I should have. We tipped her well, but I thought about sending her some flowers or a box of chocolates or something as a thank you. I've been procrastinating."

"What is the purpose of these questions?" Dan interjected. "And how does it involve my client?"

"Miss Leroix was found severely beaten last night. She's in critical condition at a hospital in Pittsburgh."

I wasn't the only one to suck in a deep breath. "Is she going to make it?"

Deputy Nelson shook his head. "The doctors aren't saying yet. And even if I knew, I couldn't tell you. Patient privacy and all that."

We all fell silent for a moment. Dan broke the quiet. "Again, Deputy, what's this have to do with my client?"

"The victim's purse was located. Although her wallet had been cleaned out, random pieces of paper were left behind. One of those scraps had your name on it, Miss Duprie."

Chapter 5

I opened my mouth, but Dan pressed on my hand, his signal to me, and I shut it again.

"That means nothing," Dan said. "Miss LeRoix might've gotten my client's name anywhere. From the newspaper, a credit card slip, or one of your co-workers mentioned her while questioning Miss LeRoix."

I wanted to ask if it had been hand-written or if the deputy had checked whether it was in Annabelle's writing. But Dan kept the pressure on my hand.

"You understand I have to follow up on all leads," the deputy said, wiping a bead of sweat from his forehead. The bright sun heralded an extra-warm day.

"Sure you do. But it's clear my client can't assist you." Dan reached into his pocket, pulled out his business card and handed it to Deputy Nelson. "If you have other questions, you can reach me at this number during the day. Have a good day, Deputy."

That's why I paid Dan the big bucks.

Deputy Nelson hesitated, then stood. He stuck Dan's card into his shirt pocket, and retrieved his card from a case on his belt. "Miss Duprie, if you think of anything helpful, please give me a call." He handed his card to Dan. "Or Mr. Albright can call me."

With the force gone from my hand, I knew I could answer. "Of course, Deputy. And if you have a way to do it, please tell Miss LeRoix I hope she gets better soon."

"I will." In an old-fashioned gesture, he tipped his duty hat, ever-so-slightly. "Have a good day, ma'am, gentlemen."

Once he left, and after letting Piper back into the yard, we all headed upstairs to my place for ice tea. While my guests chatted about the weather, I fired up my laptop.

"What are you up to?" Luke asked.

I smiled apologetically. "You know me, I want to see what I can find out about poor Annabelle."

Dan shook his head. "Let the professionals do their job, Harmony."

"It's not like I expect to find anything besides her address and phone number. Maybe she's had a parking ticket or two." I had several sites bookmarked for easy reference, so it only took a few seconds to begin the hunt.

While waiting for the results, I toggled over to the site for the license plates to see if I'd gotten a response. Nothing yet, but it hadn't been twenty-four hours since I'd put in the request so I wasn't surprised. By then, I'd convinced myself it was only a coincidence—the car sitting behind Dolores at the pawn shop.

When I flipped back to the hunt for Annabelle, I realized I needed more information to narrow the parameters. I hadn't expected there'd be as many Annabelle Leroixs as the searches turned up. They were spread across the Unites States—and the world, actually—so the search would take more work than I'd expected.

Interestingly enough, a quick scan didn't find a listing for her locally. So I started a second search for Brandy LeRoix. Not knowing how long she'd worked at The Dog House or lived in the area left open the possibility the search engines hadn't caught up to her move.

Many of the results were for social sites and had photos attached. Scanning those seemed a logical place to start, and the easiest way to eliminate some of the candidates. What I needed to do was start a spreadsheet so I could cross-reference the information for those with pictures against those without photos. But I was ignoring my guests, so that would happen later.

I pulled my attention away from the laptop long enough to realize the three guys were having an animated conversation about an upcoming NASCAR race. Not a topic I could contribute to as my interest fell more to rally racing. With my guilt assuaged, I moved my cursor to bring up another page of results.

"Holy freaking shit," I muttered softly, but not softly enough. The conversation stopped.

"What?" Joe asked.

"I'm not sure. I need more info."

"What did you find, Harmony?" Dan got up to look over my shoulder.

"We need to call Deputy Nelson and get him to come back." I clicked on a link and Dan whistled.

"What?" Luke asked.

I looked up. "If this is right, Annabelle LeRoix is a private investigator."

❊ ❊ ❊

It was fun watching people's reactions to their first glimpse of my apartment, Deputy Nelson being no exception to that. When he stepped inside some fifteen minutes later, I saw surprise flash across his face. If he'd jumped to conclusions about how I lived based on the Jaguar I drove, or because I had a lawyer that dropped everything to come to my assistance, that explained his reaction.

The place was small, only a couple of rooms, but I always kept it clean and neat. Overstuffed with books, perhaps, but Luke and Joe had built me new cherry wood bookshelves to replace the old ones I'd acquired over the years. They were crammed top to bottom with books but they matched. My other furniture was second-hand, bought from thrift shops or gifted to me.

"Ice tea?" I asked once Joe and Luke moved off the loveseat so Deputy Nelson could sit there. They dragged chairs away from the dining table to watch the anticipated show.

Despite me being in hostess mode, the deputy seemed uncomfortable as he sipped his tea. "What is it you wanted to share?" he asked. Did he expect me to spill my guts about some crime I'd committed? Boy, was he in for a shock.

I skipped right past the small talk. "Do you have a birth date or social security number for Annabelle?" Even though I'd only done a little research on her, I already felt like we were on a first name basis.

"I can't reveal that information to you," he answered in a stern tone.

"Nope." I plunked my laptop in front of him, already opened to the right page. "But if you have them, you can verify if this is the same person as Annabelle from The Dog House. If it's not the same person, they look enough alike to be sisters. All you have to do is call the licensing office in West Virginia. And then you can contact her agency and find out what she was doing here, her current case, and that will lead you to who beat her up. If she's up to talking, you can ask her if she thinks it has anything to do with the murder." It seemed too obvious. "And I'd sure like to find out why she was interested in me."

Dan cleared his throat as a signal to stop talking.

"How do you know this?" Deputy Nelson asked.

"It's my job. Research, that is. You give me a topic, I'll find out what you need to know. I try to leave the actual police work to the professionals."

Not that I was good at that. I'd stuck my nose where it didn't belong a few too many times.

Joe snorted. "You should stop letting the professionals take credit for your work."

The glare I sent across the room didn't stop him. But privately, I took credit for the raise Freddie got last spring. After all, I'd given him the leads he needed to bust a pair of thieves.

"How long have you been with the sheriff's office?" Joe continued. I gave him bonus points for picking up on the signs of the deputy's newness.

"Four months," Nelson answered. "But I had a year's experience in my hometown."

Joe smirked. "So you missed all the fun last fall when Harmony helped capture several wanted criminals. Or this past spring when she aided the Oak Grove Police in identifying and capturing the men responsible for a murder and helped the FBI bust a nationwide burglary ring. Don't underestimated this lady."

Luke nodded vigorously.

I blushed. Joe and Luke were both overly protective of me, but I hadn't realized they were proud of me. Frankly, I preferred to not share the stories of my past adventures. A muscle in Deputy Nelson's right cheek twitched several times.

"Have you upset your sergeant already?" Dan asked. "It seems as if you're on a wild goose chase."

Deputy Nelson's cheeks turned flaming red. "They only shared Miss Duprie's arrest. They didn't even tell me the results of the trial. I had to dig for that myself."

Yup, someone had it in for him. I wondered if he'd gotten hired over someone's son or other relative. Or had he come in with a chip on his shoulder and immediately alienated his co-workers?

He turned to me. "I apologize for the misunderstanding. If this was someone's idea of a joke, it wasn't very funny. It's one thing to hassle the new guy, it's another to involve an innocent civilian."

I wasn't as innocent as I seemed, but that was another story. "In this case, Deputy, maybe it was a good thing they involved me. I presume someone is guarding Annabelle at the hospital? To make sure she's not attacked again?"

"I'm not sure. I'm not part of the team that handled the call. But we haven't revealed where she is, so she should be safe."

"Unless there's a crooked officer in the department. And don't look so shocked Deputy, it happens. We had one here in town last year."

Joe grinned. "That's right. I forgot you helped the FBI flush him out."

I should have kept my big mouth shut. Deputy Nelson stared at me as if he wanted to crawl inside my brain and dissect it, hunting for more secrets. The best response was to stare back at him. I excelled at that game. He broke eye contact first.

"I'll talk to the sheriff," he said. "Directly to the sheriff. He'll make sure that all the proper precautions are being taken to protect the victim. And I'll follow up on this lead." He held out his hand. "Thank you for your help."

As I shook his hand, I noticed he'd set his glass on the coffee table, rather than using the nearby coaster. I'd need to wipe up the water droplets as soon as he left so they wouldn't leave a stain. "I'm glad I could help. If you need anything else, please let Dan know." Yeah, normally I would tell him to call me, but I wasn't going to go there. Not this time.

Chapter 6

The padded chairs in the periodical section were more comfortable than the wooden chairs in the main area of the library. I'd abandoned my books to browse through the newspapers of nearby cities, including Pittsburgh and Cleveland. The thought of moving out of Oak Grove was repugnant, but perhaps I would need to.

The non-renewable grant supporting the writers' cooperative was exhausted with no new funding sources available. The minor fees its members paid weren't enough to pay for my services, the outside research jobs I did weren't steady enough to use as my main source of income. Sure, I could supplement my earnings with the interest earned from my investments, but the idea made me cringe. I needed to do something useful with my life.

So I perused the help wanted ads for opportunities. Unless I wanted to take up long-haul trucking or nursing, the prospects were limited. I prefer my vehicles with a little more style than a box, and the prospect of spending my days with sick people made me shudder. Or I could go back to school and get a second Masters. I'd found one offered in Internet Research. Although from the description, it seemed to be aimed at students willing to work in corporate environments. The picture of me in a cubicle for eight hours a day was the makings of a nightmare.

I hadn't told Eli about the possibility yet; I knew he'd suggest I move to Florida and go to work for him. In fact, I'd told no one, and didn't plan to share. At least not until the rumor became fact or the Oak Grove gossip network got a hold of it.

"Hiding out?" a familiar voice asked as someone moved in between me and the sun shining through the windows.

I folded the paper as Jake took the chair beside me, his Amber Bay aftershave drifting my way. Had he dyed his hair again? Or was it a trick of the light? It seemed a shade darker than a few days ago. Still, it suited him, like the pale yellow polo shirt and tan casual slacks he wore. "I'm tired of Victorian England," I told him. "But I'm over the current news too. There's never anything happy in the paper. What are you up to?"

"Figured I'd stop by and say hello. Find out if you were coming by the house tonight."

"Probably. I need to water the flowers."

Jake grinned. "Already took care of it. One plant didn't survive being transplanted, so I replaced it."

"Bored, eh?"

"You could say that." His grin slipped. "It's been

a long time since I've stayed in one spot for more than a couple of months. By choice, anyway." The time he'd spent in prison wasn't his option. "Working only three nights a week leaves me too much free time. Now that the house is finished, I've got to find something else to keep me busy."

He had that goodbye look in his eyes. "Where's the job?" I asked.

He hesitated and stared at the floor. "You always see right through me. Chicago. Club there wants me to start out as a bouncer with an eye on moving me into management. It's too good of an opportunity to pass up."

"I should think so. When do you start? Two weeks? Next week?" I plastered a smile on my face. I wanted to be happy for him. I needed to be happy for him.

"Three days from now. There's an empty room above the bar they'll let me stay in until I can find a place. It doesn't have a kitchen, but it's not like I ever cook anyway."

At least he could manage something more than soup warmed up in a microwave. I'd taught him the basics but he still preferred to eat in restaurants and flirt with the waitresses.

"That doesn't give you much time to pack. We'll need to swing by the grocery store and see if they have any empty boxes."

"Everything will fit into my suitcases and a few garbage bags. I'll just toss them into the car."

"How about I take you out tonight to celebrate?" I suggested with false cheerfulness.

He agreed and we decided on Mama D's at six. My eyes tracked his path as he left and another piece of my crumbling world walked out the door.

Concentrating on my research was the best way to distract me from my problems. Either that or go home and clean. But I didn't want to return to French society during the Victorian England period and it was too early to go home so I decided to research Annabelle instead.

She wasn't a social butterfly, but someone in her position needed to take advantage of the internet to drum up business. Between her agency's website and her social media page, I found out quite a bit about her. At least, her qualifications as a private investigator.

Her specialty was collecting evidence on cheaters. It didn't matter if the wounded party was female or male; she tackled both kinds of cases. Still, Oak Grove was quite a distance from Charleston, West Virginia. I hoped her client paid her well to come here and gather dirt on a straying spouse.

I wanted to know more. The more I dug, the more I found. Her high school yearbook revealed she'd been a cheerleader and active in school clubs. She'd made the prom court her senior year, but wasn't the queen. The list of awards she received suggested she was near the top of her class, but she wasn't valedictorian or salutatorian. I tried to figure out who her boyfriend had been—she must have had a boyfriend—but there weren't any pictures to tie her to any one guy. The faces in the yearbook all seemed familiar, I guess because the hairdos and outfits were reminiscent of my high school class.

Then I hit a black hole. Nothing I found told me what she'd done in the seven or eight years between high school graduation and starting her business. She could have gone to Harvard, hitchhiked across the country, or traveled the world, and I was none the wiser.

I bookmarked a few pages online to come back to later with a fresh mind. As I checked my email, I wondered how Annabelle was doing. Had she been released from the hospital yet and gone home? Since there was no one to ask, I might have to request a favor from my favorite hacker.

Thoughts of Annabelle fled when I opened the email I'd finally received from the company researching the license plate of the mysterious car. They'd found something, and for the measly sum of fifteen dollars, they'd share it with me. I paid the invoice on a credit card with an incredibly low spending limit, worried the site might be nothing but a scam.

❋ ❋ ❋

"Are you sure this guy didn't follow you home?" Freddie asked.

I'd rushed to his office at the station as soon as the results from the website hit my email. "Absolutely. Gary kept an eye on him. And you know how paranoid I am about that." For good reason. I'd had the FBI tail me on more than one occasion, and so had assorted bad guys.

"We'll keep an eye out but those plates are likely in the trash by now." They'd been stolen near Philadelphia a few weeks earlier. Freddie's official access to the state databases confirmed the unofficial information I'd paid for. "Can you give me a better description of the car?"

"Other than dark-colored—probably faded black—and older. I didn't see much. With the storm clouds, the time of day, and the burnt-out street light, it was hard to see," I said defensively.

Freddie studied the photo on my phone. "Chevy." He passed my phone back to me. "See the emblem?"

I'd concentrated so hard on the plate itself I hadn't paid attention to anything else. I guess that's why he was Oak Grove's lead detective. "Now I do."

He leaned back in his chair. "That eliminates about two-thirds of the cars out there."

Which wouldn't be a lot of help.

Footsteps echoed in the hallway and Freddie straightened. A quick glance had me adjusting my posture too. There was something about Chief Sorenson's presence that made people do that without even thinking about it.

"What trouble did you bring us today?" the chief asked me with no hint of a smile.

"Nice to see you too, Chief. I'm just doing my civic duty and reporting a potential crime."

"She stumbled across a vehicle with stolen plates

and came in to pass the information along," Freddie rushed to defend me. Not that I needed him too. I could stick up for myself.

"And since when have you had access to the DMV databases?" the chief asked with a deep frown.

"I don't. But there are perfectly legit on-line sites that do. I used one of them."

He snorted. "Legitimate is not a word I associate with those sorts of sites, but to each his own. And since when have you started checking out license plates? Even my officers don't do that unless it's a traffic stop."

I was glad that his officers didn't have time for such trivial tasks. Or was that a bad thing? "I don't normally do it either. This is the first time as a matter of fact." *But probably not the last.* "I wanted to identify the driver of a suspicious vehicle. I didn't expect to find out it was involved in an actual crime. That's why I came to Freddie. I'm trying to stick to our agreement."

Chief Sorenson nodded his approval. We'd made a verbal pact last spring about me keeping my nose out of Oak Grove police business. He hadn't said anything about any other law enforcement agency, so my investigations into Annabelle and Tadd didn't count. "Good," he said. "Have a nice day, Miss Duprie." He turned crisply and continued down the hallway.

"That went better than I expected," Freddie said, almost whispering.

"He's warming up to me."

"Unlikely, but you never know. Miracles happen. Thing is, he's not what you call friendly to anyone on the force. He doesn't *not* like anyone, but he keeps his distance from all of us."

And the rest of the town's inhabitants. "Do you need anything else from me?" I asked Freddie.

"No. Just be careful."

I smiled as I stood. "Careful is my middle name." We both knew that was a lie. I was lucky that lightning didn't hit me as I strolled out of his office.

Chapter 7

With one final thunk, Sarah finished pounding the wooden post into the ground in front of the Aldridge house. The paperwork was signed, and with the "For Sale" sign up, it was official. Now it was a matter of weathering the wait until someone showed an interest in buying the place.

"You've done wonders here, Harmony," Sarah said as she tossed the hammer into the trunk of her car and closed the lid. "I'm looking forward to showing it."

"Luke and Joe get most of the credit. They're already making noises about wanting to tackle another project. And Jake had a lot of good ideas."

"If you want help in finding a house to renovate, I know just the person for the job." Her smile stretched across her face. "That would work out well for me. A commission to sell you a house that needs renovations, and another one when I sell it for you after it's done."

That could be my new career. 'Flipping' houses.

But first I needed to see if I would make a profit from this one. "I thought the housing market was on a downturn."

"It is. That's why I need those commissions." Sarah sighed. "But I'd never rope you into a bad deal."

"No worries. But before I'm ready to tackle anything big. I need time to recuperate." And find a new job.

"You should take another vacation. You've had a stressful year."

That was the truth. "I can't leave. Not until they arrest someone for the murder."

"Deputy Nelson still bugging you? He questioned me once and I haven't seen him since."

"I haven't seen him for a few days, I'm probably worrying about nothing. But it would be nice to know if they had any suspects other than me." Although I read it religiously, there'd been no more news about the crime in the paper.

We talked as we walked the short distance towards the house and sat on the front steps. The shade thrown by the front porch provided a hint of relief from the hot August afternoon.

"That's the second time that car's gone by," Sarah said. "I wonder if they're interested."

I looked up from my purse, which I'd been searching for a pack of gum. The onions in the salad at lunch had staying power. "Who?"

"They're gone now."

I didn't find any gum but did find a package of breath mints. I handed one to Sarah, unwrapped mine, and stuck the paper into my purse. Then I arranged my legs straight out in front of me and leaned back on my elbows. "I used to do this as a kid," I said. "Sit on the porch and watch the traffic. Haven't done it in forever. I'm always too busy."

We sat quietly and I watched a cluster of puffy clouds float by. One reminded me of a frog.

"There it is again," Sarah said suddenly.

"What?"

"That car."

I didn't bother to look. It would be gone by the time I did. "What color is it?" I asked, yawning. I imagined a hammock strung in the corner of the porch with a big pillow and a good book to read. Or pretend to read while I took a nap.

"Black. It's an older car, beat up. Doesn't fit the normal profile of an interested buyer, but you never know. Strange they haven't at least stopped and picked up a pamphlet."

The back of my neck tingled. I shot upright. "Where?"

"It's gone. But wait a few minutes, it may be back. It's circling the block."

We waited five minutes, then ten, but the mysterious car never showed again. I tried to convince myself it was a simple coincidence. There were plenty of black cars around. But my gut knew better.

❈ ❈ ❈

My meeting with the high school French teacher

was set for six that evening. Tuesday nights weren't busy at the Burger Barn and we could occupy a booth for as long as needed. Merrilee told me to watch for a guy with red hair that looked like a leprechaun.

I got to the restaurant early. No redheads in sight, either male or female. Oh, except that one guy with a Mohawk dyed in streaks of flaming red and lime green. I wondered if it was real or a hairpiece left from last Halloween because I couldn't imagine trying to sleep with that hairdo. Not a likely candidate for a high school teacher.

As I studied the menu and waited, wondering if it would be impolite to order before he arrived. This wasn't a date after all. I'd barely touched my lunch while doing the paperwork to list the house. My stomach rumbled and I took a drink of my water, hoping to fool it into hibernation.

I figured out who he was the minute he walked in the door. At six something feet tall, he didn't qualify for leprechaun status, except for that bright red hair and boyish face. He paused in the doorway and looked around. I waved and he headed towards me.

"Miss Duprie?" he asked.

I nodded.

"I'm Carlisle Buford."

I extended my hand. "Please, call me Harmony."

We shook and he slid into the booth opposite me. "And I'm Carl. What's this mystery you want my help on solving?"

My stomach growled again, loud enough for him

to hear. "Perhaps we should order first," I said sheepishly. "My treat, by the way."

"I've heard the kids talking about this place," he said looking over the menu. "What do you recommend?"

"You can't go wrong with one of their burgers and a shake."

"Have you ever tried their veggie burgers?" He grinned. "My doctor suggested I eat healthier."

"I haven't, sorry. But I haven't run into anything terrible here yet." Well, except the time they experimented with a chocolate-grasshopper shake. I never worked up the courage to try one.

"I'm surprised you want my help," he said after we'd placed our orders. "With a name like Duprie, I thought you would have studied French. Or is that your married name?" So he had been scrutinizing my ring finger. I needed to shut that down quickly. My heart belonged to Eli.

"Not married, but in a relationship. I studied Latin in high school and college. Seemed more useful for a librarian."

He blushed. "I got mixed vibes from your friend. I wasn't sure whether she was setting me up on a blind date or if you really needed help translating something."

What had Merrilee been up to? I'd confront her later. I pulled out my phone, brought up the image of the note, and handed it to him. "This is what I'm trying to decipher. That's not a clear picture, but the camera in my phone isn't very good."

Carl squinted his eyes and held my phone close

to his face. "I can make out a few words," he said. "Avec, pour, votre—is it possible for me to see the original?" He smiled. "They mean with, for, your."

I'd figured those words out myself using an on-line translation website, but I didn't want to ruin his moment.

"There's a date," he continued, "1847. And a name. It might be Louis but I'm not sure."

Our burgers arrived and he put my phone on the table with a thoughtful look on his face. "The date bugs me but I can't place why." He picked up his burger and took a bite—he'd ordered the veggie one—and covered his mouth with his hand. "That's not half-bad."

My mouth was full, so I nodded. Conversation ended as we concentrated on our food. Carl must have been as hungry as I was.

He finished first. "Where did you find the note?" he asked.

My mouth was still full, so he had to wait for an answer until I swallowed. "Stuffed inside a book." Technically, it was the truth. Just not the whole truth.

"Was the book in French?"

"No, English."

Carl frowned. "Did you see any notes in the book? Scribbling in the margins or loose pieces of paper?"

I didn't want to reveal that the only thing that made it a book was the cover and binding. "Not that I saw."

"Doesn't give me much to go on," he said. "It

could be a note from a teacher or somebody's grandmother or a kid's homework. Sorry, without a better copy, I can't help."

I put my burger down, picked up my napkin, meticulously wiped off any potential greasy remnants, and reached into my purse. I'd come prepared.

"Here's a printed copy," I said, handing him a folded piece of paper. "It's blurry, and the faded parts on the original are still barely readable on the print-out, but at least it's bigger."

"Definitely an improvement. I can almost read it." He patted his shirt pocket as if looking for something. "Do you have a pen?"

"Of course." The trick was in finding it in my purse. Pens had a habit of working their way into the folds of the lining, making them difficult to uncover. I pulled out my wallet, my eyeglasses case, and a small box of breath mints before locating the pen. I laid it on the table between us.

He picked it up and hesitated. "Can I write on this?"

"Sure," I answered, wondering what he was up to.

He traced over the writing, filling in gaps and clarifying smudged lines. It was a good thing my pen had bright blue ink because it stood out from the black copy ink. He skipped a few places because the writing was too indistinct to work with.

Halfway through the task, his eyes widened and his hand started to tremble. "I don't believe it," he said quietly.

"What?" My heart raced with excitement.

He shook his head. "I need to do more research," he answered. "I don't want to get you worked up over nothing. This could be a practical joke. Or a forgery." He tapped the end of the pen on the table.

"And if it's not?" I crossed my fingers, hoping for something spectacular.

"I'm afraid to say it out loud."

"What?" I leaned towards him.

"It's been a long time since I took those courses in French history. If my memory serves me correctly…" He hesitated. "This may have been written by the last king of France."

Chapter 8

I learned a lot about English history in school, but all I knew about French history came from old movies and novels. "You mean the guy who got his head chopped off? Marie Antoinette's husband?" Had I actually held an important historical document?

Carl shook his head. "Typical American." He smiled. "Believe it or not, there were a couple of short-term kings after Napoleon. I need to go back to my books and verify the dates. It's been too many years since I took French history courses and I've never been that great at remembering dates."

While the waitress refilled our water glasses, I picked up my cell phone. It was good for more than making calls. I rarely used its web capabilities and had next to nothing in the way of a data plan, but this was a good time to make an exception to one of my many rules. "What should I search for?" I asked.

"The last king of France or the citizen king of France. Louis Philippe. Any of those will work."

It didn't take long to find several articles about the topic. "What year is on that note?" I peered at the screen, trying to read the tiny print.

"1847."

"And we have a winner. This guy was king from 1830 to 1848." I looked up and blinked my eyes, adjusting my vision.

"France was declared a republic shortly after he abdicated. Can you find a picture of his signature?" Carl's index finger tapped his phone's screen. The race was on, but he had a head start. About the time I found a link, he declared triumphantly, "Got it!"

"Do they look the same?"

He frowned and put his phone next to the paper. With them upside down, I couldn't get a clear view to help with the comparison. "I won't even pretend I'm a handwriting expert," he said. "But in my humble opinion, no."

He slid his phone across the booth. I turned the paper so the writing was right-side-up to me. I studied the two samples and sighed.

"I hate to say so, but I agree. Oh well, it was fun while it lasted." I pushed his phone back to him. "But I'm still curious about what the note says."

"It looks like a thank you note to a guy named Antoine. It refers to invaluable services. That's why I got so excited—it reads like a semi-official document."

We both looked up as a group of teenage boys entered the restaurant, laughing and talking loudly. One of them spotted us and waved. "Hey, Mr. B.," he called, and headed our direction, weaving through the tables. He seemed unsteady on his feet.

"One of my students," Carl said quietly. He turned to face the young man. "Hey, Kody. What's up? Ready for the test on Friday?"

Kody grabbed a chair from a nearby table and plopped it at the end of the booth, the back of the chair towards the table. He straddled it, facing us.

"I still have two days to study," he grinned. "But if it's okay with you, I'll stay after class tomorrow. I need to ask you about something."

I caught the faintest hint of alcohol on his breath and glanced at Carl, whose face was expressionless. "Hey man, stop sucking up to your teacher and get over here and order," one of the other boys called.

"Yeah, I'll leave you to your date." Kody grinned. "Later."

Carl didn't bother correcting him like I expected. "See you in class tomorrow."

Kody abandoned his chair and returned to his friends. "What was that about?" I asked when he was out of earshot.

"That group has been acting oddly at school," he said, indicating the boys with a jerk of his head. "I thought they were just sneaking out for a smoke or something."

"It wasn't tobacco I smelled on his breath."

He nodded. "I caught it too. I wonder where they're getting it."

I remembered my high school days. There was always a way to get alcohol if we wanted it. I guess nothing had changed.

Carl and I exchanged phone numbers before heading our separate ways. I still wanted him to try to translate the note for my peace of mind. Plus, my innate research curiosity was still in high gear. After getting my hopes up, it was hard to accept that the note was a fake. Did that mean the cufflinks were fake, despite Gary's tests?

Back home, with a glass of ice tea within easy reach and my laptop booted, I ignored the stack of work I'd planned to do. I wanted to find out more about the end of royalty in France and my loveseat was the perfect place to do it. Sure, I knew the basics of the French Revolution and Napoleon's reign, but that was where my knowledge ended.

Several hours and half a pitcher of ice tea later, I'd learned more. Enough to wonder if the note was real after all. I'd found another picture of the signature of Louis Philippe, the last king of France, and that one looked more like the one on the note. Time to bring in an expert.

I didn't expect to find one in Oak Grove. If I got lucky I'd find one in Pittsburgh or Cleveland. I didn't want to go anywhere that required getting on a plane. Flying freaked me out.

I'd never had a bad experience on a plane—at

least not that I can remember. But there's something about hurtling through the sky at thirty thousand feet trapped in a tin can without a parachute that bothered me. If Eli lived on the West Coast, our relationship would have been doomed before it started. At least his place in Florida was within driving distance of Oak Grove.

When all the experts my first search found lived in England, I almost gave up. But one thing I've learned is by changing the words in a query different results are displayed. So, I did. And the internet gods smiled on me and I found a professor in Louisiana who specialized in French history. Made sense because so many settlers in that region had ancestral ties to France.

My email to him was cryptic. I mentioned a rare document, the last king, and the unique opportunity to authenticate a previously lost piece of French history. Every credential I'm entitled to use followed my signature. When I hit the send button, I crossed my fingers that I'd woven a fine enough web to capture his interest. Then I fell into bed.

❋ ❋ ❋

"Call me when you get there." I leaned into the Charger planning to kiss Jake on the cheek. His trunk and back seat were stuffed with suitcases, boxes, and bags of his clothes and belongings, and I worried he'd have a hard time seeing traffic around him.

He turned his head at just the wrong moment

and I ended up kissing his nose. Jake being Jake, couldn't resist the opportunity. He pulled my head down farther and planted a big, juicy kiss on my lips. "If you ever get tired of Eli, you know how to reach me," he said, grinning. "Chicago isn't that far away."

I swatted him on the shoulder. "Don't hold your breath. Besides, you'll be too busy chasing every woman in the bar to miss me."

His face turned suddenly serious. "I'll always have time for you."

If he kept it up, I might cry. I couldn't let him see that. I straightened and patted the roof of the car. "Watch out for the police. This car's a cop magnet."

He nodded and started the engine. "I'll be careful. Getting a ticket would ruin the trip." He backed out of the driveway, revved his motor and squealed his tires as he pulled away. I hoped none of the Oak Grove force was anywhere nearby. There were still a few of them who would like nothing better than to give Jake a ticket or find an excuse to arrest him.

I sat on the front steps, my coffee cup in one hand and a book I'd taken out of my purse in the other. The friends who owned the camper that Jake had been living in were due to arrive at any time to retrieve it. They had a secure storage spot to store it in, and I didn't want to risk it getting vandalized while sitting empty on the property. Besides, Sarah had an appointment to show the house in the afternoon and 'suggested' it should 'disappear' before that.

I take pride in being able to finish every book I start but this one tested my limits. I'd picked it up on a whim, but I couldn't take the idea of a billionaire vampire dinosaur shifter as a hero seriously. That may have been the point, but I wasn't in the mood for a romantic farce disguised as a cozy mystery.

Even drunk, I wouldn't be able to read it, and I couldn't foist it off on any of my friends with a clear conscience. I wondered if there was time to ditch it in the camper, buried in the bottom cabinet behind the pots and pans. If my friends ever found it, they'd never connect it to me.

The vehicle pulling into the driveway as I exited from the camper wasn't my friends' truck. It was too early to be Sarah and her potential buyers so I hurried around to the front of the house, unsure of whom it might be. I'd left my purse—and Betsy—on the porch.

I didn't recognize the shiny dark blue car parked in the driveway, and I reassured myself it was someone lured in by the "For Sale" sign. Still, I hurried to the porch, grabbed my handbag, and slung it over my shoulder. That put Betsy within easy reach. "Can I help you?" I called to the visitor, still sitting in his car.

Shock made me straighten my spine and place my right hand inside the purse. I recognized the head that stuck out of the open car window. "You the realtor?" asked Paul, one of the men from The Dog House that fateful night.

"No, it's being represented by Oak Grove

Realty. There are brochures by the sign." I was on alert status and hoped he'd drive away.

No such luck. "Hey, don't I know you?" Paul opened the car door and got out. "You're one of those stuck-up chicks that hassled us a few weeks ago."

My memory of the incident was radically different but it wasn't a good time to argue about it. "Like I said, there are brochures available by the street. I can't help you." While I wished Jake had stuck around for a few minutes longer, I tightened my fingers around Betsy's handle.

"You planning on buying the place?"

Did I want him buying the house? He didn't fit the mold of the imaginary family I dreamed of living there. If he moved in all the hard work we'd put into fixing and remodeling would get buried under an avalanche of beer bottles and pizza boxes. "It's an old house," I said with a shrug, "Something always breaking when you least expect it."

He sneered. "If you think you can talk me out of putting in a bid, you're wrong."

I faked a yawn. "Whatever." With the right to refuse any offer written into my contract with the agency, I didn't have to worry. "Not my problem."

He took several steps towards me. "What are you doing here if you aren't interested in the house?"

I raised both eyebrows. "That's none of your business," I snapped. The dude was seriously starting to creep me out. I sized him up, wondering what his weak spots were, and which self-defense moves would be the most effective against him.

"You think you're so tough." He took two more steps.

Unable to stop myself, I giggled. "You sound like the villain in a bad movie." I pointed one finger at him. "Next you'll say 'You won't feel so tough once I get done with you.' Right?"

He turned as red as the decorative bark in the flower bed. "That's not what I was going to say," he spluttered.

"I'll bite. What were you going to say?"

He turned and stomped his way back to his car like a petulant four-year-old. "We'll see who gets the house." He got back into the car, slammed the door shut and started the motor. Tires squealing, he backed down the driveway and onto the street. As he pulled away, my friend's truck came around the corner and I breathed a sigh of relief.

Chapter 9

"You can't convince me it was a coincidence." I swirled my ice tea, trying to mix the sugar in better. The ice cubes clanked against the glass even after I stopped.

"That's the way real estate works." Sarah wiped condensation from her glass before it dripped onto her pants. We sat on the steps leading to my apartment, discussing the couple she'd shown the house to earlier. "Random people drive by a house, see the sign, walk around it, and they're done. If they're curious, they might show up to an open house. It doesn't look as if we need to schedule one for your place. There's plenty of interest in it already."

"How much of that is due to curiosity? People who want to see where the murder took place?" Until Sarah told me, I didn't know we needed to disclose to potential buyers that a murder occurred in the back yard, even though *that* murder happened months ago.

"The other agents in town are aware of the history of the house. They won't waste their time showing it to people who aren't qualified to buy it. We may be competitors but we work together more often than not."

I doubted Paul met the needed financial criteria needed. That took one worry off my mind. "How long until you hear back from the couple you took to the house this afternoon?" I'd caught a glimpse of them as I drove away. They looked nice enough.

"I told you, it can take a while to sell a house. You can't expect the first people to look at it to put in an offer. Those two were looking for something more modern. They'll end up in that new development outside of town in a house they can't afford that looks like it was built in a factory. In seven years, unless he gets a promotion, they'll fight about money and get divorced."

That was a side of Sarah I'd never seen before. The cynicism, that is. She was usually all sunshine. "Are you going to tell me about it?"

"What?"

"Whatever's bugging you. If Freddie's giving you a hard time, tell me. I'll take him down a peg or two."

I was hoping for an answering giggle but I got a deep sigh instead.

"He asked me to move in with him."

Well, it wasn't quite a marriage proposal, but it was a step in that direction. "Congratulations! Why are you sitting here instead of packing?"

"We'd been talking about how bad the real

estate market is when he asked me." She finished her tea and dumped her ice cubes on the lawn. Piper rushed over to nose at them.

"So?"

"I don't want him to feel obligated. And I don't want the only reason I say yes to be the lack of money."

"If I know you, you have at least three months' worth of savings. You've been through these slumps before. What's different this time?" I reached over the fence to pat Piper, who decided the ice cubes were crunchy treats.

"Nothing, I guess."

"Then what's holding you back?"

Another long sigh. "I don't know. Fear of commitment maybe? I've been on my own for a long time. How do I adjust to being with someone all the time and having to compromise on everything?"

If I wasn't careful, the conversation could go wrong fast. The last thing Sarah needed was for me to tell her my woes. "I'm not going to be much help with that. Have you talked to Freddie about it? Seems like he'd be having the same worries."

"What would you do?"

She was hitting too close to the bone. Time to steer this another way. "Freddie and I would kill each other within a week."

This time I got the hoped-for smile. "It still freaks me out that you two dated."

"It's even freakier that we both survived the experience." Although Freddie almost didn't. Not because I tried to kill him, but because someone else tried to kill him to keep him away from me. Long story.

She grinned and shook her head. "You're no help."

"Like I'm in any shape to give advice. My track record is less than spectacular."

"At least you're doing better now you and Eli found each other."

I'd let her go on thinking that. No sense in ruining the illusion.

With the day shot as far as work went, I doubled down on my research time that evening. I decided to go for quantity, not quality. There were a few jobs that could be knocked off with only minimal time investment. They were also more boring topics so it seemed appropriate to ease the situation with a glass or two of wine. The Argentinian Malbec I'd picked up would be a fine companion for the evening. As a bonus, chilling it to the proper temperature took a matter of minutes.

The legend of Johnny Appleseed had been thoroughly researched by historians, but separating the stories from fact wasn't easy. I gathered as many sources as I could, documented their varying opinions, and forwarded the information to my client. She'd need to make the final call on truth or legend for herself.

I glanced at the clock wondering if it was a good

idea to start another project. It was midnight, and if I wanted to get back on schedule, I should go to bed. Eli hadn't called but he got as deeply involved in his work as I did mine. Then I realized Jake hadn't called either to tell me he'd arrived safely. It seemed as if he was returning to his old habits. I hoped that didn't include one particular habit that meant sneaking around in the middle of the night.

Guilt set in. We'd made a game out of him sneaking into my place when I wasn't around. He always left an obvious sign he'd been there. A cushion out of place, my books rearranged, a fresh flower on the table. He'd drill me later on the changes to make sure I'd paid attention. Keeping me safe, he said. Or had it been an excuse to keep certain skills of his fresh? Did that make me complicit in any crimes he might or might not commit in the future?

My imagination was running away with me again. Jake had been a model citizen since being released from prison. He deserved better than for me to speculate that he'd gone to Chicago for anything but a job.

But as I pulled my blankets down and got ready to crawl into my bed, I decided to text him in the morning just to say hi.

❊ ❊ ❊

I did my best to concentrate on the few remaining jobs for the writers group. With a personal goal of working three straight hours before

I took a break, I pushed myself through four books on the female "computers" of World War II. It was too easy to miss details working that way, but all my client needed was a broad overview.

To save a few dollars, I planned to go home for lunch instead of eating at the diner down the street. Even if I factored in the extra mileage and the rising price of gasoline, I'd save a significant amount over the course of a month eating at home. I'd miss the gossip from my favorite waitress but I'd adjust.

On the landing halfway up the stairs, I paused, leaned against the railing, and studied the back yard. If I moved to a big city, I'd never find an apartment like mine again. I'd be lucky to rent two small rooms for the price I paid for the entire floor. And I'd have to say goodbye to the grass, trees and flowers I enjoyed seeing from my kitchen window.

The second half of the steps seemed longer than the first. Oh, they weren't—I'd counted them enough times, but each one I climbed made me wonder how many more times I'd get to do that. By the time I got to the top, I had to blink away the tears before unlocking my door.

I flipped another page in the book I was reading—a romance novel—as I finished my sandwich. That was an added benefit to my new routine, more time to read, although I needed to expand my collection of books waiting to be read. The plot of this one was particularly predictable and each time a new sex scene started, I flipped the pages to get to the story again. As I got up to rinse off my plate, my cell phone rang with the ring tone for Joe, The Marines' Hymn.

I dug it out of my purse and answered before he hung up. "You home?" he asked. "I thought I heard you up there."

"Yeah, I came home for lunch." I should have warned the boys about my new routine so they wouldn't worry.

"Can you come down? There's a lady here to see you and I don't think she's in any shape to come to you. We're on the front porch."

"Who is she?"

His answer came in a whisper, "She won't say. But don't worry, there's no way she's a threat to you."

He may have meant that to be encouraging, but with the mood I was in, it struck me as a warning. Still, I didn't see any other rational response. "I'll be right there."

The cane leaning against the chair should have been my first clue. But my visitor's back was to me when I came around the corner of the porch, and the short blond hair didn't belong to anyone I knew. It wasn't like I was famous and got random people dropping by on a regular basis, so as I turned to face her, my nerves were on edge. Unexpected visitors usually meant bad news.

Between the recent and badly done haircut and the still healing cuts and dark bruises on her face, along with a collection of gauze wrappings on her arms, it took a minute to recognize her. The dark glasses hiding her eyes didn't help. Although I'd only met her once in real life, I'd studied her picture enough on the internet to make the connection. "Annabelle! Hi! How are you?"

I caught Joe's startled expression from the corner of my eye, but it was her reaction that stunned me.

"You!" she hissed. She raised her right arm and pointed at me, but the movement was labored. The pale green golf shirt she wore fit tightly over her many bandages. "You," she said again. "This is your goddamn fault."

Chapter 10

I must have stood with my mouth hanging wide open for a full minute before reaching into my pocket for my phone. I wanted Dan or Freddie or someone official as a witness. But I'd left it on the kitchen table next to my book. Joe and Luke would have to do.

"What are you talking about?"

"I was this friggin' close to breaking the case and then you and your friends fucked up everything." She waggled her finger at me, and the movement made her catch her breath.

"Should you still be in the hospital?" If that small of a motion hurt I was concerned for her. "How did you get here?"

"The hospital sucks. The food sucks and hell, having a cop outside my door sucks." She waved one hand towards the street. "I checked myself out and my sister came and got me. If I'm going to be miserable at least I'm going to be miserable in my own fucking bed."

I wondered how much of her bad language was due to pain or if she always cursed that much. A swear word sprinkled in here and there didn't bother me but she seemed unable to talk without using a string of them. "I'm surprised the cop let you leave."

"Shit, there wasn't anything he could do about it. I'm not under arrest or anything."

"Aren't you worried about whoever did this to you trying again?"

She eyed me before spitting out her answer. "I'll have a gun on me if they do. And I'm not afraid to use it. I hope they do show up. That way I can look them in the eye before I pull the trigger."

"Them? Them who?"

"What business is it of yours?"

None, I supposed. But that wasn't what I told her. "You made it my business when the sheriff found my name in your purse and questioned me."

She swore again, with passion. "They took every other damned thing out of my purse and left that. I don't know why the hell I kept it."

"It's almost like they tried to frame me," I said quietly. The idea had just popped into my head.

"You're a nobody. Why would anyone want to set you up?"

Joe coughed. I suspected he was covering a laugh.

"You tell me what you know about who attacked you and I'll tell you why."

She squinted her eyes, considering the deal. "You first."

I considered the possibilities and went with the easiest. "Claude Corsinski. He had a nice little scam going on, along with a nationwide string of jewelry thefts. I may have dropped a few hints that led the FBI to him. He's in prison, but he has friends on the outside." That underplayed my role in the events but bragging wasn't my specialty.

Annabelle's eyes widened. "Fuck. That's a good one. Okay, I'll tell you mine. I've told the cops this, so it's not a secret. There were two men. They grabbed me after work as I headed to my car. They didn't talk, but guys walk different than women. It probably has to do with their balls getting in the way. And they hit too damned hard to be chicks."

Nothing I could do would stop the heat rising in my cheeks so I pushed onward. "I hope you got in a few hits of your own."

She scowled. "A few. A lot of good it did me."

"Any idea who they were?"

Her frown got deeper. "No. They wore masks, so I never saw their faces. And they had on long sleeved shirts and gloves, so if they had tattoos I didn't see 'em."

I gave her points for remembering the details. "What case were you working on?" I hoped we'd developed enough of a connection that she'd tell me.

"Ha! Not happening, bitch. This case is my ticket out of that podunk town I'm stuck in. If I solve it, I'll be right up there with the big boys." Leaning heavily on the arms of the chair, she leveraged herself to a standing position and grabbed the cane.

"I'll be back. And you'd better fuckin' stay out of my way."

Like the gentleman he was, Joe jumped up and helped her wobble her way down the stairs and sidewalk to a car parked on the street. Another lady, whom I assumed was the sister, jumped out from the driver's side and came around and opened the passenger's door. He stepped back and waited while they fiddled with the seat belt.

Joe, who *never* swore around me although he knew plenty of banned words, rejoined us on the porch before they drove away. He waited until they were halfway down the block before he grinned and said, "Well, wasn't that fucking interesting? I think someone needs to buy a damned thesaurus."

It took a while for the three of us to stop laughing. When I finally sobered up, I asked the $64,000 question. "So who do I call? Dan or Deputy Nelson?"

❋ ❋ ❋

Janine was kind enough to let me use one of the library's small conference rooms. By the time Dan got back to me, and then reached the deputy, I'd returned to work. Not wanting to have the conversation where library patrons could overhear it, I'd begged her for a favor and she'd granted it.

I recited the story for the deputy, having already

shared it with Dan, leaving out the superfluous words. Other than the muscle in his cheek twitching, he didn't react. When I finished talking, he pushed his chair back, stood, and strode out of the room.

"That bad?" I asked.

Dan patted my hand. "It wasn't. You couldn't see it, but he pulled his phone out of his belt. He'll be back."

We spent a few minutes discussing this year's high school football team's prospects for winning a game. I contended, like I did every year, that they had a chance of making the district finals. Dan argued that, based on their history, a good season would be more than winning two games.

Our friendly argument was interrupted by Nelson's return. "I caught the sheriff at his desk," he said. He remained standing, so I figured he didn't plan to stay long. "The sheriff asked me to convey his thanks for your cooperation."

"That's it?" I asked as he turned to leave.

"What did you expect, Miss Duprie?"

A ticker-tape parade would be nice, but I didn't think there was any possibility for *that* to happen. "How about telling me I'm no longer under suspicion for the murder, for starters?"

He blinked rapidly several times, then stared at me for a long moment. "You are no longer under active investigation," he said. "That's as much as I can tell you."

Dan jumped in before I could get myself into trouble. "Thank you, Deputy. If you need anything all four of the men and discovered, to my surprise, they else, please give me a call."

I waited until the deputy was truly gone before I opened my mouth again. "That's it?" I spluttered. "Thank you and by the way, you're still under suspicion? What do I have to do to clear my name?"

Dan sighed. "You know how these things work, Harmony. The wheels of justice turn slowly."

I resolved to figure out a way to make them speed up. If that meant solving the murder myself, so be it.

❋ ❋ ❋

I didn't want to show up at the Dog House on my first attempt to go undercover, so I picked another bar with a slightly better reputation. With any luck, Charlie's attracted a similar crowd and the patrons' gossip might give me insight to unofficial speculations about the murder. More worried about my lack of feminine guile than my disguise, I still stopped for a second look in the mirror before leaving. If I got lucky, I'd get an inkling about Annabelle's case too.

Most of my camouflage came from thrift shops in Pittsburgh. Old jeans, tank tops, and plaid shirts, paid for in cash, to make the purchases untraceable. All except for the bright red wig. It came from a costume store. Still, it looked real.

And I'd spent far too much time watching on-line videos on techniques for applying makeup. My makeup supplies had swelled to never-before-seen proportions. I hadn't owned this many colors of eye shadows and lipsticks even in high school.

For a finishing touch, I knotted the pink plaid shirt under my breasts, exposing the black tank top underneath it. With a final fluff of the wig, I nodded in satisfaction. In the harsh lights of my bathroom, I looked sufficiently unlike myself to suit my purposes. And in the typical dim lighting of a typical bar, my alter-ego should fool everyone.

I tottered down the steps clutching my purse with Betsy stowed inside, reminding myself I was Tiffini Rain. I'd never be able to run or throw a kick in the five-inch heels strapped to my feet, so I needed protection. Hopefully, I wouldn't use it, but better with than without it.

Delores didn't lend herself to undercover work, so I left her at home and made my precarious way to the all-night convenience store several blocks away. I called a cab from the pay phone outside while ignoring the stares of men going in to buy cigarettes and snacks. I didn't know if I'd overdone the makeup, or they were working up the courage to approach the new chick in the neighborhood. Anyway, I pretended to keep talking on the phone hoping it would deter them from approaching me.

When the cab eventually pulled up, I glanced their direction to discover they were gone. It almost made me sad. Maybe Tiffini wasn't as attractive as I thought.

It was weird paying the cab driver in cash.

Although I always carried some bills, it made me uneasy leaving my one credit card at home and having only cash on me. I couldn't do anything about my driver's license, but I didn't expect to need it. No one in their right mind would think I was underage.

I gave the driver a too-large tip with the hopes that it would make him eager to pick me up for my return trip. Desperately wishing I had back-up, I strutted into the bar with an air of confidence I didn't feel. Tiffini wouldn't be nervous, would she? But Batman had his Robin, Sherlock Holmes had Watson, and I had—no one.

The booming of the jukebox greeted me as I opened the bar's front door. I needed to bone up on my country music if I was going to hang out in this type of establishment. I'd never heard the song before, and had no idea who was singing. Hopefully, that wouldn't be an issue.

The bar was mostly empty; bad for the owner but good for me. The night was meant to be a dry run. I didn't anticipate overhearing any real information. Not that I'd be able to hear much conversation at all over the blaring music. After considering the seating options, I slid onto a barstool several spots down from the nearest male patron and ordered a light beer. That's what Tiffini would drink. I'd force it down my throat somehow.

It didn't take long for a warm body to slide into the barstool next to me. The middle-aged man with a bad comb-over hairdo and bulging stomach wasn't my type at all. But Tiffini would talk to him.

"How's it going, Sugar?" he said. "Buy you a drink?" He'd already had several drinks based on the smell of liquor on his breath.

I smiled and waved my beer bottle in front of his face. "Thanks! How about the next round?"

He waved to get the bartender's attention and pointed to me. "Another of those for the lady."

I wouldn't be drinking it, but I didn't stop him.

"What's your name, Sugar?" he asked.

God help me, I giggled. "Sugar will do fine for now. What's your name?"

"Dave." He took a swig of whatever poison he was drinking. "I haven't seen you around here before."

He looked like a Dave. His wife—yes, he was wearing a wedding ring—probably called him David when she was mad at him. "I'm new in town," I said. And giggled again. "Thought I'd get out and make some friends."

Dave grinned widely. At least he had a full set of teeth. "Why don't you come over and join me and my buds?"

I glanced over towards the table he indicated. The three men looked like clones of Dave. None of them appeared to be dangerous. It would likely be a waste of my time, but I picked up my beer and slid off the barstool. "Sure."

He grabbed my second beer and his own drink and we made our way across the room. One of them grabbed an empty chair from a nearby table. "Sugar, meet the guys. That's Bill, Harry, and Lamar."

They could have been Mo, Larry, and Curly for all I cared, but I grinned as I settled into one of the empty chairs. "Nice to meet you."

"Sugar's new around here," Dave announced. "So, I volunteered us to make her feel welcome."

I fluttered my fake eyelashes and giggled. "Sure is nice of y'all to let me join you."

I did my best impression of Tiffini flirting with were actually fun to talk to. I think they were surprised at my knowledge of Steeler's football, and that made Tiffini more of a friend than a target. The chair they'd given me had a view of the front door, and as was my habit, I'd been keeping an eye on it. It had opened and closed many times, but this time was different.

This time, when the door opened, he walked in.

Chapter 11

I hurriedly turned and picked up my beer bottle. Well, truth be told, my third bottle. But I didn't want Brent to see me, not sure how well my disguise would hold up to scrutiny. From the corner of my eye, I tracked his path to a table at the back of the room. There'd be no chance of overhearing any of his conversation from where I sat.

The best bet seemed to be playing it safe and cutting the night short, trying again another night. Once I'd established myself as Tiffini—or Sugar— I'd be able to ask questions about other bar patrons without raising suspicions.

When the Steelers made a goal and the patrons of the bar cheered, I patted Dave on the knee. "I'm going to the little girls' room," I said and giggled as I stood. I'd call the taxi from the restroom where it would be quieter. He nodded, watching the action on the big-screen. The extra point kick would decide the game. That made it a relatively safe time to stroll past Brent.

The trip to the restroom went without a hitch. I kept my face turned away from the table Brent shared with a couple other men, and I didn't get that tingling sensation I get when someone is watching me. I made my call, and the taxi agreed to pick me up in fifteen minutes. Must have been a slow night.

But when I opened the restroom door to return to the table with Dave and the other guys, Brent stood at the end of the little hallway, talking on his cell phone.

"When can I expect delivery?" he asked, talking so quietly I almost couldn't overhear him. I wondered what kind of business he was in. After a short pause, he grunted. "That soon? Tell the boys to watch their speed." He guffawed, and I assumed he was being sarcastic.

I longed to hear more, but he turned and I hustled to pretend I'd just opened the restroom door. "Scuse me," I muttered, brushing by him to seek the safety of my new friends. The back of my neck tingled, but he couldn't see my face so I was good. I hoped.

Although I didn't think Dave or his friends would do anything to hurt me, I only pretended to take a drink of my beer when I got back to the table. No sense in taking any unnecessary chances. I'd been 'roofied' once in my life, and that was one time too many.

"I'm calling it a night, guys," I said.

"So soon?" Harry protested. "The game's not over and the night is young."

I grimaced. "But work starts early and the Steelers have this one in the bag." I put on my coat and adjusted my purse's strap on my shoulder. "Catch you next game night."

"You need a ride home?" Dave asked. "I'm heading out pretty soon myself."

He'd drunk too much to be driving. "Thanks, but a taxi is on the way."

Dave stood, keeping his eye on the TV. "I'll wait with you," he offered.

"That's sweet of you." And I giggled again. I was beginning to hate the sound. "But I don't want you to miss the end of the game."

He hesitated, weighing the options. But with the Steelers in possession and twenty yards from the goal at third down, the lure of the action proved too much. "All righty then," he said, and settled back into his chair.

I waved to the bartender on my way out the door, having settled my bill much earlier. Or I guess I should say, Dave had settled it. Although the taxi hadn't arrived yet, my coat was warm enough to allow me to wait outside. The fresh air would do me good after being in the smoke-filled bar.

No one hung around the front door. I huddled in the doorway, trying to find shelter from a cold wind whipping around the corner of the building. The smell of rain saturated the air and puddles glistened in the parking lot.

While waiting, I pulled out my phone to see a couple of missed calls. Both were from Eli. Would he still be awake by the time I got home? I didn't want to risk someone leaving the bar and catch me being myself, not Tiffini, so I shot him a text. *"Sorry I didn't answer. I'm in the middle of a research job. Call you in a few."*

His answer arrived as I climbed into the cab. *"I'll be waiting."*

The wig was stashed away, the makeup washed off my face and I'd slipped into a flannel nightgown before I video-conferenced him. "Hey," I said when he answered.

"You're up late. Everything okay?"

Seeing his face on the laptop screen made me giddy, but the mood was tempered by the realization that he was so far away. "Steelers played on the West Coast," I told him. It wasn't a lie.

"Research, huh?"

"I was multi-tasking. I have to do something during the commercials." To be on the safe side, I opened another window on my computer and did a quick check of the final score. Yes, the Steelers won.

Eli chuckled. "I've done that before. I negotiated a new contract while watching a Magic game."

That was new. I didn't know Eli followed basketball. "Didn't they go out of business?" I teased. He mumbled a few words under his breath I didn't quite catch. "What's that, Sweetie?"

Once he started to call me Buttercup, I needed a nickname for him too. I wasn't very creative, and after the first time I called him "Sweetie" it stuck. He didn't seem to mind, and it fit him.

"Never mind," he said. "How are the renovations on the house?"

I grinned. Safe topic to switch to. "It's done and up for sale. A couple already took a tour but Sarah doubts they'll buy it. She doesn't think it's their style."

"She's the expert. Is Jake looking for somewhere else to live yet?"

"When was the last time you talked to him?"

"A couple of weeks ago. Why?"

"He's gone. Got a job in Chicago as a bouncer. Truth is, I'm worried. He hasn't called since he left a few days ago. I figured he was busy getting settled in and learning the ropes, but he should have let me know he made it okay."

"In other words, Jake is just being Jake. Have you tried to call him?"

Eli was right, and I should have known better. "No, because I didn't want to nag him."

"I'll call him tomorrow. Will that make you feel better?"

Yes, it would, but I didn't want to sound too eager. "I guess so."

"Do you want me to tell him to call you?"

"Only if you can make him think it's his idea."

Eli grinned and shook his head. "Are you asking me to manipulate Jake?"

"No," I answered quickly. I fiddled with a stray lock of hair. "Well, yes, I guess I am. If that's what it takes."

"Remind me to keep a close eye on you."

I couldn't resist. I unbuttoned the top button of

the nightgown and coughed to make my voice sound husky. "I've got something you should be keeping your eye on."

Eli groaned. "Don't start something we can't finish. You don't know how much I wish I was holding you right now."

Actually, I did. "How are we going to fix this, Eli?" I regretted saying the words as soon as they left my mouth.

"If you want it, I can have a ticket waiting for you at the airport tomorrow morning."

I could buy my own ticket but I don't like to fly. "I'm not allowed to leave," I said as an excuse.

"No arrest in the murder yet?"

"No. They aren't even saying if there's a suspect."

"These things can take a long time."

I grimaced. "I'm running low on patience."

"Let the sheriff do his job and stay out of his way, Buttercup. I can't stand not being there to protect you."

It was a good thing he didn't know what I was up to.

❀ ❀ ❀

My phone was set on silent as it always was when I'm at the library. When I'm deep in research mode, I don't hear it ring anyway. So it wasn't a surprise that I missed a text from Eli telling me he'd left a message for Jake. I saw it when I took my lunch break. At least Jake's phone was still working.

Not like last winter when Eli disappeared and his phone broke. I had one missed call as well. No message, and from an unknown number. Probably a sales call.

I texted him back with a simple *"thanks."* I kept the phone close all afternoon and checked it numerous times to make sure I didn't miss anything else. My life was anything but orderly at the moment, and if I could tie up even one loose thread, it would help.

With that in mind, I opened my email. I hadn't heard back from that French History professor. Maybe I hadn't made my message cryptic enough to catch his attention, or too vague? I hoped he wasn't like Jake and would actually answer my inquiry.

And bingo! There it was, mixed in with my spam.

"Ms. Duprie," the message read, *"Your inquiry has drawn my interest. Attached is a contract with my standard agreement for services as well as my hourly rate. Once I am in receipt of the signed forms along with your preferred method of payment, I will contact you with further instructions."* It was signed *"Louis Bouchard, Ph.D."*

I read through the documents with interest. First, to make sure they were on the up-and-up and second, because I needed an agreement like his. I'd done a job or two I'd never received payment for. Even if the good professor couldn't help me translate the note and determine its authenticity, he'd helped me out already.

The public WiFi at the library wasn't secure

enough for me to send a response that included credit card information. I'd need to wait until I got home. Tiffini wasn't scheduled for an appearance and my dance card was empty. There was time to visit those forums I'd found last spring and see if they had any new information about Jake.

Chapter 12

Through a guy who was now in jail, I'd been introduced to the underground forums for folks who followed jewelry thieves. Jake had a loyal following, although his fan numbers had declined the last time I checked. He'd been given credit for a few new jobs that were impossible for him to have accomplished since he'd been with me, but I only read the posts and never responded to them. Which made me wonder how many of the other jobs people claimed he pulled were pure speculation.

I was looking for anything new regarding Jake—new sightings, new heists, new stories. But when I tried to get to the right location—after muddying my trail by going through several proxy servers—I met a dead end. Either the forum moved or didn't exist anymore. I no longer had contact with the 'wrong' people to find out how to reconnect.

After restarting my computer to make my trail harder to track, the next item on my to-do list was sending the agreement and pre-payment to

Professor Bouchard. That only took a few minutes. Then a quick check of my email, finding nothing of interest, not even one research request. The evening was going from bad to worse.

A quick text to Eli to see if he wanted to chat ended up depressing me even more. He went to a restaurant with some friends and expected to get home late. I momentarily considered the concept his 'friends' were attractive females but dismissed the notion. At least from the rational right side of my brain.

A walk might distract me from my misery. I pulled on my coat, yanked my door open and was met by pounding rain driven into my face by hurricane force winds. Well, they weren't that strong, but in my mood, they might as well have been. What had I done to make the universe mad at me?

After a restless night, I dragged myself to the library. Even Dolores seemed reluctant to start when I turned the key. Or it was my imagination? But before I got to work, I called the garage to make an appointment to get her checked out.

Most people find it boring, looking up insignificant details of non-important dead people, but that day I took solace in reading familiar books. One of my authors set her newest book at the Claydon House, a country estate in England, and wanted as many details as possible to make her story authentic. That was the research I was most comfortable doing, and I happily settled into my normal routine.

I buried myself deep enough into work that when a buzzer sounded, I jumped and almost tipped over my chair. I reached for my cell phone, not wanting to miss a call. But it was silent, and I realized the noise was the alarm on my laptop, reminding me to take a lunch break.

Dolores seemed to be in a better mood too and started with her usual quiet purr. The sun peeked between the clouds several times on the trip home. I took it as a positive sign. The world had returned to normal.

But my hopes were dashed when I pulled into my parking spot on the street. The sedan sporting a light bar parked up the block couldn't be good news. I grabbed my phone and scrolled through the contacts to Dan's number. Until I found out what was going on, I wouldn't hit "send."

"Hello, Deputy," I said as he stepped out of his car. "What brings you into town? And do I need to call my lawyer?" I crossed my arms but kept my cell phone where it was visible.

"No, Miss Duprie, you don't need to call anyone. I'm not here on official business."

I arched one eyebrow and pointed to his transportation. "Looks official to me."

He exhaled. "I need your help. Unofficially."

After I returned my mouth to a closed position, I jerked my head towards the stairs. "Let's take this inside."

I offered him his choice of hot tea or coffee. He

chose coffee, matching my expectation. When I brought out the freshly brewed pot, I placed several coasters on the coffee table as well, hoping he'd get the hint. He did. After adding sugar—no cream— he carefully placed his cup on one of the coasters.

"So, what is it you need my assistance with?" I asked, blowing across the top of my cup to cool down the coffee.

"First, how much do you charge?" Deputy Nelson said. "This is coming out of my own pocket."

He must have been desperate. Rookie deputies didn't earn that much. "It depends on the project. My rates are adjustable."

After stirring his coffee a little too long, he grimaced and said, "What I'm going to tell you is privileged information. You can't tell anyone."

It didn't shock me at all. I casually leaned back into my chair, coffee cup clasped in in hand, crossed my legs and waited.

"I want you to gather more information on Annabelle LeRoix."

"What kind of information are you looking for?" I leaned forward, put my cup on its coaster, and focused my attention on the deputy. "And why?"

"I think she may have information regarding the murder. My theory is that whoever beat her up is tied to Tadd Foard's death. I need to know why she won't share that information and anything I can use to pressure her to reveal what she knows."

"You want to blackmail her?"

Deputy Nelson's cheeks reddened. "It's not blackmail. It's giving her an incentive to cooperate."

Good line. "I can tell you why, and I won't even charge you for the information. She wants to make a name for herself by cracking a big case she was working on. She said so that day she showed up here. As far as the rest goes, it'll cost you. But you're law enforcement and I'll give you a discount. As long, that is, as you assure me that I'm totally off the hook for the murder."

What I didn't tell him was he'd aroused my curiosity and I would do the research for free. What was Annabelle hiding? "Why aren't you doing it yourself?" Without waiting for an answer, I started plotting which sites to visit. And a trip to her hometown, but not as myself, as Tiffini. In a rented car.

The red in his cheeks got darker. "I suggested it to the sergeant. He told me in no uncertain terms that the county doesn't have the money to waste on a wild goose chase. And that if I wasn't such a rookie, I'd know better. I was pulled off the murder case, so I have no idea what's going on with it. The investigation is locked down tight. Tight enough I'm not even picking up on any gossip."

Now, I *had* to be involved. I named my price. A very low price. And it clearly wasn't low enough, because Deputy Nelson shook his head, set down his cup, and stood.

"Sorry to have wasted your time," he said. "But you're out of my league."

I stood too. "Tell me what you *can* pay."

"I only have a couple of hundred." He adjusted his duty belt. I pegged it as a sign of nervousness. "Won't pay for much of your time."

"Let me worry about that. If I don't find anything useful, I won't charge you at all. Deal?" I held out my hand.

His hesitation lasted only a fraction of a second. He grasped my hand and shook it. "Deal."

We finished the pot of coffee before I was satisfied I understood what he was looking for. He didn't expect to tie Annabelle to anything illegal; he'd already checked her legal history, and it was clean. His assumption was a particular incident sparked her interest in becoming a private investigator. If he knew that bit of information, he might be able to manipulate her into being more cooperative with the Sheriff's Department. His theory made sense and although it skirted my sense of ethics, I really wanted my reputation cleared.

"How often do you want me to check in with you?" I asked as I walked with him to the door. He'd provided me with his personal email and I gave him my business card with the "work" email address.

"Whenever there's news, I guess."

The worry in his eyes told me he lied. He hoped for a miracle. I doubted that I could conjure up one.

"How about I update you every three or four days?" It might take several weeks for me to track down any solid information.

He let his breath out slowly. "That'll work."

I doubted he made it to his car before the computer finished booting. I usually left it behind the desk at the library when I went to lunch but, this one time, I'd brought it home. Those missing seven years of Annabelle's life seemed the logical place to start.

The hometown paper didn't reveal anything more in my second search than the first time I'd checked. Finally it struck me that the on-line archives were spotty. Not every issue of the paper was included, and not every article. Although I couldn't imagine Tiffini going to the library that would be the first stop on my trip. They were sure to have copies of the paper on microfiche.

Tiffini needed an expanded wardrobe because experience told me scanning that many years of records would take several days. I'd pass through Pittsburgh on my way and knew which thrift shops stocked what I wanted.

If I dropped off Dolores at the mechanics for a checkup, no one would question the rental vehicle. As long as I stayed in a motel with WiFi, I'd still be able to work on my paying research gigs. I'd tell Luke and Joe I was headed out of town so they wouldn't worry. I swirled my now-cold coffee in the cup and tried to think of missing details. It wouldn't hurt to get a couple of those pre-paid credit cards so I didn't have to use my own.

Too bad the trip took me away from Chicago. Maybe I'd make a trip there later. I still hadn't heard from Jake.

Chapter 13

It would be overly obvious if I took off right away. Someone might have seen Deputy Nelson at my place. So, I delayed my trip for a few days. If I dropped Dolores off at the mechanic late on Friday, it would provide an even better excuse for renting a car as the garage closed on the weekend.

The time spent waiting wasn't wasted. I still had a few jobs to finish up for the writers' group. The professor wondered if I could get a better copy of the note, which I gladly supplied. I made a trip to water the flowers and cleaned off the muddy footprints left on the front porch by a curious passer-by.

And there was the time I spent reading Chicago newspapers, looking for evidence Jake had fallen back into his old profession. The overwhelming lists of recent crimes made me thankful I lived in the little town of Oak Grove. At least he wasn't listed as the victim of any of the crimes, and I found no burglaries I could attribute to him. At least, nothing

seemed to be in the technique I thought he'd use.

The no-tell motel I pulled into at the edge Charleston was every bit as bad as expected. "One key or two?" the front desk clerk leered as I handed over cash to pay for the night. I'd changed into my newly acquired Tiffini wardrobe at a rest stop outside of Pittsburgh.

"Only one." My Tiffini persona wouldn't be bothered by his attitude, so I let it slide. He didn't ask for my ID, but a security camera behind him rotated back and forth. My visit wasn't going to be completely untraceable.

"If you have any 'guests' there'll be an added charge."

I pretended to not understand his insinuation. "Don't worry, that won't be happening." The chances of anyone I knew showing up in Charleston were slim to none. And I planned to avoid Annabelle if our paths crossed.

He grunted and pushed a key-card over the desk towards me. "You're in 212. Checkout time is eleven."

"What's the Wi-Fi password?" I shoved the key into my jeans pocket, surprised they didn't use old-fashioned physical keys.

He raised an eyebrow. "No password. You got a channel I should follow?"

I couldn't stop the heat rising in my cheeks. "No." I turned and hurried out the door, hoping he'd be gone when I checked out in the morning. Although I planned to spend more than one night in town, I planned on changing motels each day to make it harder to track me.

I hauled my suitcase up the exterior stairs to the second floor. Thankfully, the room was located away from the ice and vending machines. That was the only good thing going for it. The smell of stale cigarette smoke greeted me as I opened the door. The old quilt on the double bed appeared clean but I didn't trust it. No matter. My own sheets and a blanket were packed in a second suitcase so I didn't have to risk picking up anything from theirs. I'd seen too many news stories of the hidden dirt a black light revealed.

But changing the bedding would wait until after my trip to the main library. It stayed open until nine, and that gave me time to scope out its setup. Then I'd pick a local bar for supper. I didn't expect to pick up any information on Annabelle right away but wanted to introduce Tiffini to the right—or wrong—people.

I wanted to rub my eyes when I left the library. Reading the microfiche files while wearing contacts didn't work so well. But Tiffini wouldn't be caught dead wearing glasses, so I'd have to suffer through it.

I'd found nothing of interest. Nothing about Annabelle during those missing years. But I'd barely scratched the depths of the archives, having only made it through three months of the local newspaper. To get through two years' worth in a couple of days, I needed to figure out a different system. Concentrate on the police reports and society pages and skip everything else.

Between the long drive and the eye strain, the plan for supper at a local bar no longer seemed like a good idea. Instead, I picked up a pre-made salad and bottled water at a grocery store deli on my way back to my room. Besides, among the several calls I'd missed was one from Eli. The way I felt, even the sound of his voice made me want to cry.

At least I had a good excuse for keeping my answer to a phone call so he wouldn't see my surroundings or my tears. "Hey, Sweetie," I said when he answered after the first ring.

"Hey, yourself. How are you doing?"

"Tired." It was an honest answer. "Sorry I missed your call. I was at the library with the phone on silent." I didn't say *which* library. The bed creaked as I settled myself against the headboard.

"Big project?"

"Yep. It's a challenge. I'm trying to track down information about someone's grandmother. The ancestry sites don't have much on her besides her name and date of birth." Half-truth, half lie. Guilt would catch up to me later. Or regret.

"Sounds interesting. Anyone I might have heard of?"

"Not unless you lived in Philadelphia in the 1920's." Where that came from I wasn't sure, but it was a good line.

"Right. I actually lived in New England back

then. Did I tell you I'm a vampire and immortal?"

And that's another reason I loved him. He always knew how to make me forget my problems. I giggled. "Good grief," I fake-gasped. "How old are you? Is that why you have such a fascination with kissing my neck!"

His voice deepened and he growled, "That's not the only part of your body I'm fascinated with."

The conversation was heading into dangerous territory and I liked it. "There's certain parts of your body I'm fixated on, too."

"Oh, yea?" His voice got deeper.

I wondered if he was as hot and bothered as me. Not wanting to have phone sex in a strange motel room I wasn't completely secure in, I decided to let us both off the hook. As far as I could tell, there were no hidden cameras in the room—and I'd checked—but I wasn't taking any chances that I'd show up on a porn site later. "Your eyes," I said. "I love your eyes. What were you thinking?" Eli had the palest blue eyes I'd ever seen but they were also the most expressive eyes I'd ever known.

"My eyes? Really? I got teased so bad about my eyes when I was a kid."

"They're unique. I started to fall in love with you the first time I looked into them."

There was a long silence on the other end and then a chuckle. "You finally said it."

"Said what?"

"You said you loved me."

We'd been dancing around that word for months, neither one of us willing to be the first to use it. And I hadn't meant to say it. I frantically but unsuccessfully tried to find a way to squirm out of it.

"I suppose you're going to hold it over my head every chance you get," I said, my mouth suddenly dry. I reached for the bottle of water on the nightstand. Would he say it back? Did I want him too? I'd imagined our initial declaration of love, if there ever was one, would happen under much more romantic circumstances. Or at least face-to-face.

"I love your eyes, too," he said. "The way they light up when you open the door and see me."

I silently let out the breath I'd been holding.

"And your mouth. The way it scrunches up when you're thinking hard."

Did my mouth really do that? Still, it was nice for him to say that.

"And your hair. I love taking your hair out of the bun and running my fingers through it."

I knew that, but hearing him say so made me smile.

He laughed. "Most of all, I love that baked spaghetti dish you make."

If I could have thrown something at him, I would have.

"And yes, Harmony Duprie, I love you."

For that moment, my doubts about our relationship disappeared. "I love you too, Elijah Hennessey."

The floating-on-air feeling followed me to the

library in the morning. I hummed as I sat down at the microfiche machine, drawing a dirty look from the librarian at the front desk. I grinned at her, put one finger across my lips, turned back to the machine, and started humming again. More quietly this time, so I didn't disturb any other patrons. Not that there were any nearby. Everyone else was scattered in the stacks choosing books to read or perusing periodicals.

By noon, I still hadn't found any information on Annabelle I didn't already know. And I'd made it through six months of papers using my new system. Her name appeared in none of the countless lists of students receiving honors from their colleges in various locations. It didn't show up in police reports or any of the social pages. As frustrating as I found it, I knew anyone searching for me on the internet would fall down the same black hole. Until a couple of years ago, anyway, when Jake and I were busted on the trumped up charges of selling drugs. Which showed me the dark side of Jake and was why I broke up with him and eventually ended up with Eli.

I used my lunch break to check the Chicago papers because Eli had mentioned not hearing from Jake. Still nothing. They say no news is good news, but I wasn't so sure.

My mid-afternoon break was used for checking into a different hotel. Although this one also accepted cash and didn't ask for ID, it seemed less skeevy than the first one. The front desk clerk was an older woman who barely glanced at me during the entire check-in process. Still, I did my standard check of the room looking for hidden cameras or microphones and found nothing. That didn't stop me from putting my own sheets on the bed.

By the time the library closed, I decided I needed a totally different approach. I found no mention of Annabelle in the newspaper's archives, but the address of her office was prominently displayed on her social media page. If she showed up for work in the morning, I'd follow her around. I was willing to bet she went to the same place for lunch every day, and maybe the same spot after work. I'd make a follow-up trip to those same places after she left and talk to the employees.

Still mapping out my plans for the morning—where would I park? Did I need to buy a pair of binoculars first?—I pulled into the parking lot of the bar I'd chosen for a drink. Just one, to get the lay of the land. It looked like the kind of place where cheaters would go. A little on the trashy side, but not taken over by meth-heads. A place where a private eye might hang out to catch a straying spouse in the act.

And there, holding court at the bar, was the last person I expected to see.

Jake.

Chapter 14

He'd dyed his hair blond and wore a pair of glasses, but it was Jake. The grin was unmistakable as well as that voice. That was no doppelganger. I froze in the doorway for a moment too long. He looked up and our eyes met.

I swirled and headed back to the rental car, praying my disguise had held and knowing it hadn't. There'd been a flash of recognition in his eyes. If I was lucky, I could get the car started and pull away before he extracted himself from the grasp of the barflies hanging around him.

My hands shook as I pulled the keys out of my purse and fumbled for the unlock button. I hit the lock button first and jumped when the horn blared. Second attempt, I hit the right button and none too gracefully, yanked open the car door and slid into the front seat.

After getting the right key into the ignition and starting the car, I reached without looking to close the car door. A mistake. I should have done that first. When I pulled, the door didn't budge. Two large hands held it firmly in place. Jake's hands.

"What the hell are you doing here? And where's Dolores?"

The best defense is a good offense. "I can ask you the same thing. We aren't in Chicago."

He scowled. "I can't discuss that right now."

"Then neither can I. Let go of the door, Jake." I pulled on the handle, but it barely budged.

The overhead light of the car shone on his ghostly pale face. "I have to get back inside. Where are you staying? I'll come by when I'm done here."

"What if I don't want you to?"

"Please, Angel, I'll explain later."

I was no good at turning Jake down when he asked for things nicely. "The Starlight Motel," I said. "Room 219. I'm signed in as Tiffini Rain if anyone asks what you're doing there."

Both of his eyebrows rose and several wrinkles formed in his forehead. Then a smile took over his face. "I'll see you in a few, Tiffini. Wait up for me." He closed the car door and stepped back. Tires squealing, I pulled away. When I looked in my rearview mirror, he still stood there.

I didn't head straight back to the hotel, however. Hell, no. I needed food, and if he got to the motel before me, he could damn well wait. With little to choose from that time of night, I made do with a salad from a fast food place. It was at least partially nutritious, if not fresh.

No surprise, Jake wasn't waiting at the motel when I got there. I set my salad aside for a few minutes while going through the room one more time looking for any hidden bugs. Call me paranoid, but I had the feeling whatever he was going to tell me shouldn't be on record. My little portable bug scanner didn't find anything, assuring me we could safely say whatever needed to be said.

The WiFi in the room barely had enough speed for me to check my email, so I turned on the TV and scanned the channels while I ate. I don't watch much television, so I settled on a news channel. Somewhere along the way, I fell asleep.

And woke up to a pounding on my door. "Harm—Tiffini, are you in there?"

I rolled over to get off the bed, knocking the remains of my salad on top of my blanket. Great. I'd have to use one of the motel's tonight. Yuck. But Jake was knocking again, and I didn't want him to wake up my neighbors if I had any. I ignored the mess and opened the door, after peering through the peephole to make sure it was really him. "Quiet," I hissed.

With a glance over his shoulder, he shoved his way into the room and closed the door, locking it behind him. "What are you doing here?" he demanded.

"Research. It's my job, remember? Now it's your turn."

Jake looked me up and down. "Research? What are you researching, the undercover life of female sex workers? Is that what you were doing at the bar? Looking for customers?"

That was harsh. Too harsh. I didn't deserve that. Neither did Tiffini. "Out." I reached to unlock the door. "Now."

He grabbed my wrist. "I'm not leaving."

My self-defense training took over. I executed a perfect wrist-release move and Jake ended up on his knees. With my arms crossed and my stance widened, I waited for him to get up. "Out," I said again.

He blinked. Several times. Then he scrambled to stand. He stood with his mouth open and stared at me. "You took me down."

"You never took me seriously when I told you about the classes. How they are more than teaching us to scream and run. I'm no black-belt ninja, but I can get myself out of a few situations."

"I see that. But I don't like seeing you putting yourself in danger's way. And that getup is asking for trouble. What the hell are you up to?"

"No. You go first." I wiggled a finger in his face. "You don't get to play it off like you have a job in Chicago, not return my calls, and then show up here and get all crazy because I'm wearing makeup." And a wig, and clothes I'd never pick for myself, but maybe I could distract him from focusing on that.

He looked around the room. "Is it safe to talk?" There wasn't much to see. The bed, a nightstand, and a small desk with a chair. "Or do we need to go out to my car?"

His Charger hadn't been in the parking lot of the bar. What was he driving? "I've checked the room twice. We're safe to talk here." But my paranoia kicked into high gear. What was he doing that he was worried about being overheard? I walked over to the bed and brushed the spilled lettuce back into the to-go container. "Seating is limited, but it's halfway comfortable."

His heart-stopping grin returned to his face. Thank heavens I was immune to it. "It wouldn't be the first time we shared a bed."

I should have known better than to give him the opening, so I ignored the remark. "I'm waiting," I said as I plumped up a pillow to prop against the headboard.

Behind his cool exterior, Jake seemed uneasy as he sat at the end of the bed. The way he wouldn't meet my eyes was my clue. "Can't you trust me when I say I'm working?" he pleaded.

"I'd like to, but this isn't Chicago, you aren't driving your own car, you've dyed your hair, would you trust you?"

He squirmed, as if he was trying to get comfortable. "When you put it that way…"

I leaned back, crossed my arms, and stared at him. "Anytime, Jake."

"The boss sent me here to scout out locations to expand his holdings. He wants to buy a few more bars. It's a secret, of course."

Sounded good, but I didn't buy it for a second. "Try again."

"I got transferred here and was ashamed to admit it. I didn't want you to see me as a failure. Chicago sounded so much better."

That one almost worked. "And the hits keep on coming. Can't wait to hear what's next."

He hesitated, then reached out and rubbed my ankle. He looked up into my eyes. "I had to get out of Oak Grove, Angel, and I didn't want to hurt your feelings. I'll never be able to make anything of myself there. When I tried to apply for jobs it was as if there was a sign over my head flashing 'felon.' I had to leave."

I'd wondered about that, based on my own experience. But Jake looked away halfway through the speech, a dead giveaway. The kernel of truth the statement had made me feel guilty for what I needed to do next. Reject him again.

"I thought the third time would be the charm. How are you making these up so fast? Years of experience?"

Jake took a deep breath and exhaled loudly. "You always could see right through me." He rolled over and got off the bed, walked over to the window, and peered out between the drawn curtains. "I really wish you'd let this go. Do me a favor and put off whatever your research is and go home. I don't want you mixed up in my business." He turned back around and his eyes were heavy with sadness. "Please?"

I almost caved. Almost. "I'm your friend, Jake. If you're in trouble, I want to help you. But I can't unless you tell me the truth."

"Don't you get it? That's why I can't tell you anything."

"I understand, Jake. You're protecting me." I

brought my knees to my chest and wrapped my arms around them. "But here's the thing. How will I know who to watch out for if I don't know what the problem is? It's not like Oak Grove has a magical force field to keep trouble out."

He paced as he mulled over that idea. I watched him walk to one wall, swivel on one foot, and then head to the other wall. Not that there was much spare space in the room. I wondered if that's how he got his exercise in prison. Except for one time, he never talked about the experience.

Finally, he came to a dead stop. "Okay. I'll tell you, but you won't believe me. You'll think I'm making it up."

It couldn't be any worse than his other stories. He clasped his hands behind his back and started pacing again. I hoped no one slept in the room below us.

"I'm being blackmailed," he said, "by the FBI."

That was the craziest scenario of all. He was telling the truth. I knew it immediately. "Agent Felton? He lied to me?"

Jake shook his head. "Not Felton. Garza."

That wasn't good. Agent Garza had a personal vendetta against Jake. "What does he have to use against you?"

"He says he has connections that can change my paperwork and put me back in prison and I believe him. I wouldn't survive another stint behind bars, so I agreed to help him."

I crawled off the bed and joined Jake in pacing. He went one direction and I was going the other, so we met in the middle each lap. The space was narrow enough we had to be careful not to bump into each other. "What is he making you do?" I asked. I assumed he wasn't trying to scam Jake out of money.

"He has this theory there's a crime syndicate working out of Charleston." Jake shook his head. "He wants me to come up with information to justify a full-fledged investigation by the FBI. I don't have to go undercover because anyone checking into my background would assume that I'm less than law-abiding."

"And why doesn't he do it himself?"

His million-dollar smile returned to his face and Jake stopped pacing. "He wouldn't admit it, but I think he tried and got caught."

Chapter 15

Jake and I sat side by side on the bed, our backs against the headboard. I bent my knees while his legs were stretched out. We each held a bottle of water, with a bag of stale pretzels between us. The TV was tuned to a news channel to mask our conversation.

"Agent Garza didn't give you any idea what this supposed crime syndicate involves, did he?" I asked. "Are they stealing cars to sell overseas or selling drugs or what?"

"His theory is drugs, meth specifically, but he doesn't have enough information to be sure. There's plenty of meth available, but instinct tells me he's wrong."

Even Oak Grove had its share of drug problems according to Freddie, so it didn't surprise me that Charleston did. "Have you discovered anything?"

"No. If there's a conspiracy, the participants are damned good at keeping it quiet."

What a spider web of plots and counter-plots I'd

stumbled into. Was I the black widow in the center or the moth at the edge trying to break free of the web? "You know the research I'm here doing?" I asked.

"I wondered when you'd bring that up," Jake said.

"Here's the thing. I'm doing it for Deputy Nelson." At a ridiculously reduced rate. Because it gave me the cover I needed for my own curiosity. "He thinks Annabelle knows something about the murder that she's not sharing. I happen to agree with him."

"Annabelle?"

"The waitress from The Dog House, who got beat up and turned out to be a PI. She's from here."

He grabbed a couple of pretzels and popped them into his mouth, washing them down with a swallow of his water. "That's a hell of a coincidence."

"Even better. Annabelle told me she's working on a case big enough she'll be able to get out of here."

"And you think Annabelle knows something about whatever the FBI is interested in and it ties together with the murder."

"And they are all about grabbing the glory for themselves so no one is talking to anyone else."

"Bingo."

"And you'll play hero, rush in and figure out what's going on and save the world. Is that your plan?"

Pretty much. But Jake made it sound like a bad thing. "Do you have a better idea?"

He snorted. "Yeah. We turn this back over to the professionals and tell them to shove it. In more polite words, of course. This is way over our heads."

"And you go back to prison." No matter how I looked at it, there was a downside.

Jake shrugged his shoulders. "Better than winding up dead."

There had to be another way. I just needed to figure it out.

But by morning I still didn't have a better plan. The answer appeared to be the connection between Charleston and Oak Grove. But what was it?

Jake had left after an hour of fruitless discussion. I'd gone to bed, but not to sleep. I stayed awake trying to figure out a new approach to the puzzle. Annabelle no longer seemed to be a key player so I relegated her to the position of a cheerleader on the sidelines. And what did the local police know? I remembered how upset Freddie got when Agent Garza attempted to operate in Oak Grove without informing Chief Sorenson first.

I resorted back to my specialty—research. Only with a new topic. One I didn't need to go to the library for, but would, because their internet connection was better than the motel's. Which I decided to stay at for a second day, to make it easier for Jake to find me. I needed a good connection because I'd be pulling up a lot of web pages at the same time. Finding and comparing crime statistics, both current and historical, would be a daunting task for most people, but I enjoyed it.

I hid behind a stack of books—mostly about the history of Charleston—and switched to my glasses. They were better for reading the laptop screen. Chief Sorenson had set me up with access to several crime statistic websites when I helped him draw up reports for the city council, so I was all set.

Without the alarms I'd set before starting, I would have missed lunch. And supper. There'd be no appearance in a bar for Tiffini that night. I stopped at a grocery store on the way back to the motel and bought a pre-made Cuban sandwich, fresh pretzels and more water, getting ready for a long night.

Jake showed up around eight o'clock, to my surprise. I wasn't surprised he showed up, I was surprised he was so early. I'd figured he wouldn't put in an appearance until after the bars closed. It was my chance to show off—err, explain—what I was up to. I showed him the three different spreadsheets I'd created.

"What I'm doing," I told him, "is looking for patterns of changes. Unexplainable anomalies. For example, if there were no murders last year and one this year, that would be a one hundred percent increase. But the one hundred percent would be basically meaningless. But if there were a hundred murders last year and two hundred this year that would indicate a trend. A bad one. Now, if there were a hundred murders last year and only twenty-five this year, that would be a good trend."

"Makes sense, but how does the murder rate relate to us?"

"It probably doesn't. But the number of arrests for drug use and sales might. Then I factor in increases based on national averages for similar crimes and try to sort out what kind of drugs were involved."

"What have you got so far?"

"Not much." Because I'd gotten distracted comparing crime rates in Charleston versus Oak Grove. "It took a while to gather the data."

"Then you should take the night off."

What was I going to do, watch TV? I should have brought along some books to read, but I'd planned on spending my nights in bars. For research. "I want to keep digging," I said.

"I hoped you could be my back-up tonight." Jake grimaced. "I've been 'invited' to drop by a bar tonight and meet some people. It feels wrong, but I don't dare pass up the opportunity."

"You want me to tag along as your girlfriend?" I asked with a frown. That didn't seem like a good idea.

The grin on Jake's face was genuine. "Have you given up on Eli?"

I shoved him hard enough he almost hit the wall as he staggered backward. He held both hands up, palms open. "Hey, I was kidding!" he protested.

Maybe I'd overreacted. "Sorry," I mumbled. "I'm way out of my comfort level here." It was one thing to pretend to be Tiffini in the library, but totally different to carry on the charade in enemy territory. And that's how I saw the set-up. If Jake, with all his experience, was nervous, I had every right to be as well.

"Don't worry about it. I'll manufacture a reason to bail." He coughed. "I think I'm coming down with something."

"That's the oldest excuse in the book and it'll never fly. Besides, it would be a shame to blow off the first real opportunity you have to get any information."

"So you'll do it?"

"Act as your girlfriend? No."

He grinned. "I didn't want you to anyway. I can't bring anyone else. But if you show up to the same bar a few minutes earlier, it would be perfect."

"Do you want me or Tiffini?"

I regretted the words the moment they came out of my mouth. My Jake filter was seriously broken. He smiled broadly and shook his head and I prepared myself for the worst.

"I need the looks of Tiffini and the brains of Harmony. Oh, and the gun Harmony carries around in her purse. Is that possible?"

I'd have to rethink Tiffini's outfit if I wanted to hide Betsy. "I can make it happen. Give me a few minutes to change clothes and put on my makeup. Where am I going and what time should I show up?"

The name of the bar—The Outlaw—was enough to make me uncomfortable, but when I pulled into an almost-empty parking lot, the warning bells rang loudly. I adjusted the wig, unbuttoned another button on my blouse, and took a deep breath. I could do this.

I entered the bar with my best little-girl-lost expression plastered on my face. There were three men at the bar, and two at one of the back tables. They all turned to stare at me as I stood in the doorway. Hesitantly, I took a stool at the bar—the one nearest to the door.

"What can I get you?" the bartender asked. He was a scrawny guy with a couple of teeth missing, and his nose looked as if it had been broken more than once. His shifty eyes intensified my distrust of him even more.

"I don't know." I looked around the bar again. "Friends from work told me to meet them here, but I think they were playing a joke on me. Unless they came and I missed them. You haven't seen four women in here tonight, have you?"

He shook his head. "Nope."

"Maybe they're just running late." I bit my bottom lip. "Can I get a light beer? Whatever you have on draft. I'll give them a few minutes."

He didn't approve of my choice of beverage but drew it for me anyway. I paid, including a sizable tip, and took a chair at a table where I could keep an eye on the front door. Then I pulled out my phone and pretended to send a text. I occupied myself with catching up on email. The familiar prickle at the back of my neck told me I was being watched, but I tried to ignore it. I'd decided that no one in the room was Jake's contact.

Jake arrived about ten minutes later. That made him a few minutes early. I played it like I'd never seen him before and made it obvious I was giving him the once-over while pretending to look at my phone. He ignored me, of course, and grabbed an empty stool at the bar. I sighed and took a small sip of my beer. I needed to make it last.

He ordered a whiskey, neat, and slipped the bartender a folded-up bill. Probably much more than the price of the drink and tip. Then he started working his magic, buttering up the bartender and the other guys at the bar.

When two more men walked in, I examined them as casually as I had examined Jake. Neither was my type, but Tiffini wasn't as picky. They took seats on either side of Jake, which made me uncomfortable. It wasn't like I could do anything about it.

But he seemed unfazed. After a short conversation with the men, Jake ordered a second drink. I'd set an alarm on my phone, and when it rang, I pretended to answer it and talk to a non-existent person on the other end. As I put on my act, Jake and the two men picked up their drinks and moved to a table.

They were too far away for me to catch more than a few words of their discussion, but I did catch something about "cars" and "deliveries." It didn't matter, I'd get the details from Jake later. All I needed to know was that Jake looked comfortable sitting there and not stressed.

Out of the corner of my eye, I saw him reach up and rub the back of his neck. That was our prearranged signal. Everything was going fine, and I should take off. If he'd rubbed the top of his head, I would have stuck around.

I stood and stretched. Every male in the place stared at me, except for Jake, the only one with his back to me.

"Another beer?" asked the bartender.

"No thanks." I giggled and fluttered my eyelashes. "My friends owned up to sending me on a wild goose chase."

He grunted. "Drive safe."

"I will." I gave him a little wave and left. Outside, I took a deep breath and headed for the rental car.

Chapter 16

A flare of light caught my attention. In the mirror, I watched as a man from the bar stood in the doorway and lit a cigarette. Coincidence? I didn't think so. When he headed towards his car, he confirmed my suspicions. I didn't get a good look at his vehicle in the dim light the bar's parking lot offered, but there wasn't much traffic. He'd be easy to keep track of.

The loaner car wouldn't hold up to the demands of a high-speed chase. Besides, Tiffini wouldn't be able to handle a car that well so I had to make my escape in another fashion. Bore my follower into complacency.

It started with a stop at the first convenience store. After using the restroom, I took my time choosing a snack or two for the ride. The clerk, a twenties-something man, paid no attention to me, being too busy messing with his tablet. In fact, he seemed irritated when I approached the counter to pay for my selection—more pretzels and a package of trail mix.

When I came out, the car and driver occupied one of the few parking spots. I got a better look at the vehicle, an older dark blue sedan. The rumble of the motor didn't sound stock. But no matter how much horsepower it had, it didn't matter. This would be a test of patience and willpower, and I had an abundance of both.

I stopped next at an all-night restaurant. Its clientele were what I'd expected—everything from old men bent over their coffee cups to a group of teens rambling on about a recent movie. The waitress, who barely looked out of her teens herself, had more energy than anyone had a right to that time of the night. Her smile sparkled as she brought me a menu.

"Coffee?" she asked brightly.

I wondered if she used drugs or if this was her normal personality. "Hot tea," I answered. "And what do you have in the way of pie?"

"You're in luck. Tomorrow's pies got here a few minutes ago. How about blueberry? Made from local blueberries."

"Do you have whipped cream to go with that?"

"Absolutely."

I handed her back the menu. "Blueberry pie it is."

While I ordered, the man from the bar came in. He sat at the other end of the diner, between me and the front door. I wouldn't let it bother me. It had become a game I was determined to win.

After finishing the delicious pie and paying the

bill, I continued to sip on my second cup of tea while keeping an eye on my follower. When he got distracted by a giggling group of teenage girls coming into the diner, I made my move and headed out the door.

If it hadn't been for the semi making a slow right-hand turn, I would have made it out of the parking lot before the man—I'd named him Mr. X—got to his car. Instead, I had to wait for both the truck and the three cars behind it. My tail hung with me when I pulled onto the street. He wasn't very subtle.

The next tactic involved crawling through the neighborhood behind the diner, making abrupt right hand and left-hand turns. While I'd eaten my pie. I'd studied the street map using the GPS on my phone and knew exactly where to go. I didn't want to lose Mr. X, just confuse him enough to muddle his sense of direction.

The route took me to a major highway at the edge of town, a few blocks away from a national chain motel, my destination. I parked and went inside, hoping to get a soda from the bar, but the staff didn't look to happy to see me. The chairs turned upside down on the tables were a sure sign they'd closed. "Sorry," I said as I walked back out. "I'll catch you another night."

I exited from a side entrance and spotted Mr. X's car in the lot. In a low crouch, I moved from car to car until I reached mine, farther back in the lot. I didn't turn on my headlights until I hit the street. And voila, no one followed behind me.

Still, I chose an indirect route to my motel to make sure there wasn't a second tail. I didn't expect Jake to report in that night and I had all the time in the world to cover my tracks. Once safely in my room with a locked door, I tumbled into bed.

Despite the late night shenanigans, I woke at my normal time. The day's agenda contained only a few items. First one was to check out, second to head back to the library. Not because I needed their internet, but it felt like home to me. Plus, I wanted to be in a public location.

My research was going nowhere. No spikes in drug arrests, no rise in petty crimes, and heck, murders were down. About the only thing I found was a small increase in unsolved car thefts. FBI jurisdiction didn't cover chop shops.

The new motel made checking in harder than the previous two places. Slightly more upscale, they wanted a credit card for incidentals. But after telling the front desk clerk an elaborate story about hiding from an ex, aided by the sizable tip I slipped across the desk, he agreed to take a cash deposit. Another tip assured the private investigator—ahem, Jake— I'd be meeting with wouldn't be hassled.

The inside doors to the rooms provided an extra safety factor. And staying in a room on the third floor with no balcony meant I didn't have to worry about someone trying to get in through the windows. After completing my sweep of the room looking for hidden cameras or listening devices, I felt semi-secure.

Secure enough I decided to eat supper in the restaurant next door. I looked forward to a real meal, with a waitress to serve me and something to eat that wasn't a salad as my main course. Secure enough I considered cleaning off the makeup, removing the wig, and going as myself, not Tiffini. But paranoia can be a good thing.

The hostess took me to a booth close to the restrooms, a win-lose in my book. Being in the back gave extra privacy and on the path to the restrooms took it away again. At least I could bury my face in the book I'd bought and keep it turned away from everyone.

The restaurant's version of lasagna wouldn't win any awards, but it wasn't terrible either. Their garlic bread offered an abundance of flavor but I passed on the generic wine selection and stuck with ice tea. There were some interesting selections on the dessert platter—I noticed when a waitress walked by with it—and considered getting some to take back to the motel. I might get the munchies before—if—Jake showed up.

A family with three young children sat in the nearest booth, and I gave up my book and played peek-a-boo with the youngest. The parents didn't mind; in fact, the mother seemed relieved because it gave her a chance to eat a few bites of her own meal without interruption.

In the booth beyond the family was a couple. I wasn't sure of the relationship—at first I figured they were father and daughter because of the age difference—but the way they leaned towards each other convinced me otherwise. I couldn't see his face, just the back of his head and his short gray hair, but she was flirting with him. She fluttered her heavily-mascaraed eyelashes, pouted her lips with overly bright-red lipstick, and reached out to touch him every few minutes. The run-down chain restaurant seemed like an odd place for their date, but who was I to judge?

Based on the lack of a ring on her left hand, I assumed it was a date. Still, his left hand sported a ring. I checked when he raised it to signal the waitress.

The obvious scenario was a man cheating on his wife. Not being satisfied with the obvious, I concocted other explanations.

She was a world-class spy, and he was her handler. They were meeting up so she could pass off information she'd gathered on a Russian nuclear sub operating off the East Coast. Or maybe it was the reverse, he was the spy, and she the unorthodox manager of an unknown three-letter agency. Or instead of him being the one with money, she was a wealthy heiress and he was a down-on-his-luck old con man looking to scam an easy million to fund his retirement.

But the possibilities and the little girl amused me for only so long, and I'd eaten all the lasagna, so it was time to retreat to my room and wait for Jake.

I took a loop around smokers huddled near the front door, a minor annoyance. The lone figure sitting on the curb in a dark spot was more of a concern because the way she fidgeted made me uneasy. She raised her head and glanced my direction. I was glad I'd stayed in disguise. I didn't know who she was tracking, but Annabelle was on the job.

Casually I strolled past her and towards the hotel, fighting the instinct to give her a wide berth. The prickle at the back of my neck told me she tracked my path but I didn't turn around. However, taking the stairs instead of the elevator up to my floor allowed me to observe her through the windows at each landing. She'd apparently lost interest in me when I entered the motel alone. I, however, hadn't lost interest in her.

With nothing better to do while I waited for Jake, I found a position in my darkened room with a view of the restaurant's parking lot. I couldn't see Annabelle, but with any luck, I'd spot her as she got into her car and stalked her prey. My bet was on the odd couple.

I almost missed the lady leaving as she tagged along behind another group of customers. She headed to a sports car on the far side of the parking lot. Not as fancy as Dolores, but not bad looking at all. More importantly, Annabelle didn't follow her.

I waited in the shadows, hoping to see the man as he exited. It was several minutes later when he showed up and I wondered if he'd stopped to talk to someone on his way out the door. It turned out he was parked close to the front. He pulled out but Annabelle didn't follow, proving me wrong.

Even more curious now, I stayed in place. Apprehension flooded over me when the next patron exited. In the glare of light from the open door, I identified him. One of the men from the bar the previous night.

In my peripheral vision, I caught Annabelle sneaking through the parking lot. Her pale green golf shirt glowed in the overhead lights, making her path easy to trace. She got into a car and although I saw the brake lights flare in the darkness, the headlights didn't come on. What did she have up her sleeve?

With her headlights still off, Annabelle pulled out of her parking spot headed towards the main exit. When she got to the street, she had to wait for traffic to go by. The man from the bar pulled in behind her. At the first opening, she pulled into the street, followed by the other car. The move she pulled next was brilliant, if risky.

She swerved onto the side of the road and turned on her lights. Once he'd gone past her, Annabelle pulled back into traffic, right on his tail. It was so obvious yet beautifully innocent. He'd never guess she'd done it on purpose. I filed the trick away in my memory. Who knew when I might need to use it?

After turning on the lights in my room, I opened my laptop and found a comfortable spot on the bed. I hoped Jake would drop by soon and I might as well catch up on email while I waited.

Chapter 17

With a jerk, I pulled myself upright and reached under my pillow for Betsy. I didn't know how long I'd been asleep, but the prickle at the back of my neck told me I was being watched. The room was dark, and I hadn't turned off the lights. Blinking to force my eyes to adjust to the lack of light, I scanned the room, trying to identify the threat.

"I'd forgotten how beautiful you are when you're asleep, Angel," a familiar voice said from across the room.

Jake! I rolled over, fumbled for the switch, and turned on the bedside lamp. "How did you get in here?"

He raised one eyebrow and smirked. "How do you think?"

Damn. Sometimes I forgot he had a history as a jewel thief. I suppose breaking into the average hotel room was no problem for him.

The smirk turned into a broad grin. "I bribed the front desk clerk into giving me a spare key." He pulled a piece of plastic out of his shirt pocket and waved it in the air. "I knocked first but you didn't answer."

My laptop was on the floor beside the bed and my glasses were on the nightstand although I didn't remember putting them there. "What time is it?"

"About four, but I've only been here a few minutes." He yawned. "I need a nap."

"Did you learn anything?"

"Nada. I spent the entire night chauffeuring a bunch of drunk rednecks from one bar to another. Then I had to sit around and twiddle my thumbs while they went into the back rooms for their meetings or whatever." He sighed. "There's only so much soda a man can drink in one night and I reached my limit halfway through the evening."

I thought about offering him one of the diet pops in the little fridge under the microwave.

"My gut tells me something big's about to go down," Jake continued, interrupting my chain of thought. "But I've got no proof."

"So what's our next step? We sneak into one of the bars and riffle through the paperwork in the office?"

Jake took a deep breath. "There is no 'we.' *You* need to pack your bags and go home. Whatever is about to happen, I can't risk having you involved. These guys play for keeps, and if you get in the way, they'll do what it takes to make sure you don't interfere with their plans."

"And who will watch your back?"

"I worked alone for years. Nothing's changed."

I realized that I didn't know Jake as well as I thought I did. Under that amiable persona he displayed most of the time, there was a layer of rock-hard ice. My T-shirt did nothing to cover the goosebumps that rose on my arms.

But I wouldn't give up on him. I don't abandon my friends. Besides, I was already working on a plan.

Jake left only after we'd argued about how soon I'd head home. He wanted me to check out early in the morning, I argued that I wanted to hang out for one more day because I still had research to do. Which was the truth, but that wasn't the only reason I wanted to stay. I won. It wasn't like he could force me to leave.

Waiting until most of the business travelers left meant the slim breakfast offerings were narrowed down to stale donuts, bruised apples, and off-brand yogurt. I stuck with the ever-present coffee. If I got hungry, I'd find a restaurant along the way to my destination. Which, despite what I'd implied to Jake, wasn't the library.

The streets the GPS led me through got progressively worse. Closed stores, empty lots strewn with litter, old houses crying out to be either restored or torn down. Oak Grove had a few bad neighborhoods, but not this bad or this many streets' worth. I wondered if my electronic guide had been programmed incorrectly.

About the time I was ready to turn around, the character of the neighborhood changed again. Although it was still an older part of town, the buildings looked as if they were mostly in use and halfway taken care of. And that's where Annabelle's business was. No wonder she wanted to get out of town.

The elaborate sign on the door, out of place with its surroundings, read "Leroix Investigations." Annabelle must have started the business with high hopes. Well, I was about to help her on her way to her dreams.

I pushed open the door, expecting to be greeted by a receptionist. But the front desk was empty. "Annabelle?" I called, with no response. I waited a minute and tried again. "Annabelle?"

The door to the back office tempted me. Perhaps she was out feeding a parking meter. While she was gone, I could go back and peek at the papers on the top of her desk. If she came in, surely I'd hear her and could switch to pretending her absence worried me and I was looking for her.

Courage failed me, or my instinct for self-preservation kicked in. Instead, I studied my surroundings. Clean white walls with fading old prints hung on two of them. A minimum of furniture—an old metal desk, two standard waiting room chairs, one end table with assorted magazines. A small ivy plant that had seen better days adorned the desk. It needed to be watered.

There had to be a bathroom somewhere. All thoughts of snooping set aside, I picked up the plant and headed towards the back office.

"What the hell are you doing here?" Annabelle Susannah LeRoix snarled as she limped through the rear door.

I held up the ivy. "Your plant is in need of some tender loving care." It was ironic that someone who was so fond of wearing green had no connection to living plants.

"You came all the fuckin' way from Oak Grove to water a plant? A plant I never told you about? I told Margie to take the damned thing home."

Not in the mood to listen to a string of curse words, I interrupted. "No, I came to offer you a job."

That shut her up for a few seconds. "You can't afford me."

Little did she know. "It doesn't look like business is booming. Or you're spending so much time on your personal mission you're ignoring paying clients and losing them. Which is it?" I didn't give her time to answer. "But you can't turn down a job that will pay you to do what you're already doing for free."

Annabelle hesitated. "What do you mean?"

"That guy you followed from the restaurant last night. He's part of your personal vendetta, right?"

"Fuck, how did you know about that?"

I winced. "There's one stipulation before I become a paying customer. No swearing."

"You're not a client yet."

Easy to fix. I pulled my checkbook out of my purse, wrote out a check for a sizable sum and handed it to her. She looked at it, then at me, then at the check.

"You're a client. Have a seat." She waved the check towards an upholstered chair that had seen better days. I brushed off some imaginary dirt before settling into its worn cushion. "Tell me why you want to hire me." She put the check into the middle desk drawer and locked it.

"You want to find out what's going on here and so do I." I passed her my phone after scrolling to a picture of Jake. "And you can do that by following this guy although it will be risky for you."

Her eyes narrowed as she studied the photo. "I've seen him around."

"He's a friend. I'm worried he's hanging out with the wrong people and might get hurt. Your job is to back him up without him finding out." I didn't trust her, so I wanted to be as vague as possible.

"F…" She caught herself. "That won't be easy."

"Especially because he's an old hand at this. His name is Jake, by the way."

"That's a lot of money you're spending on an old friend."

"He's the cousin of my boyfriend." I wasn't about to tell her he was also my ex-lover.

"And what the h…" she stopped and sighed. "What is he doing here?"

"I'm not at liberty to tell you."

Her eyebrow raised and she pushed herself away from her desk. "Not even a clue?"

"Nope. What I can tell you is that his new friends are interested in Jake's driving skills. And he's good." He'd taught me, and those skills had saved my life.

She sucked in a deep breath. "That's it! They're smuggling drugs!"

I shook my head. "Not according to the stats. I've checked everything from the local police figures to the state figures and even figures from the feds. There's no indication of an increase in drug use charges and the petty crimes that accompany a better supply."

It seemed physically impossible, but her eyebrow rose even higher. "How the fuck…"

"Language," I interrupted. "You don't have to prove to me how tough you are."

"Whatever. Where did you get your info?"

"I have my sources. All legit." Well, most of them.

"What's your theory, Miss High and Mighty Internet Researcher?"

I ignored the implied insult. "Drugs were first on my list. I don't have a second suspect." Not yet, anyway. I needed to do more digging.

"That does us a h… huge amount of good…not."

"So Miss High and Mighty Private Investigator…" Two could play that game. "What's your plan?"

That earned me the ghost of a smile. "I'll follow your friend. Maybe I'll get a fresh angle on what's happening. How will I update you on my progress?"

"Jake will put too much energy into worrying if I stick around, so I'm headed back to Oak Grove. He doesn't need the distraction. Besides, I can work the case up there. Obviously, whatever is happening there ties to what's going on here. I'll give you my phone number and you can call me with updates from your end."

"I don't suppose you've run an analysis of drug usage there." Annabelle smirked as if she'd gotten one up on me.

"Last month, actually. I do a quarterly report for the Chief of Police. Drug use stats in Oak Grove have flatlined for the past year. Usage has gone up slightly for the county, but it may be a statistical anomaly. Did you discover anything while you were there?" I hoped to trick Annabelle into sharing her knowledge.

It didn't work. She turned back into nasty Annabelle.

"I was this damned close to figuring it out," she hissed, leaning forward. "And then you and your friends showed up and I became a fuckin' target."

"Language," I said. "If you don't want to work with me, give me back my check. I'll find someone else to do it."

The look in her eye was one of frustration—or was it desperation? "That money won't last forever."

"I'll sign the standard contract for services." After I let Dan review it, of course.

She re-arranged the pens laid out on her desk and scribbled something on her calendar pad. No problem, I could wait. And wait. And wait.

Finally she made up her mind and picked up a manila file and slid it across the desk. "There's not much in it. A few photos, a couple of names, and a list of bars. I can't connect the dots."

Looking through the information didn't set off any lightbulbs for me either. "Can I get a copy of that?" I asked. "The pictures, mostly. In case one of those guys shows up in Oak Grove."

"Check your email when you get home. When are you leaving?"

I didn't know if she was in a hurry for me to leave so she could go cash the check or because she wanted to jump on the new lead I'd given her. Either way, it didn't make any sense to drag our little chat out any longer. I stood, and grabbed the ivy. "Is there someplace I can get water?"

Annabelle jerked her head towards a small door. "Bathroom's in there."

The ivy cheered as I stuck it under the faucet and turned the cold water on. "So do you have any backup theories?" I asked through the open door. In the mirror over the sink, I watched her body stiffen. She was holding out on me.

"I thought about money laundering or forgery," she answered. "But the Feds would be involved with those."

The Feds were involved, indirectly, but what she didn't know wouldn't hurt her. "I can run stats on those later." I waited while the extra water dripped out of the drain holes at the bottom of the pot. "As a double-elimination."

"Okay."

I returned the ivy to the desk in the front room. It would survive a few more days. "Any of those guys in the pictures look like the ones who beat you up?" I asked, standing in the doorway between the offices.

"It was too dark when the fuckers attacked me," she said. I let the swear word slip by without pointing it out. "I never saw them. Not clearly enough to identify anyway." She chuckled. "But I got a few good punches in on them."

Well, I'd tried. Deputy Nelson would be keeping his money.

Chapter 18

My to-do list could wait. Dolores' motor purred seductively as I pulled away from the mechanic's. My favorite twisty back road called my name and I could use some driving practice. Shuffle steering went against everything they taught in driving school but was useful on tight curves. Pretending there were cones in the road made it more of a challenge.

As always, Dolores responded to the slightest nudge of the steering wheel. With no other traffic, I wove in and out of the imaginary cones, hoping no one would come speeding around a curve. Me and Dolores would be fine, but the other driver might have a heart attack. So, all too soon, I packed up my imaginary cones and headed home. There was work to do.

First on the list was letting Joe and Luke know I was back. Piper took care of that as he greeted me enthusiastically when I opened the gate. He didn't even seem disappointed that I didn't have a doggie treat to give him. The barking attracted Joe and Luke. Their greeting was lower-keyed. A simple "See you made it back" accompanied by a smile.

Next came watering the African Violets my mother left me. The ivy in Annabelle's office had reminded me of them. I even crooned a few bars of a John Denver song to them as I turned them on the windowsill so a different side faced the light.

Since I'd missed my normal weekend cleaning ritual, it became a priority. With the windows thrown open, and a set of headphones over my ears, I started with cleaning out the refrigerator. I'd moved on to scrubbing the floor when I realized the knocking I heard wasn't drums. Someone was at my door.

After several incidents of people showing up I didn't want to see, I made a habit out of checking the peephole before opening my door. It was a good habit. I should have stuck with it.

Humming along to a golden-oldie from my high school years and drying my hands off on a dishtowel, I opened the door. And stared into the face of Chief Sorenson.

All my encounters with the chief had been for official business. I'd never even run into him in the grocery store. To have him show up on my doorstep was unprecedented. I panicked. Was he here to arrest me? Had someone reported me for exhibition driving? Or had the Charleston police contacted him about me forging Tiffini's signature at the motels there? Or was there bogus evidence tying me to the murder of Tadd Foard?

But surely the chief wouldn't bother with taking me in. He'd send one of the lower level officers. Or Freddie. And no one was with him. I figured that out by peeking around his broad shoulders.

I had two options. Slam the door in his face or ask him in. Politeness and the desire to keep on good terms with him narrowed the options to one.

"Good afternoon, Chief. Would you like to come in?" I squared my shoulders, took a step back, and opened the door wider.

The chief was a big man to begin with, but when he removed his hat and stepped into my small apartment, he seemed to grow even larger. "Sorry to bother you, Miss Duprie," he said. No matter how many times I suggested he call me Harmony, he wouldn't. "But I didn't want to call you down to the station for this." He shifted his feet. "I have a favor to ask."

I needed to refill the sun ice tea pitcher. All I had to offer Chief Sorenson was coffee or ice water. He chose the water and stood awkwardly in my small front room while I headed into the even smaller kitchen to get it.

"Please, have a seat," I said when I came back carrying two glasses. I was so used to my friends making themselves at home I felt guilty for not telling him earlier.

He eyed the choices. Either the recliner of the loveseat. Not much of a choice. He picked the loveseat, so I settled into the recliner.

"What's up, Chief?" I asked, not willing to wade through social niceties.

"I'd like you to do some research for me. Off the books."

It was getting to be a trend. One I didn't like. "Oh?"

He set his hat on the coffee table and ran a hand over his crew cut. "I don't want the City Council getting wind of it. Nuisance calls are going up in the city, and I want to know if the county is experiencing the same thing."

"Define a nuisance call." I didn't want to make an assumption.

"Calls that result in no charges. NFA's and NC's. Kids skateboarding in the street after dark. Neighbors calling about loud parties. Backfires being reported as gunshots."

"Isn't that normal during the summer?"

He sighed. "This year is abnormal. My officers are spending so much time chasing the nuisance calls that it's impacting their ability to do routine duties."

That's why traffic ticket revenue had gone down last month. Was the Council giving him grief for not meeting budget expectations? "I'd like to see the reports for Oak Grove for starters." And I needed to formulate a way to get the information from the county without raising any suspicions.

"Done. My secretary will send them to you."

"What's my deadline?" He was the only one I let set deadlines for me.

"The sooner the better. How many hours do you anticipate the project will take? I'm paying for this out of my pocket."

"It's on the house." At his look of surprise, I explained, "It ties in with another project I've got going." My personal project, but that was none of his business.

"I appreciate it, Miss Duprie." He rose to leave so I stood too.

"I'm curious about one thing, Chief. What do you think is going on?"

His face darkened. "That's the problem. I've been a cop for a lot of years and I've never seen this happen before. Normally these calls can be traced back to something. Increased drug use, a flare in racial tensions, or even something as simple as the public pool being closed for repairs. Not this time. It's got me puzzled and I don't like it."

So much for cleaning house. Or doing laundry, or any of the other chores I'd planned for the evening. The quick trip to the grocery store to stock up on fresh fruits and veggies along with my favorite late night munchies couldn't be put off, however. I needed brain food to pull an all-nighter.

By the time I got back and had put everything where it belonged, the email from the chief's secretary had arrived. As much as my fingers itched to hit the keyboard, I took the time to prepare a tray of cheese, vegetables and ranch dip and then plugged in my laptop. Not until I poured myself a glass of white wine did I stretch out on the loveseat and go to work.

Statistics are dry to begin with, but these were worse than usual. No names; only dates, times and the barest of details. A gang roaming the streets at 10 AM turned out to be kids playing hide-n-go-seek. The neighbors arguing at noon was a loud TV tuned to a talk show. A call at 4 PM about drag racing was no more than an old man working on his '56 Chevy.

Hanging out with Freddie had taught me the officers of the Oak Grove Police Force took pride in being ambassadors to the community. That meant each call took far too much of an officer's valuable time. The kids playing? The responding officer probably joined in for one round of the game. And the officer likely hung around and talked shop with the old man. Under normal circumstances that would be part of the job.

But Chief Sorenson's concerns were valid. Over the course of the summer, the calls had doubled. And no matter how hard I looked, what factors I figured in or excluded, I couldn't find a common thread. Not age or sex or time of day. I even mapped out the addresses. Although a few neighborhoods had a heavier concentration of calls, no area of town was excluded.

By the time Eli pinged me for a video call, I had

three spreadsheets going and was getting ready to open a fourth. I wanted to see if there was a connection between the nuisance calls and calls that resulted in arrests. But I was ready for a break and talking to Eli would give my brain a rest. Besides, I flat-out missed him because every time I'd looked at Jake, I'd seen the resemblance to Eli.

"Hey, Sweetie," I said when we connected. The impatiens that decorated his patio created a colorful red, purple and white background, in stark contrast to my boring brown loveseat. "You're actually home and not at the office."

He chuckled. "Yeah, how about that? We finally nailed that contract. Now I'm waiting for final approval from our legal department and theirs. I expect that to happen by the end of the week. You should fly down and help me celebrate."

"That sounds wonderful, except for the flying part."

"One of these days, I'll get you up in the company jet so you can see how much fun flying can be. Better than a first-class seat on a commercial flight."

I wouldn't know, never having spent that much money on a plane ticket. "I might take you up on that offer." Fat chance.

"Are you free to leave town yet?" he asked.

"Unofficially, yes. They still don't have a suspect, but I'm no longer on the list."

"Good. Then pack a bag."

I'd have to wash my clothes before I could re-pack them. "Why?"

"When the contract is signed, we can take the jet and go celebrate. I don't know exactly when it will happen, so you'll need to be ready."

I'd walked right into that one. After a moment of panic in which I found myself unable to come up with a good excuse, I lamely answered, "We'll have to see what's going on. I am trying to sell a house."

"One of these days you're going to tell me," Eli said.

"Tell you what?"

"Why you're afraid to fly."

It was a well-kept secret. Why I was afraid to fly. Only me and the therapist I'd visited a few times knew the reason, and it was long enough ago that she'd likely forgotten. And that's the way I liked it.

It was one of those nights when conversation seemed forced, probably because I was tired and, at the same time, anxious to get back to my spreadsheets. Eli was relieved that I'd heard from Jake, although I didn't tell him how. Jake and I had agreed to use the excuse that he'd lost his phone charger in the move and it took him several days to replace it. A believable reason and Eli didn't question it.

After we had said our good-nights and I'd refilled my wine glass, it was time to get back to work. I hoped it would distract me from the guilt I felt for lying to Eli. Spider graphs are not the easiest thing in the world to create, as they chart data in unique ways, but they can reveal hidden connections. As I stared at the web on my screen, trying to find a previously unseen correlation, the thought hit me again. Was I the spider creating the web or the hapless fly being drawn into the trap?

Chapter 19

All the law enforcement types coming to my apartment made me nervous, so I arranged to meet Deputy Nelson at the restaurant down the street from the library. He showed up in nicely fitting jeans and a polo shirt. Was that good or bad? My gut insisted on bad, but logic called it good. I'd wait and see.

"Your day off?" I asked as he settled into the booth.

"After the weekend, I deserve it." He looked at me over the menu. "I half-expected you'd be mixed up in it somehow."

"I don't have the foggiest idea what you're talking about."

"We had fights at several different bars. Nothing too bad, just a bunch of drunk guys throwing punches and missing for the most part, but the deputies on duty couldn't be everywhere at once. We called in backup from the State Police." He paused while the waitress brought his coffee, refilled mine, and took his order. "The

Sheriff doesn't like to do that. Ask for help, that is."

A lightbulb turned on. Not only did I need to see the reports from the Sheriff's Department, the State Police might have pertinent information. This was getting way deeper than anticipated.

"How many arrests did you make?"

"Me? Personally?" he asked as he dumped three packets of sugar into his cup. "None. No one wanted to give a statement or press charges. The department, total? Four. And that's standard for a Saturday night."

"How can the public see how many calls deputies go on? Even if they don't result in an arrest?"

"You mean under the Sunshine Laws? The clerks at the office deal with those requests. I think you can walk in and request to see the logs. Why?"

"Just curious. Overheard a couple of Oak Grove officers complaining about nuisance calls. Wondered if you guys got them too."

"I haven't been here long enough to answer that question."

Conversation stopped while the waitress brought his food. A vegetable omelet and whole wheat toast, and not a doughnut in sight. I let him eat in peace for a few minutes while I drank my coffee and checked my phone for messages.

"Now you mention it," he said after finishing a third of the omelet, "some of the guys were talking about not having time to do paperwork. I didn't pay much attention, figured they were complaining to hear the sound of their own voices."

"Your workload hasn't picked up?"

"It has, but nothing I can't handle."

While he concentrated on his food, I digested the minimal information.

"Did you have anything for me?" he asked before taking a bite of toast.

I frowned and shook my head. "A whole lot of dead ends. If Annabelle has ever been in trouble, she's hidden it well. I won't be charging you."

"But…"

I held up a hand to stop him. "No results, no charge. That's the way I work."

"How many hours did you spend doing the research? That should be worth something." Deputy Nelson leaned forward and his neck muscles tightened.

If he only knew. "Enough to make sure I didn't miss anything. Because I don't give up easily, I'll do some random searches off and on. If I find anything, I'll update you. We can talk money then."

"That seems fair." His words didn't match the tight line his lips formed and I wondered what was bothering him. I sipped my coffee and waited for him to decide if he wanted to tell me.

"Have you ever felt…" he asked. "Like things are about to explode?"

I couldn't remember the last time I *hadn't* felt that way.

But I played dumb, not willing to reveal how

deep the trouble went. "Anything in particular setting your copdar off?"

A small smile replaced his frown and the lines in his forehead disappeared. "Copdar? Like gaydar? Can I borrow that?"

"Go for it." I waved a hand in the air. "I didn't invent the phrase. Freddie must use it."

"Cool. Well, my *copdar* says everything is too quiet, too normal. I'll admit to being an action junkie and maybe the area is always this way, but I keep expecting something big to happen. I just don't know what."

"A man was murdered and a woman beaten up. You think that would be enough excitement."

"And we haven't caught the perpetrators yet." Deputy Nelson sighed. "We don't even have any new leads on either case."

So why are you looking for trouble? "If I get wind of anything, I'll get in touch," I assured him, "but things should calm down now kids are in school."

"From your mouth to God's ears."

I hadn't heard the expression for years and fought back tears. The last time was when I wished my folks a safe trip. The one they came back from in coffins.

Deputy Nelson accepted my lame excuse about needing to water the flowers at the house before it got too hot. On my way out, I paid for both my coffee and his breakfast. It never hurt to stay on the good side of the law.

It had been years since my parents died in a freak accident while mountain climbing, but now and then the depth of what I'd lost hit me hard. Sure, I didn't have it as rough as some people. I was a senior in college when it happened, but they still had a lot of good years left. Or so I thought. There was a time I would have denied my grief, but no more. So the flowers got more water than what came from the garden hose, tears mixed in.

With the house to myself—at least, Sarah hadn't told me she'd be showing it—I decided to check inside and make sure everything that had needed fixed or repainted had been. With all the lists I'd created to work from, I don't know how anything would have been missed, but it never hurt to take another look.

Freshness filled my lungs as I wandered through the rooms. Gone the stale, closed up atmosphere that used to haunt the place, replaced by an aura of waiting. All it needed now was a loving family to bring it back to life.

Somewhere along the way, I lost track of my original task and started planning the furniture each room needed. After adding bookshelves and deep upholstered chairs, the living room could double as a library. A farm-style table in the kitchen would be great for casual breakfasts. The master bedroom, already painted a deep blue, needed a sleigh bed topped with a coverlet with a red rose pattern.

Then there was the smallest room on the third floor. The one I'd use as a home office. An old-fashioned roll-top wooden desk would face the window, and a papesan chair could go in one corner. There'd be room for an old-fashioned stereo to play my collection of vinyl. With the extra space, I'd have room to store all those records I'd wanted forever. Jefferson Airplane, Pink Floyd, and if I got lucky, some original Beatles.

I stared out the window, daydreaming, hearing the sound of children playing in the back yard. Not *my* children, but kids from the neighborhood, playing tag or hide-n-go seek. Or were they the youngsters of years before?

A stand of trees on the property line provided shade for the edge of the lawn and a home for birds and small animals. My reverie was interrupted when a larger than normal body broke through the underbrush. Not a rabbit or a large bird and not a figment of my imagination. No, a real-life teenage girl, followed by another. After them came two teenage boys.

Instinctively, I moved to hide behind the curtains, but there weren't any. Embarrassed, I chuckled to myself. There was no need to hide anyway. It was my house and my property, and the chances of them spotting me on the third floor slim. Likely they were just out for one last adventure before the end of summer.

Laughing wildly, they stumbled to the ground beneath the largest tree. One boy pulled a bottle from his backpack and passed it around. They were smart to stay hydrated. It wasn't good they tossed the empty bottle aside instead of taking it with them to dispose of properly. I'd need to take a walk around the yard to make sure they didn't leave behind other garbage.

Which made me think of Jake, because he used to do that. No surprise he hadn't been in contact since I left Charleston, but I hoped Annabelle had news. The cell phone signal was better on the other side of the house, so I walked down the hall and typed up a text to send. I didn't want to appear overly-anxious so I kept it simple. "*Any updates?*"

While waiting for a response, I returned to my original task of inspecting the house for flaws. All I discovered was a small spot in the upstairs bathroom that needed a second coat of paint. The leftover paint was stored in the basement but I'd worn my best jeans for my meeting with Deputy Nelson, so I'd come back later to fix it.

By the time I completed the inspection and headed towards the back yard to pick up trash, the kids had left. A few candy wrappers nestled among the bushes, hidden like left-over Easter eggs, and a single sheet of newspaper fluttered at the base of the steps leading to the back porch. An empty tobacco can marked the spot where one of the boys had sat, and I shook my head as I picked it up. The kids were too young for any of them to start such a filthy habit.

The water bottle was just out of reach and as I stretched and picked it up, a trickle of liquid ran out. *Water for the lawn.* Then the odor hit me, and I sniffed the bottle. Alcohol. Strong alcohol. Even as I ran my finger around the lip of the bottle, I realized it was a stupid thing to do, but I did it anyway. I lifted my finger to my lips and licked it. And gagged.

Rotgut. That was the only way I could classify the vile liquid. Hell, I'd drunk some nasty stuff in my life, but it was the worst thing I'd *ever* run across. And the kids sucked it down like water. I shuddered as I tossed the bottle into the garbage bag.

As I threw the bag onto Dolores' floorboard, the sound of an engine revving caught my attention. I glanced up, expecting to see a friend pulling into the driveway. Instead, a black sedan tore down the street, turned the corner, and disappeared.

The next stop was the sheriff's office. It served a double purpose. First, to request the weekly reports Deputy Nelson told me about. Second, to scare off anyone who followed me. Although I didn't spot the black car again, my nerves stayed on edge.

The reports weren't free but I convinced myself they were an investment. Unfortunately, I couldn't check right away how big my return would be by adding the information to my graphs. I still had a real job to do, one I'd get paid for. The ladies-in-waiting of Queen Victoria's court were the research topic of the day.

Chapter 20

Normally calm, cool and collected Sarah fidgeted with the collar of her blouse as she ordered lunch. I couldn't imagine what had changed since Girl's Night Out at the Burger Barn. Or why she would want to brave the Friday lunch crowd instead of telling me what was up over the phone. As we waited for our food, she avoided the topic, repeating a story about kids who set up a lemonade stand in front of the real estate agency.

When she switched to describing the flaws found in some new listings, I figured we were getting closer. One house had termites and needed major reconstruction. Had termites been spotted in mine? But, no, I'd had a termite inspection done so that wouldn't be right. Another house had several broken windows that needed replaced. I *knew* that wasn't a problem. What was she hinting at?

Once we'd finished eating, she pulled a stack of paperwork out of her briefcase and put it on the table. "Remember, I'm just the messenger. I didn't even do the showing. That was Carla from our competitors."

"What am I looking at?" I didn't have the patience to read through the legalese on the top sheet.

"It's a bid for the house." She flipped to the third page and laid her hand over the middle. "As your realtor, I pass on all offers. That doesn't mean you have to accept the first one."

"And as my friend?"

"I'll let you see it first." Sarah's lips formed a tight line and she moved her hand.

It took a moment to process the information. "Are you kidding me?"

"Is that a no?"

"Even better, it's a hell no. Are these fools serious?" They'd offered $100,000 less than the asking price.

"I figured that would be your reaction. Do you want to make a counter-offer?"

"Sure. Request $100,000 over the current price. Will that send the right message?"

The corner of Sarah's lips curled. "Nice. I'm tempted. Better than rejecting the offer."

Idly I flipped through the rest of the paperwork. It was my first offer, after all, and I wanted to know what to expect the next time. The name of the potential buyer caught my eye.

"Paul Zavari?" I raised my eyebrows. "Is he who I think he is?"

Sarah sighed. "I hoped you wouldn't see the connection. Yes, it's one of the guys from The Dog House."

I didn't want him anywhere near my house let alone have him buy and live in it. "Reject the offer," I said crisply. "No counter offer."

"I thought you might feel that way. That's why I didn't tell you up front."

I didn't like being manipulated but Sarah was just looking out for me. "The house has only been on the market for a few days. I'm not even close to being desperate." I'd never be so desperate I'd sell to Paul.

"It's good you feel that way. Still, I want it to sell quickly at your asking price."

Of course she would. The more it sold for the bigger her commission would be. "You have any more showings scheduled?"

Sarah shook her head. "Nothing." Her face brightened. "I received an interesting email from a law firm in Pittsburgh. They wanted more information about the house for one of their clients. I'll go out this afternoon and take more pictures."

I stewed over the information as we paid our bills and left the restaurant. "Does that happen often?"

"Once in a while. When someone is looking to move a long distance and wants to have a place ready for them. Or they're buying it as an investment or for another family member."

That made sense, but I didn't like the idea of selling to an unknown person. "Do I get to know who's buying it before the final paperwork is signed?"

"Why is that important? Look, Harmony, I understand you like to control things, but let me do my job. I have your best interests at heart, I promise you."

I took a deep breath. "Joe and Luke and I put so much work into the house, I want to make sure whoever buys it will take care of it."

"You have to let go. Once you sell the place, it's not yours anymore."

I knew that. Intellectually, of course… Emotionally was a whole different game.

"I've never done this before," I said with a shrug. *Is this what it felt like to be a parent and watch your children grow?*

She opened the door to get into her car as I turned to walk back to the library. "Harmony?" she asked, pausing halfway in, "Are you all right?"

That stopped me in my tracks. "Yes. Why? Do I look sick?"

"More tired than sick. Even your glasses don't hide the bags under your eyes. Are you having trouble sleeping? Are you that worried about the house?"

I worried about a lot of things… Like my entire future. And the law enforcement bomb due to explode. "I stayed up too late last night working on a project." In fact, for the last three nights I'd gone to bed way past my normal schedule. No matter what info I fed into the computer, or how I manipulated the data, I couldn't find a root cause for the increase in calls to the various law enforcement agencies. But it was there, somewhere, and I'd stumble across it eventually. I crossed my fingers behind my back and lied, "I'll get to bed early tonight."

I vowed to not touch the charts all weekend. I'd come back to them after a few days for a fresh look. My weekend cleaning ritual was what I needed to relax and cleanse my mind. It started off well enough as I vacuumed and dusted while listening to a playlist of hits from the disco era.

Cleaning the refrigerator was next on the list. Since I hadn't done it the prior weekend, I put extra effort into the job.

But as I watered the African violets on the kitchen windowsill, my mind wandered back to the ivy in Annabelle's office. And as I scrubbed the front door around the handle, I worried about Jake. It wasn't the same coming home knowing he hadn't been there. The last I'd heard from Annabelle, she had nothing to report. Jake was still acting as a chauffeur.

I may have cast longing glances towards my laptop while straightening the books. Each one had to sit at the edge of the shelf, its spine aligned with every other book and in a strict Dewey Decimal formation. Jake loved to rearrange one or two books to see how long it would take me to catch they were out of place.

The bedroom seemed like safer territory. Piper greeted me cheerfully as I made the trip to the basement to wash the sheets. Luckily, I'd remembered to stick a doggie biscuit in my pocket.

As I pulled fresh sheets out of the linen closet, the memories of sharing those sheets with Eli crept into my brain. It would be easy enough to send a video conference to him, but that would mean touching the laptop. So I settled for sending him a quick text message. *"I love you."*

Clearly, I needed to get away from the apartment. Maybe an impromptu movie day with my friends would help. But realtors are busy on weekends, Janine had mentioned going to visit her aunt, and Merrilee had a date. It was just me, and a solo trip to the theater didn't sound like any fun.

While I mulled over my lack of options, I tackled the bathroom. Scrubbing the tub was cathartic but the lack of mental stimulation meant my mind had the freedom to roam over the many problems at hand. I raced to answer when my home phone rang, but the person at the other end hung up by the time I got there. Sales call, likely. I'd been getting too many of those.

"This is ridiculous." I threw the sponge into the tub and sat back with my back against the wall and my knees tucked into my chest. A stiff drink or two was in order, but nothing was more pathetic than the vision of me getting drunk all by myself. There was only one solution—a long drive in Dolores with the windows down, going as fast as I dared.

A flip of a quarter determined I'd head south. West might have been better with less traffic but I wouldn't fight fate. With Betsy tucked under the driver's seat and a full tank of gas, I headed towards Pittsburgh.

Dolores always drew stares but I'd gotten accustomed to ignoring them. With the radio tuned to classic rock, turned up as loud as I could stand it, and not a cop in sight, I blew past both the north and south Pittsburgh city limits barely slowing down for the heavier traffic.

At the West Virginia Welcome Center, I stopped for a break and a soda. A couple of truckers discussed the construction down the road. Bridge repair or something, but I rejected the hint to head home. It was still daylight.

Between the gravel on the road, the lower speed limit and the fact that the construction narrowed the interstate down to two lanes, I regretted my decision soon enough. Especially as I got stuck behind a mini-van whose driver couldn't keep a constant speed.

Just before Morgantown, a vehicle coming the other way flashed its lights several times. Nice guy, warning drivers of a speed trap ahead, but I wasn't worried. Not with Miss Mini-van in front of me.

As the car sped past me, I caught a glimpse of the driver. My plans changed immediately and I thanked the gods there was an exit a mile down the road.

It was Jake.

From the quick glimpse I'd caught, he didn't appear to be in distress, so this wasn't a rescue mission. But he'd *wanted* me to see him. I wouldn't be able to follow him without being noticed, so as I waited for my chance to pull back onto the interstate headed north, I devised a plan.

The two-lane traffic pattern meant I'd have no possibility of catching up to him until we got out of the construction. Since Dolores wasn't built for stealth surveillance, I'd have to use a different approach once I got past the road work. Hopefully, Jake would cooperate by not speeding up too much once he got clear of the construction and make my task easier.

A major challenge would be identifying the car from a distance. Every black or dark blue vehicle ever made was on the road that day. Unless Jake made the car stand out somehow, I'd zip right by it.

Happily, I didn't get stuck behind another soccer mom when the road returned to a normal traffic pattern. With the gas pedal pushed a little farther than it should have been, I zig-zagged my way north, keeping one eye on traffic while the other kept watch for law enforcement. The last thing I needed was to be stopped for speeding or failure to maintain my lane.

Ahead, a car flashed its brake lights. My first thought was there had been an accident but no one else slowed. The lights lit up again and I tried to tell if they were in a particular pattern, but they seemed random. And that's what convinced me it was Jake signaling.

I settled into a spot three cars back. Close enough to track him, but not so close to seem that I was following him. There was no hope that Dolores wouldn't stand out amid all the generic cars that filled the road.

When his right turn signal came on, I wasn't sure if it held a message or if he was pulling off the road until I spotted the sign for the rest stop. Luckily, the car in front of me also decided to make a stop and gave me some cover. Jake pulled into a spot near to the main sidewalk, but as normal, I guided Dolores to a stop as far away from other vehicles as possible. The precaution added extra steps for me, but helped avoid scratches from people carelessly opening their car doors.

I got out and, leaning against the car, pretended to make a call. In reality, I watched to see what Jake and his passengers were up to. And where was Annabelle? Shouldn't she be around? What was I paying her for?

Two of the men went inside, while one, a balding overweight man, stayed outside with Jake. So much for my chances of talking to him alone. I shot off a quick text to Annabelle. *"Target in sight. Where are you?"*

I opened the trunk and stuck my head inside, pretending to re-arrange the several boxes I kept back there. If Jake saw an opening, he'd find a way to get a message to me. I tried so hard to not pay attention that when a man walked up behind me and said "Nice car," I almost hit my head on the trunk lid as I straightened.

A normal person would have apologized for startling me. Not this guy. He laughed. Which made me angry. And when I recognized him as the guy who'd been with Jake, I got mad. But I couldn't do anything about it which made me even angrier. I shoved the anger into a tiny corner of my brain to store for later and pretended I was a meek little librarian.

Chapter 21

"The car is pretty, isn't it?" I tittered. "It was *so* nice of my brother to let me borrow it." I stroked the trunk lid before gently lowering it. "Even if it's way too powerful for me." I maneuvered around him to shut the driver's side door. The new position gave me the ability to see Jake by glancing over the man's shoulder.

"How fast can it go?" the man asked.

"How would I know? The speed limit is 65. Most of the time, I don't go that fast." I flashed an apologetic smile.

He waggled an eyebrow and jerked his head towards Jake. "My buddy over there is a professional driver. He could test it for you."

I made a big show out of looking towards Jake. "You mean like a race car driver?" I added a touch of Southern Belle to my act. All I needed was a fan to wave in flutter in front of my face but I settled for fluttering my eyelashes. "Oh, no, my brother would *never* forgive me if I let someone else drive his baby. Even someone as good-looking as your friend."

There was no way that Jake would have suggested he wanted to drive Dolores. Was the guy looking for a way to hijack her? He had a surprise coming his way if he tried. First, I needed to get back into Dolores to get my gun from under the seat.

The buzzing of the cell phone in my pocket gave me the perfect excuse. "Excuse me," I said with another flutter of my eyelashes, "I have to take this." Without giving him a chance to protest, I slid into the driver's seat and shut the door. He had no excuse to stick around and with my peripheral vision, I watched him leave.

Annabelle had texted me back. *"*#&** Broke down near Clarksburg. You?"*

"Rest stop near the border. Jake and three more."

"That's one too many."

Which of the three men was the extra? The whole setup made me nervous. Since they knew what Dolores and I looked like, there wasn't any way I was going to be able to tail them.

But if I left now, and drove slow, they'd catch up and pass me. Then I'd hang just a little way back and pray that Jake would warn me of any changes. As far as plans went, it was weak, but no other alternative presented itself. Before starting Dolores' engine, I reached down and found Betsy and set her on the passenger's seat.

I wasn't sure whose eyes burned a hole in the

back of my head as I pulled out. Or how many sets of eyes tracked my passage. I prayed the ploy would work.

In the slow lane, I puttered along at the leisurely rate of 60 MPH, annoying those who fought traffic to pass me. While keeping an eye out for Jake and his companions, I broke my rule of no phone calls while driving and called Annabelle.

"Any idea who those guys are?" I asked without even saying hi, assuming her phone had identified who it was before she answered.

It didn't seem to bother her. "Not a f… clue. He picked them up at one of the normal clubs. They stuck a sh… bunch of boxes in the trunk, but didn't let Jake carry them. Where are you now?"

"Headed north, waiting for Jake to catch up." I explained the situation. "Hopefully they won't take any of the exits I've passed."

Annabelle grunted noncommittally.

"How bad's your car?" I asked. Before she answered, I quickly added, "And watch your language."

Another grunt. "It's fixable. Belt snapped. I'm waiting for the tow truck."

In my rear view mirror, I spotted the car Jake drove pull into the passing lane. "There they are," I told Annabelle. "Gonna hang up. I'll update you later." I wouldn't be able to concentrate while talking to her.

To make it look as if I was nervous, I adjusted my posture, leaning forward and gripping the steering wheel at ten and two. The man from the rest stop waved as they pulled past me. I nodded my head but didn't wave back.

The two men in the back seat turned and craned their heads, clearly studying me. I dropped back and let another car take the spot in between us. Repeating the maneuver provided an even better safety net. To make it less obvious, I waited a few minutes before allowing a third car to slip in between us.

By then, I hoped they'd lost interest in me. All but Jake. He'd flashed his brake lights each time the space between us got bigger. I'd flashed my headlights in acknowledgment the first time, but only once. He knew me well enough to know my actions were deliberate.

I assumed we were heading for Pittsburgh. I was wrong. As we blew by exit after exit, I started to worry. If they pulled off onto one of the roads leading to a residential area, I'd stick out if I followed. But they drove right past Pittsburgh.

At first, I thought the sirens I heard came from the radio, part of whatever rock song was playing. As they grew louder and more urgent, I kept a watch on my mirrors. Everyone started pulling over from the left lane into the right one, and I let one more car slip in front of me. But a car farther up seemed determined to be the good neighbor and allowed four or five cars to squeeze in. And I had no way of knowing just how many other cars had moved in between me and Jake.

As I tried to figure out my next step, two highway patrol cars screamed by. Drivers started moving back to the fast lane, but then squeezed right back where they'd come from. It wasn't long before a fire truck, sirens wailing and lights flashing, tore down the road. I sent up a small prayer for whoever had been in the accident, then cursed, because I didn't see any way I'd catch up with Jake.

Even with the emergency vehicles out of sight, people seemed reluctant to move back into the passing lane. Maybe they expected an ambulance or two, or were afraid to change lanes and then find themselves stuck as the odd man out closer to the accident. So we crawled along single file, craning our heads to spot the cause of the holdup.

Finally, a black SUV that had been behind me for some time pulled into the left lane and hit the gas. The move broke the spell, and other drivers copied the maneuver. Soon I was able to speed up as well, and traffic resumed its normal flow. By that time, the black SUV had been lost in the traffic ahead. Which made me happy. Something about it gave me the creeps.

The accident turned out to be a few more miles up the road, but on the other side of the interstate. By the time I got to the exit for Oak Grove, I still hadn't seen any sign of Jake. Reluctantly, I gave up the chase and headed home.

❀ ❀ ❀

Sunday was my day to relax. Kick back and catch up on my reading list or talk to friends. Help Joe and Luke with yard work when they needed it.

But to start the day, I sat with my cup of coffee at the bottom of the steps, patted Piper, and read the comics. The birds sang, the wind blew gently, the early morning sun sparkled in a cloudless sky. It was perfect enough that I relaxed for the first time in days.

Until Piper rushed the gate, barking furiously. Which meant it was someone I didn't want to see. With Betsy upstairs, locked into her case, I looked around to find something to use for protection. The Sunday paper wouldn't cut it. Running upstairs would leave me with my back to the intruder. At least my cell phone was in my pocket, with 9-1-1 on speed dial.

With my phone in my hand, I stood, planted my feet shoulder-length apart in a defensive posture, and waited.

When the man came around the corner of the house, I took a moment to search for a new contact. I didn't need to call the emergency line, but I might need to contact Dan. Not what I wanted to do on Sunday morning.

"Agent Garza," I acknowledged, speaking loudly enough to be heard over Piper's barking. "What brings you here?" Especially on a Sunday. And obviously on the clock because he was dressed in the traditional black suit. I wondered how many of them he owned.

"I should arrest you for interfering with a federal investigation," he growled. "But I'm here to give you a chance to explain yourself."

He'd find out I didn't blackmail as easy as Jake. Maybe I could pry information out of him that would be helpful to my research. I put my phone back in my pocket—after starting the voice recording app—picked my coffee cup from the stair and took a sip. "What investigation would that be?"

"You know what I'm talking about."

Sure I did, but I wanted it on record. "Enlighten me."

He glanced around frowning. "Are your landlords home?"

They were probably still asleep. "It's not my day to keep track of them."

His frown got deeper. "Don't play games with me, Miss Duprie."

That was ironic, coming from the man who was playing with Jake's life. The Southern Belle took over. "Why, whatever are you talking about, Agent?" I asked with as much innocence as I could muster.

He tired of the circular questions first. "Yesterday," he snapped. "On the interstate. What were you doing there? And explain to me your use of the crime statistics database. I've been tracking your usage."

That did it. I was over being stuck in the middle. It was time for all these law enforcement types to start talking to each other. "Have you read the morning paper?" I asked. "Because I'll give you your answers, but not until a couple of other people get here. You can either wait here, or go sit in your car. I promise I'm not going to try to escape."

Piper had stopped barking but eyed Agent Garza with a threatening look. "Can't I wait in your apartment?"

Vampires couldn't enter your home unless you invited them in, but that rule didn't apply to the FBI. They needed a warrant, which I was sure Agent Garza didn't have. I didn't want him overhearing my phone calls or leaving behind one of his listening devices. Still, it wouldn't be polite to leave him cooling his heels outside while I made my preparations. "Fine. Follow me. But don't even bother asking me any questions until I say you can."

I made my phone calls in order of distance—the farthest person away got called first. Then I made a fresh pot of coffee while waiting for my guests to arrive. I put Agent Garza to work after that, helping me to hang a white sheet over the curtain rod of the windows in the front room. It would act as a screen for the projector I'd attach to my laptop for the meeting. There wasn't room for everyone to huddle around my laptop screen.

The invitees arrived in opposite order of their calls. That meant Chief Sorenson was first. He was dressed in a nice suit and I wondered if I'd pulled him out of church. I'd have to make it up to him somehow. He glared at Agent Garza and followed me into the kitchen when I offered him a cup of coffee.

"What's he doing here?"

"If you can wait a few minutes, I'll explain." I wanted to wait until everyone arrived, so I only had to tell the story once.

Next to arrive was Deputy Nelson. He was in full uniform and I apologized for pulling him off patrol but he assured me he had permission from the Sheriff himself. After making introductions all around and getting the deputy something to drink, we went into waiting mode. I needed one more person there.

Joe came up the stairs first, alerted to the unusual activity by Piper's behavior and, as he told me, the number of cars parked along the street. After one glimpse of the front room, he offered to call Dan for me and to stick around. I sent him away, assuring him everything was okay, not wanting him to be dragged into the mess.

I wasn't sure how long it would take my last guest to arrive, so I turned on the TV and tuned it to a weather channel to break the heavy silence. Let them discuss the potential tornadoes in the Midwest before I unleashed my own storm of information.

But before long, the three men got restless. If my last guest didn't show soon, I'd have a rebellion on my hands. I was already nervous, and the delay wasn't helping to sooth my fears.

Finally, I heard them. Footsteps on the stairs. Purposeful, but not hurried. I flung open the door as he raised his hand to knock. "Glad you could make it, Agent Felton."

Chapter 22

"This is quite the gathering, Miss Duprie," Agent Felton said, scanning the room. "But you're missing Captain Hodges of the Highway Patrol. And I don't believe I've met the deputy."

I'd fix that, although I couldn't fix the glare he sent Garza's direction. "Agent Felton, this is Deputy Theo Nelson. Deputy, Agent Marcus Felton of the FBI."

The two men shook hands while I poured Felton a cup of coffee and started a new pot. Once he'd settled into the last available chair, I handed the cup to him and plopped down on the floor by the coffee table. It was funny to see all four men get to their feet simultaneously to offer me their seat. "No, I'm good," I said, waving my hand towards the laptop, strategically placed on the coffee table. "But please take your seats and let's get started."

"Can you give us a clue what this is about?" asked Chief Sorenson.

"Agent Garza has taken offense to the time I've

been spending in various crime-related statistical databases," I explained. "I'm going to show all of you what I've been working on. And he seems to think I'm interfering in a federal investigation. Were you aware of any such investigation, Chief?" The more honey I poured into my voice the redder Garza's face got.

Felton shot another glare at Garza before answering. "There's nothing going in Oak Grove that I'm aware of." He raised his cup to his lips and took a swallow. "But I'd like to see what you been up to."

I started with the simple stuff. Basic bar charts of arrests in Oak Grove, then comparing last year to the current year. Barely the hint of an increase.

Then I jumped to the county. Same setup. When I overlapped the county and the city, there was amazingly little difference. That drew murmurs from the audience, but if I didn't show them something good, they'd lose interest.

The next slide was a chart of the "nuisance calls" in the city. Chief Sorenson hadn't seen it yet, so I studied his reaction when the image showed up on the makeshift screen. "That's just the numbers," he said, setting down his cup and leaning forward. "Do you have a breakdown in reasons?"

"It's coming. But first, the county." With the click of the mouse, I brought up the next chart and left it up long enough for Deputy Nelson to get an eyeful. The next chart compared the city and the county.

"Same pattern," Deputy Nelson murmured.

"Exactly. Now here's a pie chart with the reasons for the incident calls for this summer." Noise complaints had the highest piece of the pie for the city, and reports of speeding cars for the county.

"Where are you going with this, Miss Duprie?" Chief Sorenson asked impatiently.

"And what inspired you do it?" Felton added.

"I asked her to," Deputy Nelson and Chief Sorenson said at the same time.

"Exactly." I grinned and bypassed several slides to get the spider chart. The number of lines and colors were enough to cause a major headache. "I've overlapped our local statistics with national ones," I explained. "Oak Grove is green, the county is blue, and red is the national figures."

All four men leaned forward to try to make sense of the display. "We look good compared to national averages," Chief Sorenson said. "But what's the purple? Or are my eyes imagining something that's not there?"

There were a lot of lines in the chart, and the sheet wrinkled, so I didn't blame him for second-guessing himself. "Charleston. West Virginia," I said and waited for it.

Garza's reaction was more subdued than I expected. He hissed. Loudly. But at least he didn't jump up and threaten to slap the cuffs on me.

Deputy Nelson nodded while Chief Sorenson looked thoughtful. The question came from Agent Felton. "Why Charleston?"

"Annabelle," I answered promptly.

"Annabelle?

I nodded. "Annabelle LeRoix. The PI who was beat up a few days after the murder."

"I don't understand."

"She's from Charleston. She was up here on a hunch. It didn't work out for her."

Nelson cleared his throat. "I asked Miss Duprie to research Miss LeRoix, to look for information that would convince her to help our investigations. Both the beating and the murder. She drew a blank."

"Except I think that she knows more than what's she's saying." I grinned. "So I hired her."

"To do what?" Nelson asked.

I left the question hanging in the air for a few seconds, hoping Garza would speak up. His continued silence made me lose any remaining shred of respect I might have had for him. "She's following Jake," I said.

"Jake? Jake Hennessey?" The Chief blurted. "What's he doing in Charleston?"

I crossed my arms over my chest and stared at Garza. "I can't tell you. I'd be interfering in a federal investigation. Right, Agent Garza?"

He paled under the stares of the other three men. "I don't know anyone in the Charleston office, so I asked him for a favor. Heard rumors about something big going on there, but it's out of my territory."

Asked Jake for a favor? Not the way Jake told the story.

"He was under strict instructions not to tell anyone. Why did he tell you?"

I knew the game. Garza was trying to shift the blame away from himself.

"Jake didn't reveal that you'd blackmailed him until I went to Charleston last weekend," I said, as matter-of-factually as possible, "and ran into him there. He told me because he was trying to convince me to leave town."

"Garza blackmailed Hennessey?" Felton asked. His eyebrows twitched and I wondered how hard he was working to control himself.

"According to Jake, your co-worker said he'd cook up paperwork to send Jake back to prison."

If I'd had a clock on the wall, we could have heard it ticking like a time bomb in the sudden silence. The two federal agents engaged in a stare-down and I wasn't sure who was winning. Deputy Nelson and the Chief pretended to study the spider graph still on display.

Finally, Felton jerked his head and stalked to the door. Garza, studiously avoiding looking at the rest of us, followed him. The yelling didn't start until they were too far down the stairs to overhear the conversation.

Chief Sorenson cleared his throat. "Let's see what you've got going, Harmony."

Once I got over my shock at him using my first name, I swung into researcher mode. "I'm looking for variations in patterns," I explained. "Inconsistencies. Something that doesn't quite fit."

"And?"

With a grimace, I stood and walked over to the sheet, tapping several spots where the lines overlapped. The sheet shimmered at my touch, causing the display to distort. "I've got nothing. No matter how I manipulate the data, nothing sticks out. Except, that is, for the murder and Annabelle's beating." I tapped the two peaks that indicated those events.

"Why did you bring us all here, if that's the case?" Deputy Nelson asked, frustration evident in his voice. "I could be out trying to chase down leads and protect and serve."

"Agent Garza forced my hand. I planned to go through these figures one more time before I talked to you." Or maybe two or three times. I still felt as if the answer was just out of my reach. "And I hoped fresh eyes would pick out what I'm missing. You've got a different perspective than me. And in the Chief's case, years of experience in law enforcement."

"She's right to bring us together," Chief Sorenson said. "We're better off combining our efforts."

"The way I see it," and I tapped the sheet again, "is that figures don't lie. But they also don't replace your gut feelings. Something is going on and we have to figure out what it is."

It's not like the two of them hadn't been trying already. And when Felton returned—minus Garza—he wanted to be involved too. He even gave me permission to talk about Jake and Charleston and said he'd take responsibility if the

Special Agent in charge of the Pittsburgh office got upset.

Not that there was much to share. I explained that Jake was being used as a chauffeur and he hadn't learned anything important. But he thought something was up too. And that we weren't in contact because he didn't want to risk blowing his cover. I left out the part about me being in Charleston as my alternate personality. The fewer people who knew about Tiffini the better.

It didn't take long until the discussion turned into a testosterone match as each man tried to outdo the others with stories of their crime fighting abilities. I turned on hostess mode and kept the coffee and ice tea coming. Around noon, I ordered Chinese for all.

After lunch, we got back to work. For real. I took their suggestions and questions and re-graphed the same information I'd already graphed four times. Even with their suggestions, I couldn't get the charts to reveal any secret, hidden nugget of information.

We gave up in the middle of the afternoon. They had other places to go, things to do. In the aftermath, I had cleaning to tackle.

Chief Sorenson, the last to leave, stopped on his way out the door. "Thank you, Harmony. Your instincts were correct. Sometimes we in law enforcement get territorial. We didn't resolve anything today, but now we're cooperating. That will go a long way."

My cheeks burned, and I made a show of leaning over to pick up a napkin from the floor to hide my reaction. "It makes me feel safer. Besides, I had an ulterior motive. I didn't want to be the only one with access to the information." And I hoped it would end up in protection for Jake, too. Felton had promised to do what he could to bring Jake home.

Although I had my doubts Jake would want to come back to Oak Grove. Not long-term, anyway. He wouldn't stick around once he found out I was leaving. It wasn't his home. As far as I knew, he didn't really have a home. Besides, he was an adrenalin junkie. The thrill of the hunt would keep him distracted. Temporarily, at least.

❁ ❁ ❁

Even though three additional sets of eyes hadn't found any gold in the crime data, I didn't want to give up. But I was forced to take a break by the need to finish up the projects for my authors. We were having our final get-together at the Wrangler Buffet on Thursday. They might still have meetings, but unless I decided to write a book, there wasn't a reason for me to go anymore.

Buried behind a stack of books at my favorite table in the library, I delved once again into Regency England. The information I needed was easy to find but I was reluctant to put the books away and turn off my laptop. I wasn't ready to accept that my 'job' had run its course. When I got home, I couldn't gather the enthusiasm to do much more that stretch out as much as possible on my loveseat and read. I put on a happy face for my call with Eli, using every ounce of my limited acting skills.

Tuesday and Wednesday were repeats of Monday. Different topics, but the same routine. I'd miss the routine. Even my 'outside jobs' were drying up. I understood because college students wouldn't start writing papers again until the middle of the semester. What was I to do for money until then?

Granted, it was a silly question. I had money. I just liked to live on what I earned, not spend the money I'd inherited. Becoming a lady of leisure wasn't in my future. Being forced to take a break was, however.

Chapter 23

Girls' Night Out did nothing to shake my mood. Sarah had a headache after having one of her panic attacks, Merrilee's latest special friend moved out of town for a new job, and Janine—she wouldn't say what was bothering her, but something was. The restaurant—one of those chain ones off the interstate—didn't help. The waitress didn't understand the concept of sitting around and talking after a meal. Even though the dining area was mostly deserted, she kept cleaning around us, trying to get us to leave.

So, we left. And went home. Separately. No drama, no lingering in the parking lot making other plans.

The apartment seemed emptier than usual when I unlocked and opened the door. I was tempted to transform myself into Tiffini and go back out. But I didn't have the energy required to get all dressed up and do the makeup. Instead, I slipped into my old bathrobe and turned on my laptop. Maybe checking email would provide the needed distraction.

The one message asking for research assistance wouldn't support me, but I accepted it anyway because it sounded interesting. The requester wanted information on her great-grandparents during the Great Depression. She thought they lived in western Pennsylvania, but wasn't sure.

With the 'real' email taken care of, I moved on to my spam folder. No, I didn't need to re-finance my student loans or buy any male enhancement treatments. Or invest in penny stocks. But it turned into a good thing I took time checking instead of mass-deleting the entire list, because that's where I found my response from Professor Bouchard.

He'd passed on the copy of the note to several acquaintances to verify his results and would get back to me. Sounded encouraging. At least, I took it that way, needing any good news I could get. I thanked him for the update, turned off the laptop, and tumbled into bed.

Someone would be taking pictures, I figured, so I wore my contacts, dress slacks and heels, and even makeup for the last meeting. And I was right. But I cried and my makeup smeared. I forgot to bring tissues and resorted to using the restaurant's rough napkins to wipe away the tears.

I caught several of my authors wiping their eyes too. Their promises to keep in touch were sincere, but I knew how those things went. They'd get busy, and I'd never hear from them again. But that was life, and I planned a quiet exit into the sunset.

Because just like Jake, there was no reason for me to stay in Oak Grove anymore. Once I sold the house, I'd be gone.

With that in mind, I swung by the house to make sure no more garbage had accumulated in the yard. With the weekend coming up, it was likely there'd be a showing or two. Besides, I didn't want to show up at the library with my mascara smeared and my nose red or go home.

As I sat on the corner down the block waiting to make my turn onto the street that ran by the house, I saw an older black sedan pull into the drive. Huh. Sarah hadn't mentioned any new potential customers and they would have come in her car anyway. Maybe it was someone wanting to check the outside of house before contacting a realtor. That made sense, but I couldn't convince my gut it was the truth. Too many similar vehicles haunted my life.

I backed up enough to park Dolores where the hedges hid her from the house. After tucking Betsy in my waistband and my cell phone in my pants pocket, I headed up the street, darting from tree to tree, wobbling in my heels. Whenever a car drove by, I dropped to a normal walk and pretended nothing was going on. I convinced myself I needed to do this on my own. It wasn't like I could call Freddie and get the police involved. It was perfectly legal for someone to stop and take a gander at a for-sale house.

The journey between the edge of the drive and the house presented a problem. The long driveway and open yard I was so proud of offered nowhere to hide. Sure, I could circle around and come through the woods at the back, but that would take too long.

I stopped by the big old oak tree marking the edge of the yard to study the situation. Three cars, not one, sat in front of the house. None of them belonged to Sarah. Three men stood on the porch, one waving his arms wildly in the air. I sucked in my breath. Him I recognized. Paul Zavari.

Had he put in another bid on the house? Were the other two men interested as well? If I got lucky, they'd start a bidding war against each other.

Paul waved his hand towards the cars. Worried they'd see me, I flattened myself against the tree and waited a few seconds before sticking my head back out. Then ducked right back into my hiding spot. If they glanced towards the road as they headed towards the cars, I'd be caught. I needed a new way to conceal myself.

The large azalea bush a few feet away held potential, *If* I sprinted there and crouched low enough to hide behind the thickest cluster of leaves near the bottom. It seemed like a solid plan.

Except for my heels. I forgot I wore heels. At each step, my heels dug into the well-watered ground. I lost my left shoe first. By the time I made it to the azalea, my feet were covered only by shredded hose.

But I made it safely and knelt in the grass. I'd hoped to get close enough to overhear what they discussed but they talked quietly and I only caught occasional words.

Peeking between the leaves of the azalea, I watched as Paul moved a box from the trunk of his dark blue car to the trunk of the black sedan. Then another one. They looked heavy, and I wondered why the other guys didn't help. And darn my luck, they still had their backs to me.

I used the opportunity to snap a few pictures of the men and the cars. What I wanted were pictures of the license plates, but the cars were parked at the wrong angle. I'd have to wait until they left and try to snap pictures as they checked for traffic before pulling onto the street.

A landscaper's old pickup rattled down the street. As it turned the corner, it backfired and released a belch of black smoke. As I turned to look, I almost missed my chance, but turned back to the men just in time.

But in my surprise, I almost dropped my camera. They also turned at the loud POP and I got a glimpse of all three faces. The second man I didn't know, but the third one, the one that seemed familiar—I'd eaten supper with him not too long ago.

It was Carlisle Buford. Carl. The French teacher.

The red hair should have been a giveaway, and I don't know how I missed it. School was out for the day, but Paul seemed like an unlikely person for Carl to hang out with. They didn't seem interested in the house itself, so what were they doing there? And if they were having a clandestine meeting of some sort, why didn't they do it behind the house instead of in front of it? Nothing made sense.

I snapped one picture before they turned back to their project. Paul closed his trunk and the men moved to the next car, an old beige beater. It was Carl who pulled out his keys and opened the trunk. Two boxes were transferred from the blue car into the trunk of the beige car. Ordinary cardboard boxes, the ones grocery stores give away, so they didn't provide any clue to what was inside.

When they shook hands and appeared to be ready to leave, I realized Carl would recognize Delores. I needed to leave before they did. I crouched low, and headed back to the street, retrieving my shoes on the way. Once I got back to the sidewalk, I slipped them on and rapidly walked back the way I'd come.

I'd gotten into Dolores and was sitting at the stop sign when the blue sedan drove down the cross street. With the tinted windows rolled up, I couldn't see if the driver glanced my way or not. I pulled in behind him, but didn't follow him very far. Two blocks down the street, before he had a chance to get nervous, I made a left-hand turn. Paul and Carl must have headed the opposite direction because I never caught sight of them in my mirror, and I checked. Frequently.

On the drive home, I mulled over the incident.

Although it was odd—strange, even—nothing illegal occurred. It certainly didn't rank a call to Freddie. Which led me to wonder if the Chief had shared my charts with his lead detective. I'd been half-expecting Freddie to show up on my doorstep all week long, wanting to discuss the information.

Deep in thought, I didn't pay as much attention to traffic as I should have. So, when I stopped at a red light and glanced behind me, I was startled to see a black sedan. A second look told me it wasn't Paul driving and I relaxed. Still, when the light turned green, I proceeded, staying diligent.

The chances of it being random when the car followed me through the right hand turn two lights later were fifty-fifty. The odds of it being a coincidence when they followed me into the parking lot of McGrady's Grocery were slim. When I parked as far away as possible from the store, and the car pulled into a slot three rows away, the likelihood of it being unplanned shrunk to next to nothing.

Without turning Dolores' engine off, I stepped out of the car and pretended to search my purse for something. Her motor's purr was soft enough I doubted they could tell that she was still running. In my peripheral vision, I saw someone step out of the other vehicle. It didn't look like one of Agent Garza's cronies. I held up my phone, as if taking a selfie, but in reality I used the picture to study my tail. At that distance, however, the details blended in with the background.

I pretended to make a call and waited. And

waited. Finally, a man stepped out of the driver's side and shut the door. That was the opportunity I'd been waiting for. In a flash, I jumped back into Dolores, snapped on my seat belt and took off. Simultaneously reminding myself to breathe and keeping an eye on my rear-view mirror, I pulled onto the street in front of a slow-moving Buick driven by a little old woman. She honked her horn at me, and I gave her an apologetic wave,

The black car got stuck behind her and a dually pickup. When the opportunity arose to make a left-hand turn as the traffic light switched to orange, I took it. At the next intersection, I made an abrupt right. And decided it might be time to have a talk with Freddie.

Chapter 24

"If you were anyone else," Freddie sighed, "I'd say they were experiencing paranoid delusions. But this is you, and somehow you attract trouble." He leaned forward and put his ice tea on the coffee table. On a coaster, of course.

He'd come by my place after he got off work, having been out on a call when I dropped by the police station. "Thanks, Captain Obvious," I said with a sigh. "Thing is, I don't know if it was the FBI, someone interested in Dolores, or something else." My pictures turned out blurry and useless.

"And all I can tell you is to be vigilant. Watch your surroundings when you come and go, keep the doors locked when you're in your car, lock the door when you get home, and always check to see who it is before you answer your door."

A very good habit I'd gotten careless about recently.

"Can I convince you to go stay with a friend for

a few days?" he asked, "Or visit Eli? At least until the task force figures out what's going on."

Yes, the sheriff and Chief Sorenson put together an impromptu task force to share pertinent information. I figured they'd meet a few times and get nothing accomplished, but it would look good on paper.

"You know me better than that." Particularly as I wasn't willing to abandon Jake. "But I promise to be careful. I came to you, after all, instead of trying to convince myself it was a coincidence."

He grinned. "Baby steps. Are you still taking those self-defense classes?"

Between the trip to Florida and the time spent working on the house, I'd stopped. "I took a break."

"Hmm. And the last time you shot your gun?"

Even longer. Not since the day Eli and I argued at the range. I kept Betsy cleaned and oiled, but I'd lost my taste for target practice. With a shrug of my shoulders, I answered. "It's been awhile."

Freddie shook his head. "Not good. I'm only asking because I care about you."

Sometimes having a cop as a friend was inconvenient. Especially when he knew too much about my personal business. Granted, other times it had its advantages. Like when he was willing to drop by to talk to me after work.

"I'll try to work it into my day tomorrow."

Did I really believe he wouldn't be able to tell I was lying? "Don't blow it off, Harmony. It's important to keep your skills sharp."

My instructor had drilled that into my head.

"You're right. And I promise I'll try." I'd have plenty of time, but wasn't ready to reveal my situation to him, or any of my friends. Not yet.

❊ ❊ ❊

Friday morning, I got up, took my shower, made coffee and took a cup with me when I went downstairs to retrieve the paper and sit on the bottom steps to read it. A perfectly normal day. Except I was unemployed.

Piper seemed to sense my mood, and after getting the standard treat, lay as close as he could get. If it hadn't been for the fence, he would have been in my lap. It was good to have a friend who couldn't pester me with a zillion questions I didn't want to answer.

Not being motivated, I got to the library late. Well, late based on my normal schedule. The only reason I even went was to check for new job opportunities. Sure, I could have stayed home and perused the various job sites, but some places didn't post their openings until they'd been advertised locally. The periodical room at the library would see a lot more of me than usual.

To my surprise, Janine didn't accost me when I walked in and bypassed my normal table. In fact, I didn't even see her. She was probably at a meeting or buried in her office doing paperwork. I considered tracking her down to say hi, but didn't want to interrupt.

Instead, I ensconced myself in a soft chair with

the daily newspapers of the five nearest cities. If I moved to one of them, I'd be able to come back to Oak Grove to visit my friends at a moment's notice. But the help wanted ads mocked me. If I'd been a nurse or a truck driver, lots of opportunities would be available. Not so much for a librarian.

Even expanding the geographic area didn't help. The only opportunities were in places I didn't want to live. New York City wasn't my kind of town.

Accepting temporary defeat, I fired up my laptop. Time to resort to the on-line job sites and update my resume.

Despite my conversation with Freddie, I decided Tiffini needed to make a reappearance. Or maybe she was Tiffini's cousin, because I swapped out the wig to a short blond one, did my makeup differently and modified my outfit to be more sedate. Slightly. I named the new version Rainey Peaters.

I checked my outfit in the mirror one more time—a tight sweater, short skirt and leggings—and wondered why I was taking the risk. All the available information was in the hands of law enforcement. But there was a piece of the puzzle missing and no one else could go undercover like me. They'd have to bring in someone from out of town.

Besides, it was a way to work off my frustrations.

I slipped on a pair of over-sized sunglasses before leaving my apartment. With the sun setting, I wouldn't be able to wear them for long, but they'd provide extra cover for the short trip to the convenience store. The sandals I picked featured a shorter and broader heel, so walking down the steps became easier.

During the walk, I debated my choice of destination—either back to Charlie's or hit up The Dog House. Although it was more likely I'd get some real information at The Dog House, the other bar would be a safer choice. I chose The Dog House.

The cab driver kept checking me out in his mirror. Enough that it made me squirm. When I handed him the cash to pay for my ride, he sniffed it! I hoped I'd get a different cabby for the ride home.

Wolf whistles greeted me as soon as I walked in the door. I considered turning around and heading back outside. But I figured I only had one chance as Rainey, and I didn't want to blow it. With a sickeningly sweet smile for the bartender, I settled onto an empty stool.

He raised an eyebrow. "A light beer," I requested.

My choice clearly disgusted him but he drew it and slid it across the bar. The large tip I included in my payment ensured he'd keep an eye on me. That was my theory, anyway. He wasn't the same guy who'd been tending during my last visit. I didn't recognize the waitress on duty either.

It didn't take long for the man on my left side to turn and strike up a conversation. "Nice night."

He eyed me as I studied him. Younger than many of the others in the bar, he didn't seem to fit in. For one, he was much better looking than everyone else. He didn't have the rough look desperation etched on many of the faces.

"Yep," I answered.

He lifted his glass my direction. "And it's getting better."

Did he really think that old line would work? Well, this time it would. With a smile, I lifted my beer mug. "Could be."

Then the guy on my right got in on the action. He was older, had a pot belly, and the way he was going bald reminded me of a monk from the Middle Ages. "A pretty girl always makes the night better," he said.

Great. I was surrounded by males with no imagination. I smiled at him, figuring if anything bad happened, at least *one* of the men would watch out for me.

"You two know each other?" I asked, trying to get a feel for the lay of the land.

They grunted simultaneously. "Not really," said the guy on the left.

I needed to find out their names. Or make some up for them. Tweedle Dee and Tweedle Dum would work as long as I never called them by name.

"I've never seen you here before," said Dum, the guy on the right.

"You new around here?" Dee asked at the same time.

I'd planned my cover story in advance. "Only in

town for one night," I told them. "The clerk at the motel told me this was a good place to get a drink."

"You can hardly call a light beer a drink," said Dum.

"Let me buy you a *real* drink," said Dee.

"I'm good. Thanks anyway." I took a small sip of my beer. "I have to pace myself, ya' know."

Both Dee and Dum chuckled, and I relaxed a tiny bit. Still, it was time to switch the attention off of me and on something else. "What are the Steelers chances of making the playoffs this year?"

That's all it took. All I had to do was nod at the right time and let them argue the merits of the new quarterback. I got a kink in my neck from turning my head back and forth as they took turns talking. But paying attention to Dee and Dum meant I couldn't keep an eye on the rest of the bar.

After draining my beer—I didn't trust either of them enough to leave them alone with my drink—I headed for the ladies room. It was a single stall setup, and I ended up in a small line that formed in the hallway. While we women waited, three men pushed by us to enter the men's restroom.

With my head down I dug into my purse, pretending to hunt for something. I didn't want Brent to have the chance to get a good look at me.

I considered leaving, but I really needed to use the facilities. Besides, the night was just getting started. I pulled out my cell phone and shuffled through old messages, mimicking the woman in front of me.

By the time Brent and one of his companions exited the men's room, I'd made it to the front of the line. My nose still buried in my phone display, I barely glanced their direction. That didn't stop me from overhearing a snippet of conversation.

"… late," Brent said. "Road construction."

"Can't be helped." The other man shrugged his shoulders and they returned to the main bar.

My mind immediately jumped to the road work I'd run into the previous weekend. But my logical side scolded me for making assumptions. It was construction season. Road repairs were happening all over the place.

I was still wondering what—or who—was late after using the restroom. On my return to the bar, my ego took a big hit. Dee had abandoned his seat to go flirt with a newcomer. Dum barely nodded at me when I slid back onto the barstool as he and another man discussed politics. I was so easily dismissed and replaced.

The bartender noticed my predicament and held up an empty mug. With a lopsided grin, I nodded. I didn't want to be too noticeable by leaving so early in the evening.

Then Brent came and stood at the bar a few feet away from me. The bartender leaned over and they held a quiet conversation. Not quiet enough that the background noise drowned them out.

"You have enough for a day or two?" Brent asked.

The bartender grunted. "Enough for tonight but not tomorrow."

"I'll see what I can do to get you more."

"Hopefully it'll be better. That last batch tasted off."

"What do you think?" Dum asked, breaking my concentration.

I didn't have the foggiest idea what he was asking about. "I haven't made up my mind yet," I said. Brent and the bartender moved away, and any chance of figuring out what they were discussing vanished. "I don't think we've got all the facts yet."

Dum and the other man expounding on the evils of a new bill being debated in the state legislature, one to increase the penalties for possession of small amounts of marijuana. I concentrated on my beer and nodded every once in a while. My instincts had been wrong—I wasn't going to learn anything interesting. I'd be hitting the internet again in the morning, trying to find data I'd missed along the way.

Chapter 23

I stood at the darkened corner of the building waiting for the cab to show up, avoiding the haze surrounding the smokers near the door. The odor of tobacco and weed would be next to impossible to remove from the wig. Even if I never appeared as Rainey again, it would be a great addition to a Halloween costume.

The men passed around a flask, each taking a swallow. They coughed, shuddered and sighed before passing the flask along. I kept my eyes on my cell phone, pretending not to watch them, but in reality, I was trying to figure out what they were doing. Surely they wouldn't bring along their own supply of liquor to a bar.

Each time a car pulled in off the road, I looked up, hoping it would be my cab. The dispatcher had promised it would only be a few minutes, and I'd already waited fifteen. My feet hurt, and I shifted my weight from side to side to relieve the pressure. I wasn't use to wearing heels.

The uncomfortable prickle at the back of my neck told me I was being watched, too. I couldn't catch any of the smokers casting their eyes my direction, so the perceived threat had to come from another direction. Half of the lights in the parking lot were out, so someone might be in one of the cars and I'd never spot him. Or her.

If I called the cab company again, would they get upset? It was a risk I was willing to take. I moved a few steps away from the building, hoping to get more than two bars worth of signal.

"You waiting for someone?" a gruff voice asked to my right.

"My ride," I answered blandly, without looking up. I didn't want to show any interest.

"The night is young," came a second voice from my left.

I was in trouble. The voices held no hint of helpfulness. "And I have an early morning. So it's time for me to go home."

"Don't you want to party with us?" The smell of alcohol lingered heavily on the first man's breath.

"No thanks."

The man on the left reached out and grabbed my arm. "Sure you do."

I didn't even think about it. Although I was out of practice, the move was ingrained. I brought the side of my hand down on his lower arm near the elbow and pushed him away, dropping my phone in the process. Better to lose the phone than a fight. He staggered backwards, missed a step, and fell on his ass. The next step was to run. My shoes weren't made for running. I whirled to face the first man, my hands in tightly balled fists.

He backed away, hands held at shoulder height. "It was a joke!" He pointed somewhere behind him. "They dared us!'

What were they, twelve? I didn't have time for their nonsense, nor the inclination to deal with it. "I'm not in the mood for games," I snarled.

"We're sorry!" He backed away two more steps, accompanied by the snickers of the men near the door.

Time to make a graceful exit. But the taxi still hadn't shown up. The parking lot was no safer than where I stood and I didn't want to force my way through the group of men blocking the front door. I was stuck.

A sudden flare of bright light illuminated the front of the bar, and I raised an arm to protect my eyes. I hadn't even seen the car pull up. "Sorry I'm late," a deep voice boomed.

I recognized the voice. I casually reached down and scooped up my phone. "Later, losers," I said, stepped off the front sidewalk and headed towards the passenger's side. I yanked open the door, slid into the front seat and reached for the seat belt.

The driver threw the car into reverse and gunned it before I had the belt fastened, forcing me against the seat back. With one hand, I braced myself against the dashboard, preparing for his next move. As he twisted the steering wheel, he braked, then shifted into drive. The tires squealed and he burned rubber as he tore out of the parking lot, pulling in front of an oncoming pickup. I wasn't worried because I knew his driving skills. He'd taught me, after all.

"Good timing," I said, finally getting my seatbelt fastened.

Jake turned with a big smile. "Nice getup. I almost didn't recognize you. Wasn't sure if you wanted my help or not. You handled yourself pretty good for a girl."

Was that a compliment or a dig? I didn't want to get into an argument. "So what are you doing here?"

He glanced at the rearview mirror, then the sideview mirror, then back at the rearview one. I twisted as far as possible in my seat to look out the back window. "Are we being followed?"

"No."

I took his word for it and faced forward.

"No," he repeated, "I lost my tail outside of Charleston. She's not as good as she thinks she is. Just making sure I didn't pick up a new one here. You wouldn't know anything about that, would you?"

I covered my mouth to hide my grin and pretended to cough. "Me?"

"That's what I figured. I didn't tag her as FBI. I thought you trusted me, Angel."

"You, I trust." Well, mostly. He knew far too much about things he shouldn't for me to trust him entirely. "The situation is another story. I thought a little backup wouldn't hurt. Did the guys you are working for make her?"

"Not yet, but she's getting sloppy."

"I'll call her off."

Jake nodded once. We rolled up to a red light and he tapped the steering wheel impatiently. "She should have gotten the message tonight. To get one flat tire is coincidental, but when you get two the same night..." The light turned green and he stepped on the gas. "Don't be surprised if you hear from her in the morning."

No loss. Annabelle hadn't provided me with any useful information anyway. "So what are you doing here?"

He grunted. "Playing errand boy. I visited three different bars and picked up an envelope from each, including The Dog House. I went in and out the back doors so the customers wouldn't see me."

"What's in the envelopes?"

"No idea. They're padded and sealed." He jerked his head towards the back seat. "See for yourself."

They were basic shipping envelopes and I figured the internet would reveal ways to open them without leaving any trace of surreptitious activity behind. Home would be the perfect place to try. If we could get there with no one seeing us. Or...

"Any chance there's a tracker on the car?" I asked.

His lips tightened. "I didn't have the opportunity to check. I'm operating under the assumption there is because they don't trust me yet."

Well, there went my plan and I didn't have a Plan B. It was discouraging being so close to a potential clue and not being able to do anything about it.

"In that case, you'd better drop me off a few blocks from home," I suggested. "Plausible deniability." And that was even more frustrating, because we had so much to talk about. At least, there were things I needed to tell him.

But Jake, being Jake, reacted in his own unique way. He flashed that overwhelmingly sexy grin of his and asked "You sure you don't want me to walk you to your door? And invite me in for a nightcap?"

Actually, I did, yes, but not for the reason he hoped. But he knew that, and that I wouldn't take him seriously. "Not tonight, I said regretfully.

"I don't want you walking home by yourself. So how about I pop by the convenience store and get a drink for the trip home. Then just happen to go by your place on the way back to the highway."

The plan seemed flawless on the surface. "Okay."

"I'll leave the empty cup in the console." Another of his trademark grins. "Plausible deniability."

Several cars occupied spots in the parking lot of the convenience store, but none I recognized. Jake pulled into the darkest space available and turned to me. "Are you going to be alright waiting for me out here?" he asked with real concern.

I snorted. "Me? Go on, go buy your drink."

He got out and glanced around. "Keep the doors locked," he whispered, before closing his.

Good advice, but before I pushed the switch to do just that, he locked the car from the key fob. That was fine with me.

I waited until he was in the store before unfastening my seat belt and twisting and stretching towards the back. I picked up the envelopes to examine them. The store's outside lights provided enough illumination to give them a good looking-over.

It wouldn't be an easy job to break into them. There was a possibility I could steam them open, but the plastic exteriors might melt. At this time of night, I couldn't buy new ones to replace them. Besides, I wouldn't be able to duplicate the scrawled names on the outside.

I fondled one of the envelopes, looking for clues to the contents. It was stuffed full, but weighed next to nothing. Was it filled with paper or feathers? When I prodded the package, the crinkling sounds came from the packaging itself. What seemed to be a layer of cardboard on either side blocked me from deducing anything based on the shape or size of the contents.

Carefully, I tried sliding one fingernail under the glue strip to pry it loose. If I got lucky, it hadn't been secured tightly. A flash of guilt, and I looked towards the store's entrance to see if Jake was on his way yet. If I damaged the envelope, he'd be the one taking the blame.

The glare of headlights as another car pulled into the parking lot drew my attention. I stopped messing with the envelope and looked down so my face couldn't be seen. Not that I expected to see anyone I knew, but better to minimize any chance of being recognized.

I waited for someone to get out of the vehicle so I could resume my work on the envelope. When I didn't catch any movement in my peripheral vision, I ventured a glance that direction. And immediately crunched down as far as possible into my seat.

The darkness made it hard to tell, but that sure looked like the same car that had followed me a few days back.

Where the hell was Jake? What was taking him so long? Knowing him, he was inside flirting with the clerk. I couldn't even text him to tell him to hurry his ass up. And what were the guys in the other car doing? Yes, my quick glance confirmed two people occupied the vehicle.

But there were a lot of black cars in town. Paranoia was the only thing connecting this one to the others.

The click of the door unlocking alerted me to Jake's return. It was followed almost immediately by the driver's side door opening. "What the hell, Angel?"

"Get in, quick,' I hissed. He slid into the driver's seat. "Take a gander at the car beside us. Just a quick one. Don't be obvious."

"Okay," he said, stretching out the word. "And?"

"Do you recognize them?"

"No."

` "Get us out of here."

He started the motor and turned his head while he backed up. "Do you know them?"

"No. But black cars seem to be showing up no matter where I go. One even followed me about a week ago. It makes me nervous."

"Who have you told?"

I straightened up as he pulled into the street. The muscles in my back had started to cramp, and I needed to stretch. "No one. I can't prove it, and don't want to look like a fool."

He kept his eyes on the rear view mirror. "They haven't moved."

"See what I mean? My natural instincts have gone haywire."

"So they didn't pan out this time. That doesn't mean they haven't been right every other time." He turned the car down the street towards my place. "Keep your eyes open. I wish there was a way to keep in touch."

Me too. But it was too risky for him.

"Did you make any headway on the envelopes?" he asked, glancing down at my lap.

I sighed and tossed them into the back seat. "No. I can't break the seal."

"If I see what's inside, I'll find a way to pass the information along. Maybe I can get a message to your PI."

She wouldn't be my PI much longer. "Don't take any risks, Jake," I said as he pulled up to the curb near the back of the house. Not that I had any hope he'd take my advice.

He reached over and patted my thigh. "I'll be careful. Now get out of here. I have to hit the road."

I couldn't help myself. I leaned over and kissed him on the cheek. Then, before he reacted, I flung the door open and jumped out of the car. "Good night," I said pushing the door closed.

As I rushed up my stairs, I scolded myself for playing with fire and half-expected Jake to follow me. I even paused at the first landing to check. And he must have considered it because it wasn't until I reached the second landing I heard the car pull away.

Chapter 26

Three nights of tossing and turning and worrying did not a rested Harmony make. I was a pro at staying up for caffeine-fueled nights of research, but not being able to sleep when I wanted to was a new experience. Especially that many nights in a row.

Still, I managed to drag myself out of bed on schedule Monday morning, make my coffee, and head downstairs to pick up my paper. After giving Piper a doggy treat, I sat on the next-to-bottom step and turned to the comics. Usually a good way to start the day, but sometimes social commentary overwhelms humor and this was one of those days. Either that or my brain was too sleep-deprived to get the jokes.

Heading to the library and faking I had a reason to be there didn't seem to be a good plan. More out of curiosity than real expectations of finding an interesting post, I flipped to the help wanted ads. The offerings were few and pitiful, but one particular picture in the real estate section at the bottom of the page grabbed my attention.

I didn't realize there was a 1950's A-frame house in the Oak Grove area. It had been used as a vacation home, according to the description. Unfortunately, it looked as if that meant no one had put any money into its maintenance. It needed help, big time. And it called to me.

It was too early for Sarah to be at the office, and I wouldn't call her about business at home. The ad listed the address of the house however, so I could drive out and take a look at it without talking to her first. One quick trip and I'd be able to decide whether it was worth the effort or too much for me to handle. I wouldn't dare ask Luke and Joe to help me with a building that needed torn down and replaced.

Had my GPS steered me wrong? The ad hadn't mentioned a dirt road, especially not one in as rough of a condition at this one. Which explained why I'd never seen the house before. As much as I liked exploring the back roads around Oak Grove, Dolores didn't handle well on dirt.

I gritted my teeth and prayed I wouldn't lose a hubcap as more dips and ridges rattled the car. Fixing an entire road just to get to the house was not in the budget. It doomed the project before I even submitted an initial bid. But I still wanted to see the house so I kept driving.

The road trailed up and down hills and followed

the path of a small creek. After crossing a trembling bridge and steering through a sharp curve, I spotted it. Situated halfway up a hill, a large overgrown yard spread from the tattered front porch all the way to the road. The view of the little tree-filled valley from the picture window would be spectacular in the fall. Despite the ratty appearance of the porch, the rest of the house seemed in better shape than I'd anticipated.

What I didn't expect was the cluster of cars near the detached garage. Was the home occupied? The cars didn't look as if they belonged and were as out of place sitting in the driveway as Dolores would be.

My plan to wander around the property and peer through the windows of the house disappeared into the cloud of dust rising from the dirt road behind me. I wasn't comfortable using the driveway to turn around and head home, feeling like I'd be intruding. I'd need to forge on down the road and hope it didn't dwindle into a wagon path or a cow trail before I found a spot to turn around.

As I drove past the house, slowing so I wouldn't make too much dust, several men came out of the garage and pointed my direction. Typical reaction to Dolores, but they seemed more excited than normal. For maybe two seconds, I thought about honking and waving. When I recognized one man, the plan changed again.

What the hell was Jake doing in the middle of nowhere?

As I glanced over my shoulder towards the house, I saw several men headed for the cars.

Shit.

On a paved road, Dolores was a goddess. On the dirt road, not so much. If they followed me, I didn't know if I could evade them.

My best strategy was to get a flying head start and pray. And I didn't have time to pray. With one foot on the clutch and the other on the gas, I shoved the gearstick into second and stomped on the pedal. The bumps in the road smoothed out as Dolores' wheels barely touched most of them.

The cloud of dust in my wake prevented me from seeing how many cars followed behind me. Even with the windows closed, particles of dirt crept into the car. I coughed to clear my throat. The GPS kept intoning "at the first opportunity, make a legal U-turn." I didn't dare take my hands off the steering wheel to silence it.

Then the unprayed-for miracle happened. The road turned into rough pavement. Not city street or interstate smooth, but not ridges and depressions either. Dolores' tires hummed on the surface, and I shifted into third. And then into fourth.

Two cars appeared out of the dust cloud. If Jake drove one of them, he wouldn't take it easy on me. He couldn't, not if he wanted to keep his reputation. And his life. Without knowing what kind of engines or suspensions the cars had, I didn't dare make assumptions about their capabilities.

My best shot was a game of hide-n-seek. But doing sixty on a road posted for thirty didn't leave me much room for sightseeing or scanning for side roads. Hell, we were on a side road. The only cutoffs I expected to find were driveways, and they wouldn't do me any good. I needed to find a major highway. One I was familiar with and Jake wasn't. *If* such a thing existed. And still the GPS unit droned on about correcting my route.

I spared a sideways glance to locate the button to turn it off and saw it displayed the map of my route. A second glance confirmed what I thought I'd seen. The bad news was the road ended soon. The good news was it ended onto a bigger road, and that road joined a major highway, all within a few miles. I had this.

The stop sign that marked the end of the road couldn't come soon enough. Jake was closing the gap between us. I didn't make a complete stop. With no trees blocking my view of the intersection, I blasted through a small gap in the oncoming traffic. Instinct screamed at me to make a right-hand turn, so I swung hard to the left. *Do the unexpected.* That had been one of Jake's rules. Would he remember it?

He wasn't so lucky with traffic. When he reached

the intersection, so did a slow-moving farm truck followed by a string of cars. I'd be a mile or more down the road before he ever made his turn.

I wouldn't wait for him to catch up either, so I floored it, getting up as much speed as possible in the short distance to the major highway. Luck stayed with me because the traffic signal turned green as I pulled into the line with three other cars. The few seconds I had to wait for them to clear the road took forever, but then it was my turn. And still no sign of Jake in my mirror.

This time I took a right. Then another right, into the entryway to an outlet mall. I'd been here once before, shopping with Janine, so I was in semi-familiar territory. All the roundabouts and heavy traffic slowed me down, but also gave me abundant opportunities to make myself scarce. I could slip into the alleyway between stores and hide. Which I did. What it didn't do was give me a clear view of the highway so I could watch for Jake to drive by.

Then I waited ten minutes. Hopefully, Jake would be able to use the excuse of losing me in traffic to end the chase. I dismissed the niggling worry that he'd turned traitor and would try to find me. Although the parking spot was shaded, I turned the air conditioning vents to blow on me when a few droplets of sweat trickled down my forehead. Even my palms were damp.

While I waited, I reset the GPS to take me home. The nagging message was replaced by a new one, telling me which direction I should drive to get back to the highway. At first, I thought it had messed up, because it seemed to be directing me the wrong way. But studying the map, I realized there was a back entrance and that's where it wanted me to go. Perfect.

As always, Dolores drew a few stares, but nothing out of the ordinary. With the ten minutes over, I crept from my hiding place. Plenty of black cars circled the parking lot, but none seemed to be looking for me. No one followed me as I turned onto the highway and nothing suspicious happened on the way home. Still, I tucked Dolores into the garage, closing and locking the garage door behind me,

I contemplated my next move as I climbed the stairs to my apartment. Should I call one of my law enforcement contacts? If so, which one? As far as I knew, the group hadn't been doing anything illegal. Well, except for exceeding the speed limit and I was guilty of that too. I wasn't even sure if the house sat within our local county or in another one.

That left only my favorite FBI agent. He'd have the contacts to keep an eye on the place if he deemed it important. I'd give him a call and update him, leaving out a few minor details.

My next call would be to Sarah. Not to tell her what happened, but to get more information on the property. Did someone still live there? And what shape was it in? Any give in the asking price? Simple questions any prospective buyer might ask their real estate broker. It would also be a great excuse to see if there'd been any showings on my house.

Beyond that, I'd hibernate for the rest of the day. Stay out of the public eye. Read a book and relax. Have a couple of beers or a glass of wine or two. Break into my emergency stash of chocolate. Yep, that sounded like a plan. At least it stood a chance of keeping me distracted.

Chapter 27

Agent Felton didn't laugh at me. In fact, he took me seriously. He didn't tell me what he planned to do with the information, but I expected that. One thing I'd figured out was he didn't share his plans with unnecessary people.

The conversation with Sarah took longer. Of course, part of the discussion was her and Freddie's plans for the evening. He was taking her to an upscale restaurant in Pittsburgh for supper followed by a drive to a park along one of the three rivers. It sounded romantic, and I wondered if he'd present her with a ring. But I kept my mouth shut and didn't mention my hunch.

I remembered to ask her about the house. As far as she knew it was empty and shown on an appointment-only basis. But as part of an estate, family members could use it.

I'd barely settled into my easy chair with a book in hand and a beer within easy reach when I heard the distinct sound of a pair of heels walking up my stairs. I didn't make it to the window in time to peek out to see who was coming before my visitor knocked on the door. At least I remembered to look out the peekhole. What was Janine doing here on a Monday afternoon?

She turned down my offer of a beer but took me up on a glass of ice tea. It could have used a drinking partner, but it wouldn't do to have her show up at work with alcohol on her breath. Based on the dark circles under eyes, she hadn't slept for days, so beer wasn't the best thing for her.

We chitchatted for a few minutes about Sarah's date while Janine made up her mind to reveal what had brought her to see me. If tonight turned out to be the night Freddie asked Sarah to marry him, Janine would win our bet. I didn't mind, even though it meant I'd have to pay for her drinks at the next Girl's Night Out.

Halfway through her second glass of ice tea, Janine broke. "I need a favor," she said, her voice so quiet I almost missed it.

"All you need to do is ask."

"You remember my mother moved to Florida a few years ago?"

"Of course I remember." I'd gone to the party her friends had thrown to tell her goodbye. "Didn't you go to see her last winter?"

"Yes. And I'm going back."

"You need me to water your plants? I'll be glad to." I'd done that for her before.

"I need more than that." Were those tears

glimmering in her eyes? "I've talked to the board of directors and they've agreed with my recommendation."

What was she talking about?

"My mother has been diagnosed with stage four breast cancer." The tears ran freely down her cheeks and I rushed to pull her into my arms. I rubbed her back as she sobbed. "I'm going there to be with her. The doctors gave her only a few months to live."

I reached for the box of tissues I kept by the loveseat. We both needed them. After my own parents' death, Janine's mother helped me with arranging the funeral and had been a shoulder to cry on. In a way, she'd been a second mother to me. No matter how much I did for Janine, it wouldn't be enough to pay back all the help her mother gave me.

"What can I do?" I asked, once I'd regained my composure.

Janine blew her nose and sniffed. "I don't know how long I'll be gone."

"That's not important. It's not like I have any big plans." And wasn't that just the truth.

"I'm worried about the library. We're in the middle of so many changes."

Some of which I'd suggested. "Won't someone cover for you?"

"There's only one person I trust to do that."

Normally, I'd be much faster on the uptake. Not that day. Blame it on the lack of sleep or the stress or the morning's activities or whatever. I didn't even think before I opened my mouth. "So ask! Whoever it is, I'm sure they'll be glad to help out."

Janine took a deep breath and blew it out quietly. "Harmony, will you be acting chief librarian while I'm gone?"

I wanted the job. Lord, I wanted the job. But not this way.

Janine caught the hesitation in my eyes. "The Board of Directors has agreed to pay you full salary and provide benefits except for vacation pay. You'll have the same authority I do."

It was a generous offer. One I wouldn't refuse, but not because of the money. It was all about friendship.

"Of course I'll help. Anything for you and your mother. But whose arm did you have to twist to get them to agree to it?"

She grinned through her tears. "It was easier than I expected. I believe several of the board members feel guilty about the way they treated you and they did the hard work for me, pressuring the others to endorse the decision. In the end, they approved it unanimously."

Only because Mr. Randall no longer sat on the board, I was sure. He'd disliked me even before my legal issues. There's no way he would have agreed to the scheme.

"You need a ride to the airport?" I asked. "It'll

be tight, but I'm sure we can get your luggage into Dolores."

"Are you in a hurry to get rid of me?" Janine laughed shakily. "I haven't even bought a ticket yet."

Three days later I sat at her desk and stared at the stack of paperwork waiting for me, wondering what I'd gotten myself into. I'd spent twelve hours a day with Janine for the last two days, but it wasn't enough time to prepare me for the task ahead. At least it had distracted me from thinking about Jake. And the murder. And the house not being sold yet.

I'd come in early—ridiculously early—to have time to myself and settle my nerves. The cup of coffee I'd brought with me sat cooling near my right hand. I'd only taken one or two sips of it before setting it aside. Caffeine wouldn't cure stage fright.

Obviously, Janine had told the staff I was covering for her, but I wasn't sure what their reactions would be. So, I stood by the back door and greeted each one as they arrived for work. Then I got out of their way and let them do their jobs. They didn't need me hanging over them.

Secretly, I hoped for the kind of welcome that Janine received when she started the job, but I didn't expect it. Still, I was disappointed when no one knocked on the office door to welcome me. Or even acknowledged my presence. Maybe the citizens of Oak Grove hadn't truly forgiven me for my perceived failings. Or word just hadn't gotten out about the arrangement. I could hope.

So late morning, when I was engrossed in studying the list of recommendations from the volunteer committee for book purchases, I jumped at the loud knock on the office door. The cold cup of coffee on my desk almost got knocked over but luck stayed with me and it wobbled but settled back in place. "Come in," I called, picking up a large stack of papers, trying to appear businesslike.

"Flowers for Miss Duprie." I couldn't see the face behind the large multi-colored bouquet, but the voice was familiar.

"Eli? What are you doing here?"

The flowers moved and his faced peeked around them. "I couldn't resist," he said. "I've been missing you and this seemed like the perfect reason to show up."

He didn't need a reason, but I wasn't going to ruin the moment. "I can think of something better for you to hold in your arms than the flowers, even though they are beautiful."

He set them on top of a novel on one corner of the desk, but I was too busy being kissed to scold him.

In what seemed like only a few seconds later, there was a timid-sounding rap on the door. We broke apart, somewhat guiltily. I was supposed to be working after all, and had a lot to prove. "Come on in," I called after straightening my blouse and patting the back of my head to make sure my bun was secure.

Eleanor, one of the long-time volunteers, stuck her head into the office. "Sorry to interrupt, Miss Duprie," she said with a broad grin that told me she was putting on a show. "But there's a *patron* out here requesting we remove a book from the shelves."

That wasn't going to happen. I didn't believe in censorship. And from the tone of Eleanor's voice, I guessed the *patron* to be someone who never actually used the library. "Ask them to have a seat," I said. "I'll be with them in a minute."

Eli winked at me. "Go get 'em, Buttercup."

It was too easy, dealing with the complainant. Mrs. Pohl had a reputation for complaining about adult books. It didn't matter that adults were reading them—we had a policy that children and young teens couldn't check out adult books without written permission from a parent. I handed her yet another copy of that policy as well as the official statement on censorship and sent her on her way. Even so, she'd be back in a month or two with a new complaint.

The incident seemed to break an unseen barrier between me and the staff, perhaps because it showed I wasn't going to change the way the library operated. The rest of the day, they trickled in in one's and two's to tell me they were happy I'd been picked to fill in during Janine's absence. What touched me the most was the high school volunteers. They came in as a group—even the ones not working—to make sure I knew they'd be glad to help me with whatever I needed.

Eli set up his temporary office at my favorite table since I wasn't going to be using it. Every so often, I found an excuse to walk through the main room and stop by to exchange a few quiet words with him.

It was frustrating, not being able to call it a day on my schedule instead of one set for me. Eli's presence was both a comfort and a distraction. There was so much I wanted to tell him but the library wasn't the proper place to have the conversation. Since I hadn't expected company, we went out for supper, and I still couldn't tell him what I wanted to. By the time we got to my place, we had better things to do than talk, and all my worries disappeared—at least for a while.

❆ ❆ ❆

Eli's side of the bed was empty when my alarm clock went off in the morning, but the sweet-sharp smell of coffee hung in the air, telling me he wasn't far away. I stretched, rolled over, and slid out from the warmth of the light blanket I used during the cool late-summer nights.

I considered padding my way out to the kitchen just as I was to surprise him, but thought better of it and tugged on my robe. He might have pulled open the curtains in the front room, and I didn't want to parade my naked butt in front of the window.

Instead, I stopped in the bathroom long enough to tuck a few stray hairs behind my ears. "Good morning, Sweetie," I said, admiring his shirtless body as I walked into the kitchen.

He turned with a big smile on his face and a cup of coffee in his hand. "Good morning, Buttercup." His free hand snaked around my waist and he pulled me close. "I missed this," he said as he lowered his lips to meet mine.

"Me too." The doubts I had about our relationship disappeared the moment I saw him in the office. They might come rushing back when he left, but for the moment we were good. Especially then, when his warmth enveloped me.

I reluctantly pulled away before things got too interesting. With my head against his shoulder, I whispered, "I need to get ready for work."

"We don't want the new chief librarian to be late on her second day, do we?" He squeezed me tighter. "It's going to be strange, knowing you can't pack up your laptop and spend time with me whenever you want."

It would be an adjustment for me, too.

"Don't get me wrong," he added, "I'm proud of you. I understand the position is temporary, but look at all the obstacles you've overcome to get this far."

"You don't think it looks like I got handed the job just because Janine is my friend?"

Eli ran his fingers through the hair at the back of my neck. "There's always going to be someone who tries to put you down. Don't listen to them. I know and you know that you are the best person available to fill in for Janine, and the fact that she's your friend has nothing to do with it. If you'd said no, where would the city get someone to relieve Janine? Out of Pittsburgh or Cleveland? And how much would that cost?"

I'd considered those same ideas, but it was comforting to hear someone else say them. I stepped back, regretting that I had to leave his arms and asked, "What are your plans for the day?"

He poured a second cup of coffee, added just the right amount of cream and sugar, and handed it to me. "If it's all right with you, I'll hang out here and work for a couple of hours." I translated that to mean all day. He continued, "I have a phone call to make I don't want anyone to overhear plus your WiFi is more secure than the library's." True, because he and his cohorts had set it up for me. "And then I'll take you out to dinner."

I would have loved to stay home and spend the day close to him, but dinner would be a good consolation prize. "Works for me," I said. "Now I have something to look forward to all day."

Chapter 28

It didn't work out that way. I got so overwhelmed I didn't have more than a moment or two to think of anything but business. One of the staff members called in sick, and I needed to rearrange the schedule. After that crisis was resolved, I met with the teacher from the high school to set up informational meeting times for students interested in volunteering as part of their graduation requirements. Finally, half the board members showed up—not in a group—and I had to spend time with each and every one.

Thank heavens Janine caught up on most of the paperwork before she left because if every day turned out like this I'd have to use a lot of early morning hours to do everything I needed to. Or late evenings. Or both. And I'd committed my nights to a more pleasurable interest, at least as long as Eli stayed in town.

But it had been a long time since I'd needed to be so sociable for so many hours in the same day, and by the end of it, I was worn out. In fact, when I parked Dolores along the curb by the house, I wondered if I could talk Eli into ordering supper in to give me time to relax and recuperate. When he met me at the door in a perfectly fitting deep gray suit, I gave up that idea.

"Looking good." I eyed him up and down. "You going somewhere important?"

"Since I'm escorting the best looking lady in town out to supper, I dressed for the occasion."

Heat rose in my cheeks. Eli didn't throw out compliments easily and I appreciated every one of them. "I'm not sure I can meet your expectations."

He grinned. "You do every time you smile at me."

I didn't know I could blush that hard.

"We have reservations at The Grove in an hour. Is that enough time for you to get ready?"

The Grove was the finest restaurant in the city. An hour should have been more than enough. But I wanted to put in extra effort to do him justice. I wouldn't have time to do anything fancy with my hair but didn't want to wear it in my typical bun. And what dress would work? My normal wardrobe was pants, although I had a few dresses in the back of my closet. "An hour should be good. But what are you going to do in the meantime?" If he got busy, I'd sneak in extra time for myself.

"A little reading. I've got contract revisions waiting for my signature."

He'd never called me for a celebration of his last

project, and I hadn't brought it up in conversation. "Something big in the works?"

"A couple of old ventures I'm still trying to close. It's like someone is leaking information to our biggest competitor and making negotiations rough."

I couldn't imagine how hurt Eli would be if that were true. He'd built the company from scratch and personally hired each employee. I'd met—and liked—most of them. If one of them was betraying him… "Are you sure?" I asked.

"No. For all I know the leaks are coming from customers. I'm working on it." He sighed.

That explained a lot. Like why he seemed stressed when we talked. And why we didn't talk as much as we used to. "Anything I can do to help?"

"Yes. You can go get ready. I need you to distract me tonight."

My mouth twitched. There were several ways to do that but most of them would have to wait until we got back.

The knee-length dark blue dress with the plunging neckline was a good start. The sparkling necklace that glittered against my skin added a nice touch. When I sat beside Eli on the loveseat to strap on my stiletto heels, pulling my dress up around my hips to do so, his eyes nearly popped out of his head. Good. The plan was working.

Wordlessly, he set his laptop on the coffee table and stood, extending his hand to help me. With as much grace as possible, I took his hand and wobbled to a standing position. I was worried about making it down the steps safely but that was my secret.

"Shall we go, Miss Duprie?" he asked, offering his crooked arm.

"But of course, Mr. Hennessey. Let me grab my purse first."

The purse didn't match the rest of the outfit, but that's where Dolores' keys were stashed. They were another part of my plan. After all, I didn't let just *anyone* drive her.

Eli almost dropped them when I tossed him the keys. His smile stretched across his face. "Do we have to go straight to the restaurant?" he asked.

I planted a peck on his cheek. "You're driving. Your call."

The drive to The Grove was uneventful. Except for the preponderance of black cars on the road. Which I didn't mention because I didn't want my paranoia to cast a shadow across our evening. We barely got there in time for our reservation. Yes, Eli took the longest possible route to the restaurant and I didn't mind.

We ate, we drank, we talked. We even danced. It was the perfect evening. I was determined that no one and nothing would ruin it. He needed it and I did too. So it was late when we finally left. Late enough I suspected our waiter was tapping his foot in the kitchen, anxious for us to settle the bill and leave.

There were still a few cars in the parking lot when we left, but truthfully, I was too wrapped up in Eli to pay any attention to them. He opened the passenger's side door and held it for me while I settled in. "In one way I want to head straight back to your place and in another I want to take you somewhere else," he said.

I knew how he felt. There was magic in the air. "Want to go star-watching at the point?" I asked. "If we get lucky we might catch sight of a meteor or two."

"Oh, I'm planning to get lucky tonight." He snapped on his seatbelt. "But that will wait. Tell me where to go, fair lady, and we'll ask this trusty steed to take us there."

He wanted to play, did he? "If thou wilt take a right at the exit, Sir Knight," I said, "And follow the path northward, the gentle Dolores wilt be headed the right direction."

Eli snorted. I swear, it was an actual snort. "The good Dolores is a demon in disguise, with fire in her hoofs. But she has never done us wrong, and verily, I trust her to take care of us now. So I will do as you ask, Lady Harmony."

We kept the banter going all the way to Oak Grove's make-out spot. On a cliff above town, the lights of the city laid spread at our feet and the stars glittered overhead. We lowered the roof and reclined our seats as far as they went. I took off my shoes to give myself more room to stretch out.

We held hands but neither of us spoke for a long while. "There goes one!" I said excitedly, raising my free hand and pointing when I caught a flash from the corner of my eye.

"Where?"

"Oh, it's gone."

Eli sighed. "I missed it."

"Maybe you'll catch the next one." I patted his hand to comfort him.

"You know, I've never done this in Florida. I don't think there's any place dark enough. There are lights everywhere. Unless you're in a swamp, and mosquitoes make putting down the roof impossible."

"But you have rockets," I said. "We don't." He'd taken me to a launch during my trip to visit him. I'd been properly overwhelmed.

"True."

We lapsed back into silence and studied the sky. Around us, the other cars were leaving, one by one, as curfews approached for the teens inside them. I eventually drowsed off, not meaning to, but it had been a long couple of days.

The glare of a flashlight shining in my face woke me. I blinked rapidly and rubbed my eyes like a child does upon waking from a nap.

"A little old to be out parking, aren't you?" a voice asked from somewhere in the vicinity.

I sat up and blinked more, trying to adjust my vision. It helped when the light was no longer in my face. Beside me, I sensed Eli performing similar actions.

"Didn't expect to find you here when I made my rounds," the voice chuckled.

Recognition slipped in between the cracks of post-sleep obliviousness. "Still on the Captain's black list, Deputy?" I asked, remembering from my high school days that the sheriff's department patrolled the area at night to send kids home. But Deputy Nelson seemed like an unlikely candidate for the job. He switched the flashlight off and tucked it into his duty belt.

"Not sure if it's the Captain or the Lieutenant," he admitted.

"Eli, this is Deputy Theo Nelson. I believe I've mentioned him. Deputy, Eli Hennessey."

Eli reach across me and extended his hand. "Pleased to meet you."

In the dim light provided by the almost-full moon, the deputy studied Eli. "You aren't from around here, are you?" he asked.

"No, I'm from Florida. The Orlando area." When the deputy released his hand, Eli draped his arm across my shoulders. It looked as if another testosterone battle was shaping up. "I'm up visiting and staying with Harmony." And whoop, there it was.

The perfect evening had lulled me into complacency, however, so I didn't object. In fact, I may have found it a bit funny. Didn't Eli realize that he had no competition?

"Then I won't tell you to get a room. But if you're tired enough to fall asleep here, I suggest the two of you head back to town." Deputy Nelson shook his head and grinned. "Can't have you setting a bad example for the kids."

And I couldn't risk getting caught in a compromising situation now that I was acting Chief Librarian. "Thank you, Deputy," I said demurely, covering my mouth and yawning. "We'll head back to my place. The moon is too bright for star watching anyway."

"Is that what they call it these days?" He winked, tapped on the car door, and returned to his cruiser.

He'd barely pulled away before I looked over at Eli. The expression on his face was either embarrassment or consternation. I wasn't sure which. And, God help me, I giggled. Just a little, at first. Then it turned to laughter. Eli got over himself and grinned. Then he laughed. Soon I was laughing so hard I couldn't catch my breath and I straight-up snorted. More than once. Whatever tension we felt disappeared. When I got the hiccups, it made Eli laugh even harder which made me laugh harder. Which didn't help me get rid of the hiccups at all.

It was a good thing I'd put on waterproof mascara because I was laughing so hard tears dribbled from the corner of my eyes. Which made me worry that my contacts would slip out of place. So I resorted to holding my breath. Which mostly worked. And as Eli was also sobering up, it made it easier for me to get control of myself.

"Oh, man," he said, taking a deep breath. "I haven't laughed that hard for ages."

I nodded in agreement. "Grade school, maybe. But I needed that."

Eli pulled his ever-present cell phone out of his suit coat pocket and glanced at it. "It's after one. I guess we should head back to your place."

Sadly, I agreed. "Yeah, I have to be at work in the morning. Or, I should say, later this morning."

"Well, I hope you can put off sleep for a little while." Eli's hand strayed to my knee and wandered under my dress and then northward. "I had one more thing planned."

"Thought you were going to get lucky? Maybe you will and maybe you won't." But since I chose that moment to run my hand over his upper thigh, it was clear I was teasing him.

He groaned and withdrew his hand from my leg. He started the car and raised the roof. "I'm already lucky, having you in my life. Now I need to show you how much I love you."

And here I thought I couldn't get any luckier. Maybe he'd prove me wrong.

Chapter 29

That time of the night, the streets of Oak Grove were empty. Still, I didn't think much of it when a car pulled up beside us at a stoplight on the main drag through town. You never knew when someone might make a late-night run for munchies or diapers to one of the convenience stores. Besides, my attention was focused on Eli. Yet, I could hardly ignore the revving of an engine in my ear.

"Do they want to race?" I asked.

Eli glanced out my window. "That car doesn't stand a chance against Dolores. Just an ordinary black sedan."

"There are a lot of those around if you pay attention. I feel like I'm being followed every time I go anywhere."

I sensed the change in Eli's demeanor. He tightened his grip on the steering wheel and straightened his back. "How long has this been going on?"

"Since the murder, I suppose."

"Why haven't you mentioned it?"

The light changed and Eli allowed the car beside us to go through the intersection first. He switched lanes and dropped in behind it. `

"What are you doing?" I asked.

"Turn around is fair play, right?"

"It's probably some kid who borrowed Daddy's car, but if you want to give him a run for his money, go for it." I reached out and patted Dolores' dash. "Just be careful."

The car made an abrupt left turn without signaling first. With the speed limit a measly thirty-five mph, it wasn't a problem for Eli to stay close. The other driver seemed to have an issue, however, as his brake lights flashed in an erratic pattern.

"Do you think he has a bad bulb or a loose wire?"

"Or he's not familiar with the way the car handles," Eli replied.

"Should we drop back and go home? I'd hate to see him get in an accident if he doesn't know what he's doing."

The other car's taillight's flashed again. We headed down a straight stretch of street and I wondered why the driver rode his brakes.

"Did that look like a pattern to you?" I asked

"Yes, but I can't tell you why." Eli slowed. "Let's give the driver some space and see what happens. Is he by himself?"

I hadn't looked. "Can't tell."

The car made a right-hand turn, heading for the

interstate. Again, the brake lights flashed and this time the pattern was clearer. It tickled my brain as I tried to place it.

Three short, three long, three short.

"SOS!" Eli and I shouted in unison.

I reached for my purse on the floorboard of the car. Who should I call? We were out of city limits. That meant the sheriff's department. Good thing Deputy Nelson was on duty. Better that I had his cell number in my contacts.

I left the driving to Eli, hoping his skills were up to the task. "By any chance, did Jake teach you how to drive?" I asked. Jake had been the one who taught me my more advanced skills.

"I taught him. One of my biggest regrets. That's a story for another time. Make your call, Buttercup."

Why didn't I know that already? One way or another, I'd find out later. My phone was already to my ear. Deputy Nelson's phone was ringing. Would he answer?

Eli swore under his breath as the brake lights of the car in front of us flashed again. Not the whole sequence to make SOS, only SO. What did it signify?

Deputy Nelson's voice mail picked up. "Theo Nelson. I'm not available. Leave a message." And I thought my voice mail message was curt.

"Deputy, this is Harmony Duprie. We're headed towards I-95, following a car that's flashing SOS with its brake lights. It's a black sedan, number of occupants unknown. I'll call 9-1-1 next."

I hung up and Eli said. "Hold off on the call to 9-1-1. There's a passing lane just ahead. Try to see if you can tell how many people are in the car."

I could do that. The sedan maintained the speed limit going up the long hill. Eli floored it and Dolores easily overtook and zoomed past it. There were no street lights, and the windows of the car were tinted, but I made out two people in the front seat. A truck coming from the other direction lit up the interior just as we went by, and the driver turned his head at the perfect time.

Until that moment, I was treating this whole thing as a lark, a string of coincidences. We were having a little fun, that's all. At that moment, everything changed. I filled my lungs with air to chase away the sudden sense of panic.

"Pull off!" I screamed.

Eli didn't question me until he found a wide spot to get off the highway. The other car zipped by us, its brake lights flashing a short and long and short sequence.

"Harmony?"

I took several deep breaths to drive away the dread. "Jake," I breathed out. "The driver. Was. Jake."

I grabbed the dashboard as Eli hurled Dolores back onto the highway. "What haven't you told me?"

"Long story. It involves the FBI. A PI. Assorted bad guys. And Jake's in the middle of it."

"Whose side is he on?"

His own, I suspected. "The good guys."

Eli's glare burned my face. There was too much of the story I wasn't telling. But I stared straight ahead, watching the black car. My phone ringing gave me the out I needed.

"Hello?"

"Miss Duprie? You called? What's this about a car flashing SOS?"

I put him on speaker. "Deputy Nelson. Good timing. We're almost to the interstate. Jake's driving."

"Drop off. Now."

Eli shook his head. I shared his feelings. "Not happening. We can't abandon him."

"You're with your boyfriend?"

I glanced at Eli. Boyfriend didn't seem to be the right word to describe him, but it would work for now. "Yes."

"Where exactly are you? I'll call for backup."

We'd almost caught up to Jake. Eli slowed down. He needed to maintain some distance between the two cars.

"County Road 30. We're about five miles from the interstate." And if Jake got to the interstate, there'd be heavier traffic and our options would be limited.

From a side road, a set of headlights illuminated Dolores. The car pulled in behind us. Just what we needed. An innocent bystander.

"Stay on the phone."

"Roger." Was that the right terminology? I should have stuck to normal English, but too late.

From the dead air emitting from my phone, I

surmised the deputy had put me on mute. "Do you think the guy with Jake knows what's going on?" I asked Eli.

"Jake's not pulling any evasive maneuvers, so I'd say no. But he knows. He's not flashing SOS anymore, but the lights flash when there's no reason for him to be using the brakes."

A car came barreling down the road from the opposite direction, going too fast to make the curve we'd just slid through. I turned and watched, fearful I'd need to report an accident. Instead, it braked and pulled off the road, then turned and joined the procession. "Eli? Did you…"

He nodded. "I saw."

"Deputy," I said into the phone, "If you can hear me, is that one of yours? The car that pulled a U-turn to follow us?" I hadn't noticed a light bar or any markings.

There was a delay before he answered. "No."

Well, shit.

"Mute it," Eli whispered.

I punched the button on the phone.

"You have your gun?"

That's the other reason my purse didn't match the rest of my outfit. I'd needed one big enough to stash Betsy in. "Yes."

"Good."

"Do you have yours?" If gunplay would be involved, two handguns were better than one.

Eli nodded. "Yes."

In the not-too-distance I saw the lights that marked the on-ramp for the interstate. If Jake could make a move, now was the time. His brake lights flashed the entire SOS sequence.

Eli flashed the bright beams in acknowledgment. This was all on us. And whatever cavalry arrived in time. He sped up to close the gap.

"Miss Duprie? Are you still there?"

I'd forgotten the deputy. "Still here," I said, unmuting the phone.

"I've got a car headed your direction. And I've alerted the Highway Patrol. I don't have an ETA."

Unless it was five minutes ago, it wasn't soon enough to do us any good.

"Thanks, Deputy." I muted the phone again. "What's the plan, Eli?"

"How much to you trust Jake?"

It depended on my mood. But because I couldn't imagine he was drawing us into a trap, at the moment, a lot. "Enough for whatever you want to do."

"Before we get to the interstate, I'll get ahead of them and slow down, try to find someplace where they can't pass us. Force them to stop. Hope that Jake doesn't ram us and he has a chance to bail. Are you good with that?"

No, I wasn't. The risk to Dolores was huge. But what choice did I have? "What about the cars behind us?" I asked.

He glanced in the rear-view mirror. Sometime in the last minute or two, a third car had joined the procession. If I squinted hard enough, I could pretend to see a light bar on its roof. "Let's hope this does the trick." he said as he braked and flipped on the four-way flashers.

The reaction was instantaneous. The entire chain slowed. A second later, Eli hit the gas.

Dolores responded in her typical fashion. We absolutely *flew* by the car Jake drove. I braced myself for what was coming next. And for the possibility of a crash as a car came towards us in the other lane.

Eli cranked the steering wheel hard to the right. Tires squealed when he braked. The headlights from the black sedan were too bright and too close for my comfort. I reached for the door handle to hop out, ready to rush to Jake's aid.

I didn't know if the tap was on purpose or Jake really couldn't stop in time. It was hard enough that my still-fastened seatbelt saved me from being thrown against the dash but would leave a bruise. I was more worried about Dolores's bumper. Had it crumbled from the impact?

What I should have been worried about was Eli. I glanced over and realized he'd already taken his seat belt off. When we'd been hit, he'd been pushed against the steering wheel. "Eli?" I asked tentatively.

Eli waited for the three other cars to stream by, faces peering out the windows with curiosity. Typical looky-loos. "He'll pay for that," Eli muttered as he thrust open his door. I took it to mean he was all right, so I followed suit. The rough surface of the road bit into my bare feet.

The doors on the other car swung open and Jake and the other man jumped out. I recognized the second guy immediately. He was the bald man from the rest stop, the one who had wanted me to let Jake drive Dolores. Even if he didn't recognize me, he'd remember her. The situation couldn't get any worse.

I hadn't counted on seeing light reflecting off a gun, half-concealed in his hand.

Betsy was still in my purse, laying on the floorboard. Although Eli normally carried his gun in his pocket, I had no way of telling him what I'd spotted.

"Idiot!" Jake screamed. "You almost killed us!"

For a moment, I felt guilty. Then reminded myself it was all a show. Eli needed to be as good of an actor as Jake to carry on the performance.

"And you're drunk. Or the worst driver in the world," Eli yelled back. "Or are you too stupid to be behind the wheel?"

Road rage. That was a plausible explanation and a good delaying tactic until a deputy showed up. Would the bald guy fall for it?

Jake took two steps forward, clenching his fists and sparring with the air. "Just because you have a fancy car doesn't mean you can drive like an asshole."

Eli put one foot in front of the other, bent his knees slightly and raised his own fists, reminding me of pictures of old-fashioned pugilists. "You want to try me?"

I was so busy worrying that they might attack

each other—all part of the show, of course—that I forgot to keep track of the bald man. Footsteps crunching in the gravel drew my attention back to him. He leaned on the hood of their car, apparently as enthralled by the display as me, his gun firmly grasped in his hand.

Desperate to get to my purse and my phone, I used the moment to gracefully slide back into Dolores' passenger seat. At least, that was my intention.

As I swiveled on one foot, a rock bit into my heel and I turned my ankle. I half-fell, catching myself with one hand on Dolores' roof. With all eyes now on me, I sobbed and sank into the seat.

Eli bent over and stuck his head in from the other side. "Are you all right?"

"I twisted my ankle," I said louder than needed. Then, much softer, "He has a gun."

His head disappeared from my view as he straightened up. "Talk about clumsy…"

He never got to finish the sentence because Jake pounced. They ended up on the ground, wrestling to get on top and throwing punches. "Stop!" I screamed not knowing what else to do. Then I noticed most of the blows missed their target. Tension drained from my body.

My relief proved temporary because through the rear window I spotted the bald man holding his gun out, waiting for a clear target. With Betsy in my left hand and one of my shoes in my right, I hopped out of the car without a conscious thought. I didn't want to shoot him. The black stiletto flew through the air in my attempt to hit him with it and make him drop his gun. When I missed, I switched Betsy to my right hand, raised both arms, released the safety and put one finger on Betsy's trigger. "Drop it," I ordered in my best cop voice.

He fired a round in answer. I didn't wait to see if he hit anyone before I let Betsy do my talking for me.

Chapter 30

"I know I'm supposed to aim for center mass," I explained again. "But I didn't want to kill the guy, just put him out of business."

Which I'd done. My first bullet struck him on his gun arm. He'd dropped the handgun, which was now in Deputy Chard's possession. The second shot hit him in the upper leg, so he wouldn't run away. I'd restrained myself from firing another time.

This was the third time I answered the same questions. Once for the State Police, and now for both Deputies Chard and Nelson, who'd finally arrived. They'd taken pity on me and let me sit in Dolores. Eli and Jake—both unharmed—sat in separate vehicles, undergoing similar grillings. I hadn't talked to Jake so I still didn't know his story. If he thought being questioned by the police was bad, he'd hate what I planned to put him through.

They'd been checked out by the ambulance

crew. Both got a few bruises during the fight but were otherwise all right. The crew gave them ice packs before the ambulance left for the hospital with the guy I'd shot.

"How much longer is this going to take?" I asked, not for the first time.

"What's your hurry?' asked Deputy Chard.

"I have to get home, get cleaned up and go to work. The library won't open itself." I wouldn't go straight to the library because I needed shoes. The one I'd thrown disappeared, likely buried in the drainage ditch. The hospital-type slippers the ambulance crew gave me fell off my feet with each step. There'd be no sleep for me. I'd have to run on caffeine all day long.

"You'll need to make other arrangements. Is there someone you can call to do it?" Deputy Nelson asked.

There was, but I didn't want to wake anyone at this time of the morning and try to explain why I wouldn't be there. I considered pulling the damsel in distress act, go for the sympathy factor. Pout, make my lower lip tremble, force tears from my eyes. But it was too late in the game for that ploy to work, and I wasn't that good of an actress.

"You realize," Deputy Chard said, "Based on your own words, there is a litany of charges we could take you in for. You have more pressing problems to worry about than getting the library opened on time."

In the confusion, I'd never once thought about it

that way. And there I was, stuck in the middle of a crime scene, surrounded by law enforcement, and me without my lawyer.

The interview rooms at the sheriff's base were in worse shape than those at Oak Grove's police station. To the amusement of Deputy Chard, I pulled a tissue from my purse and wiped off the hard metal seat before I sat. They'd taken Betsy but allowed me to hold onto my purse after checking to make sure it didn't contain any surprises.

"Let's go over this one more time," he said.

"Not until my lawyer gets here." I'd already placed the call to Dan.

Deputy Nelson set a bottle of water in front of me. "I'm sure he'll be here soon. We'll come back then."

Dan wouldn't be here soon enough. Left alone in the room with nothing to do but twiddle my thumbs did not make Harmony a happy person. I welcomed the sound of the door being opened, expecting it to be Dan. Not even close. Not either of the deputies either. No, Agent Felton had arrived to join in the fun.

He didn't look like he'd been dragged out of bed in the middle of the night, but in jeans and a pressed cotton shirt, he didn't appear to have been on duty either. "What are you doing here?" I asked.

"News gets around fast." He looked around and shook his head. "I'll be right back." Then he disappeared back out the door. Well, that distraction lasted all of thirty seconds.

He must have pulled some strings because in a few minutes Deputy Chard returned and escorted me to an empty office. Dan showed up a few minutes later. I filled him in on the night's happenings and waited for him to scold me. Instead, he sighed. "How do you get yourself mixed up in these things?" he asked.

I needed to figure that out.

It wasn't too long until Agent Felton came into the room. "Just so you know," he said after I introduced him to Dan, "I'm here because Hennessey—Jake-—was involved. Deputy Nelson alerted me to the incident. I can't do anything about charges at the county level, if the sheriff chooses to file them."

"I appreciate your honesty," Dan answered for me. "But I understand that any information you get you'll share with local officials. That's why I'm here. To make sure that Harmony's interests are represented."

"Someone needs to watch out for her." Felton grinned. "I've never known someone who can attract trouble like she does."

Both men laughed. I wanted to protest, but couldn't. The words were the truth.

"Anyway," Felton continued. "I want to hear your take on what happened tonight."

Was that normal procedure or was Agent Felton

trying to soften me up in a bizarre strategy to get me to incriminate myself? I didn't care. There were a few things I *had* to ask.

"Who was that guy?"

Agent Felton wasn't fazed by my impatience. "The suspect wasn't carrying Identification and provided a fake name. Mr. Hennessey knows him only by a first name, Zeke. Did you run across him in your investigation?"

I glanced at Dan and he nodded. "Twice. Both times he was with Jake. Once at a rest stop outside of Pittsburgh and once at a bar in Charleston. Never got a name."

Fenton reached into his pocket and pulled out a phone. "This belongs to him. Do you recognize anyone in the pictures?"

"Do you need a warrant to let me see this?" I waited for Dan's approval before taking the phone.

Felton grinned. "We found it on the road. It might have fallen out of his pocket. That allows us to examine the contents to try to identify the owner."

I took his word for it and tapped on the screen to light it up. The first few pictures were of a cute little boy, about two years old. I took my time looking at his sweet smile and hoping the guy I'd shot wasn't his father. Then I flipped to the next picture. "I saw this guy at a bar in Charleston. Didn't talk to him."

I didn't have to glance twice at the face that came up next. "Paul Zavari. He's one of the guys who caused a ruckus at The Dog House that night me and the other ladies were there." The bald man had his arm around Paul's shoulder as they posed for a selfie.

Agent Felton nodded. "Deputy Nelson recognized him."

I looked twice at the next picture, then a third time. "This can't be right."

"What can't be right?" Felton asked, leaning forward in his chair.

"I know this guy. He can't be involved in whatever is going on."

"Why not?" The simple question was weighted with suspense.

A glance at Dan told me he could offer no assistance. "It must be his evil twin or something," I sputtered.

"Who's evil twin, Miss Duprie?"

"Carl. Carlisle Buford. He's a French teacher at the high school."

It was as if an electric spark shot through the room. "How do you know him?"

"I needed a note in French translated. Merrilee put me in touch with him. He was able to help me a little." Which reminded me, I'd never heard back from the professor about the note. Had he forgotten me?

"Is that the only contact you had with him?"

I scowled. "One day I was up at the house and Carl got a couple of boxes out of another car and put them in his. I took a few pictures. One of the guys with him was Paul Zavari."

"The plot thickens," Dan muttered.

"The pictures are still on my phone if you're interested. They aren't very good."

"Let's see them," Felton said.

It only took a few seconds for me to retrieve my phone and find the pictures. Wordlessly, Felton studied them. "Did you notify anyone about this at the time?"

"No. I mean, it was weird, but as far as I could tell, nothing illegal happened."

The agent nodded. "Will you email these to me please? When you're done here."

I slid my finger across the screen of the bald man's phone, passing by pictures of scenery and pretty women. None looked like candidates that could be his wife although several looked young enough to be his daughter. I stopped at one. The face tugged at the edges of my memory. "Is there another picture of her?" I asked.

"Why?" Felton tensed.

"She seems familiar. The hair is wrong," I mused to myself. "It should be blond, not brown. I wonder if that's a wig.

"And the makeup. How much makeup does she have plastered on her face?"

"Who is it?" Felton asked.

I shook my head. "I don't want to say because I'm not positive."

"Tell me anyway." I recognized that tone of voice. For a minute, Felton sounded like Chief Sorenson in command mode. It might work on someone else, but not on me. Well, not totally.

"I'm surprised Deputy Nelson didn't recognize her. That's Annabelle."

"The PI from Charleston?"

He impressed me, remembering her name from the meeting in my apartment.

"Who is she?" Dan asked.

I didn't know if I could answer without breaking the confidentiality of several law enforcement agencies. Most notably, the FBI. Dan noticed my hesitation and asked "Do you and I need to discuss this in private, Harmony?"

"It's not him I'm worried about, it's you."

"Huh?"

Felton coughed. "Miss Duprie did some research work for the Agency. However, it's safe to assume that everything you hear in this room will be covered by client-attorney privilege. Correct?"

"Absolutely," Dan agreed. "So what's the story, Harmony?"

I gave him a run down—Jake being railroaded into working undercover, Annabelle's interest, my hiring of her to act as backup for Jake. "Jake caught on to her last week," I told them both, "and I meant to take her off the case. But I got distracted and forgot." What was her picture doing on the bald man's phone? After flipping past a few more men I'd never seen before, I ran out of photos to examine—random shots of flowers didn't count—and handed the phone back to Felton.

Dan had other fish to fry. He pointed two fingers at Felton. "So Harmony is unofficially working with the FBI and you can't do anything about the potential for her being charged? She was within her rights defending her friends."

"As soon as my supervisor can get through to the Sheriff it will be straightened out. Unfortunately, the Sheriff claims he's too busy to take phone calls. So my apology for the delay, but rest assured the Agency is working to resolve the issue. Ms. Duprie is too valuable of a resource to allow her work to be put at risk."

Talk about flattery! I wondered what favor Felton wanted next. But speaking of work… "That reminds me," I interrupted, "I have to get to the library to open up soon."

I didn't understand the look Felton sent to Dan. "What's going on?" I asked.

"Has anyone told you yet why Hennessey—Jake—bailed out of the investigation after all this time?"

"No. I figured when I got out of here I'd ask him."

Felton's lips formed a tight line. "According to his story, they were going to 'initiate' him tonight. He didn't have details, but it involved beating up a guy the group he's been ferrying around was mad at. After that, he had another 'test' to go through and they wouldn't give him the details. He overheard something about running a gauntlet and decided he didn't want to take the double risk."

"What does that have to do with me going to work?"

"A call was placed from this phone during the time you were following them. We called it and got the answering machine for a bar in Charleston. You could be in danger. I'd like to put you in a safe house."

My mouth fell open. "I can't lose this job. I can't let Janine down," I pleaded.

"Can't something be arranged?" Dan asked. "What evidence to you have that Harmony won't be safe in public?"

Felton sighed. "None, really. Call it instinct."

There was no prickle at the back of my neck. Either my sensors were off or Felton's were.

"If you have no justification for depriving her of her freedom, I insist that she chooses whether to go into hiding or not." And that's why I paid Dan the big bucks.

"My apartment is plenty secure," I said. "We've upgraded the locks and they're unpickable." Except by Jake, of course. "No one will bother me at the library."

Felton's lips tightened. "Have you forgotten your own experiences over the past year?"

No, but I was determined not to live in fear. "I've taken precautions to insure things like that never happen again."

"What do you call last night?"

"Proof that I can take care of myself. After all, Agent, I'm not the one in the hospital."

"I could ask the Sheriff to hold you until charges

are determined. Until you're charged, you won't be eligible for bail."

Dan leaned forward. "Are you threatening my client, Agent?"

"If that's what it takes to protect her."

The two strong-willed men glared at each other. I wouldn't place a bet on the winner.

"If you're worried about protecting me, don't. Eli will be glad to volunteer his services."

"How long is he going to be here?"

I had no idea. We hadn't talked about it. With a shrug, I said "As long as he can or has to." He was a participant in the night's events, too. Although he hadn't shot anyone.

Felton wasn't satisfied. "He's not a professional."

Eli didn't like to tell people about his background as a Ranger, so I wouldn't either. "I trust him."

"You don't understand the seriousness of the situation."

"A bunch of middle-aged men going from bar to bar to get drunk doesn't sound that serious to me." He stared at me and I stared back.

"What *is* going on?" Dan asked.

"We aren't sure yet." Felton frowned and blinked. I won. "Your friend has a couple of theories, but until we get a search warrant nothing is confirmed."

Finally! "What does Jake think is going on?"

The agent studied us as if trying to decide if we could be trusted with the information. I wanted to shake it out of him but placed my hands in my lap and waited.

"A raft of federal laws and regulations," Felton said. "Mostly falling under the jurisdiction of the TTB."

I didn't have a clue what he was talking about and it must have showed on my face.

"The Alcohol and Tobacco Tax and Trade Bureau," Felton explained. "Hennessey thinks they're running moonshine."

Chapter 31

Moonshine? No wonder they wanted Jake in on the action. He'd be the perfect delivery man with his fast talking and fast driving skills. "I thought moonshine disappeared after the Twenty-First Amendment passed," I said.

"It went deeper into hiding, that's all," Felton said. "It never stopped."

Little pieces of the puzzle clicked into place. Random incidents over the last few weeks started to make sense. I reviewed the crime statistics in my head. Had there been a small spike in driving under the influence arrests?

At least I understood why Jake bailed from the investigation. "What can I do to help?" I asked.

"Nothing. We'll turn over what limited information we have to the TTB."

Felton's phone buzzed, and he glanced at the screen. His face grew serious and he stood. "I'll come back if I can," he said. "In the meantime, sit tight. At least until we can straighten out your situation."

The level of stress in the room didn't decrease with his departure. "What now?" I asked Dan.

He shrugged his shoulders. "Like Agent Felton said, sit tight. You might want to close your eyes and try to catch some sleep. This could take a while."

It was sound advice, but I doubted I'd be able to fall asleep. Not in the uncomfortable straight back chair I sat in. Not with the fear of losing my job because of it. Not with the threat of being charged with a crime—or several of them—hanging over my head.

I could do something about one of those fears. "I need to call Marcie to ask her to open the library." I picked up my phone from the table and glanced at Dan for approval. He nodded, and I steeled myself for the inevitable storm of questions I was sure to face.

❄ ❄ ❄

"Half an hour," Dan whispered.

I raised my head groggily and blinked my eyes. They'd only been closed for a minute. "What's up?" I asked, wiping drool from the corner of my mouth.

"Time to go home," Eli said.

Eli? When had he come into the office? "Can't. I have to go to work," I insisted.

"Not today, Buttercup. The library will have to do without you for today. You need to get some rest."

"So I'm in the clear?"

"The Sheriff's office hasn't decided yet," Dan said. "But they've agreed to release you pending their decision. Under the usual rules, of course."

How much did Dan have to do with it and how much was Felton's influence? I stretched and yawned. "Any chance of getting Betsy back?"

The look on Dan's face gave me my answer. "I thought not. But you can't blame me for asking."

"Don't worry, they didn't confiscate my pistol," Eli grinned. "But I didn't shoot anyone either. And no, you can't borrow it."

It was childish to pout, but I did. Oh well, if that helped to ensure Eli would stick around, I'd live with it. For as long as possible.

"Where's Jake?" I asked once we were outside, the sun warming my face, and Eli's arm around my waist warming other parts.

Eli pulled away. "I'm jealous," he said. "First you ask about Betsy and then Jake. When are you going to pay attention to me?"

I was torn between punching him and pulling his arm back around me. With Dan only a few feet away, neither seemed like a good option.

"It's just odd," I explained. "All of this was for him, and now we're walking away and leaving him."

"Don't worry. He's waiting for the TTB guys to show up, that's all. They want to talk to him. In the meantime, he's being treated like a guest. Last time I saw him, he was in the break room, drinking coffee and swapping stories with a few of the deputies."

That made me feel better but not good enough. I missed Eli's touch so I reached down and took his hand. To my relief, he didn't pull away. Instead he gave it a squeeze.

"I'll give you guys a lift," Dan said. "That way I can make sure you go home."

I'd forgotten Dolores had been towed off to my mechanic's to be checked for damage. So much for my plans for stopping at the library, hospital slippers and all.

"We can take a cab," I suggested. But Eli knew me too well.

"We'll take you up on that offer," he said to Dan.

I opened my mouth to protest, but his lips crashed into mine and any thought of objecting disappeared.

"We have unfinished business back at your place. And the sooner we get there, the better," he whispered into my ear when we stopped to catch our breath.

He was right. The library could wait, just this once.

❄ ❄ ❄

I woke to a bed that didn't hold Eli, but the aroma of coffee coming from my kitchen almost made up for it. With coffee being the limit of his culinary skills—he'd proven that one unfortunate meal in Florida—any real cooking was up to me. His idea of preparing a meal was cold sandwiches or taking me out to a restaurant. So I didn't expect much when I stumbled into the kitchen, wrapping my short silky robe—the one only he got to see— around my body.

With his phone pressed to his ear, he one-fingered pecked on his laptop's keyboard. He looked up, smiled and blew me a kiss.

My hands were free, so I did better than that. I wrapped my arms around his chest and kissed the top of his head. He leaned back into me but kept on talking to the person on the other end of the phone. Although I didn't understand half the acronyms he was using, the conversation sounded important. I gave him a quick squeeze before releasing him.

After pouring myself a cup of coffee, I turned on my phone. Eli and I had a policy of turning off our cell phones when we were about to get busy. There were too many instances of a moment being ruined by a call.

The messages from the news organizations were annoying but easy to delete. How did they get my number anyway? The sheriff's department had put out that the incident was a fender bender so the calls came from local reporters. Different library staff called asking if I was all right. The Oak Grove rumor mill must have been in overdrive. At least the news hadn't got relayed to Janine yet because there wasn't a message from her.

The one message I wanted wasn't there. I hoped to hear from someone, anyone, at the Sheriff's Department telling me common sense prevailed and no charges would be brought against me. No such luck. Or would a deputy come by in person to deliver the news?

No sense in holding my breath and waiting. With Eli occupied, I needed to stay busy so I wouldn't go crazy worrying. One task in particular shouldn't wait.

The portable scanner, stashed in the hall closet, beeped faintly when I powered it on. The batteries needed replaced. Luckily, I had the right size stashed in the junk drawer in the kitchen. With it fully operational, I started the sweep in the front room, not expecting to find anything.

Eli's eyes followed me. At least, every time I glanced his direction, he was looking at me and not his laptop's screen. I wasn't sure if he didn't know what I was doing or was getting a kick out of watching me. "Scanning for listening devices," I whispered as I moved by him into the kitchen.

He nodded and mouthed "I know." Well, if he wanted to watch me while I worked, I'd put on a show for him. Every chance I got, I wiggled my hips or bent to show off my minimal cleavage. I thought about letting my robe drape open, but didn't have the courage. The curtains were open, after all.

As I swept the scanner around the kitchen window, there came the sound I never expected. A beep. A solitary beep, out of cycle. I retraced the path, holding my breath. Nothing. I released the air from my lungs and drew in a fresh supply. It must have been a malfunction. I repeated my actions, just to make sure. Another beep.

"Let me do some digging and I'll get back to you," Eli said in the background. I ran my hand over the window frame, but didn't find a telltale bump on the surface.

Then he was beside me, taking the scanner out of my hand. He ran the device around the window and was rewarded with a faint beep. He leaned across the sink and pressed his cheek to the glass, examining the wooden frame. "Have you had a false positive with your scanner before?"

"No. Let me hop on the company's website and see if they have any information."

I signed into my laptop while Eli carried the scanner into the front room to recheck where I'd already been. As he waved it over my easy chair, it beeped. He cursed under his breath and tried again. Nothing.

The manufacture's front-page extolled the virtues of their products. Not surprising, but I dug deeper. Still no information that would explain the strange behavior of the device. I abandoned the official site and started a search for user forums.

And found an answer immediately. "You got a new cell phone, didn't you?"

"Huh. Yeah. I didn't even think about that. Go ahead and turn it off."

Cell phones, laptops connecting wirelessly and radios all interfered with scanners, according to the forums. But mine had never caused a problem, so Eli's was the likely suspect. I turned off his phone but didn't touch his laptop in case he had unsaved work. At my nod, he moved the scanner over and around my chair. I let go an audible sigh when there was no reaction from the scanner.

"On to the window," he said.

I crossed my fingers. On both hands. The first pass resulted in dead air, and I uncrossed my fingers ever-so-slightly.

"Now we try again," Eli said, matching his actions to his words.

Damnit, there it was. A beep, faint as ever. He grimaced. "Take our laptops into your bedroom. And leave your phone in there, too."

It took me two trips because I didn't want to close the lid on either of our laptops. If I could have crossed my toes as well as my fingers when he raised the scanner for another pass, I would have.

It didn't take two tries. We got a beep on the first one. Eli's lips tightened and I clenched my fists.

"There's nothing there," he said, once again examining the area around the window. "Nothing. So why is your scanner reacting?"

Chapter 32

We spent the night in Eli's favorite suite at The Towers, Oak Grove's best hotel. The company from Pittsburgh I used last fall to make sure my place was 'clean' couldn't get someone out until the next day and neither of us wanted to stay in my apartment. So after we 'swept' the hotel rooms—and found nothing—we called both Deputy Nelson and Agent Felton to let them know where to find us. We asked them to pass the word along to Jake because he was still talking to the TTB agents. At least that was the story we got. I half-expected to run into them in the hallways, because where else would federal agents stay?

Even with Eli's arms around me, I didn't sleep well, but then, he didn't either. Around three in the morning, he tried to slip out of bed without waking me. I was already awake, so it didn't work. "Where are you going?" I asked as he headed for the adjoining room. He'd grabbed his pants but not his shirt so he wasn't leaving.

"I didn't mean to wake you." He shrugged his shoulders and the muscles in his chest rippled. "But I couldn't sleep, so I'm going to work.

"If I had any work to do, I'd join you," I said, sitting on the edge of the bed. He caught the implication, even as I tried to engineer an excuse for my slip.

"How's that possible?" He crossed his arms and waited for my answer.

I couldn't lie to him in person. "The grant ended. I don't have any good independent research gigs lined up. The library job is my only job. Before it came along, I didn't know what I was going to do. I've been looking, but librarian openings are scarce."

"Why didn't you tell me?" He sat beside me and ran his fingers through my hair. Before we went to bed, he'd freed it from its bun. "You can come work with me any time."

I liked how he said 'with' instead of for, and I rested my head against his shoulder. "You know me, I'm an independent old cuss."

"You're not old, Buttercup." He kissed the top of my head. "Independent, yes. One of the many reasons I love you."

No matter how many times he said it, I never tired of hearing it.

"I'm scared, Eli." I forced the statement out, hating to admit it. "If this situation makes me lose the library job—even if it's temporary—I'll have to resort to living off of my savings. I don't want to do that."

"Can you get a job in one of the local schools?"

"If one of the librarians ever leaves. They don't have any openings right now. I checked." The only chance of that happening was if Sue, the elementary school librarian, got pregnant again and took maternity leave. The others were years from retirement and not going anywhere.

He sat quietly for a moment, stroking my hair. "Anything I can come up with, I'm sure you already thought of. Don't go borrowing trouble when you don't need to. Oak Grove is lucky that you're willing to fill in for Janine, and I'm sure they'll understand why you took the day off. You're a hero, after all."

I snorted. "Not according to the sheriff."

"He doesn't like all the agencies encroaching on his territory. You're an easy target. He'll give into the pressure to clear you."

"Not soon enough for me."

"You'll feel better after you get some sleep. Crawl back into bed."

At that point, sleep was a dream. "Are you going to be my pillow?" His chest wasn't all that comfortable, but I liked listening to his heartbeat.

He hesitated. "For a couple of minutes. I've got an idea I need to jot down before I lose it."

"How about I keep you company?" I liked watching him work. His mouth would scrunch up as his fingers traveled so quickly across the keyboard I couldn't keep up. When he stopped to think, he'd turn his eyes to the ceiling, as if the answer to his question would be written there. "I didn't check my email yesterday."

"This won't take long." He stood and offered me his hand. Not that I needed the help, but I never passed up a chance to hold his hand.

My in-box contained the normal assortment of authors' newsletters and sales pitches. I deleted the sales pitches and saved the newsletters for later. I might buy some of their books. It wasn't until I'd scrolled to the second page I found it. An email from the professor.

"*Dear Ms. Duprie,*" it read. "I *am greatly interested in seeing the original of the note. Can you arrange to bring it to Baton Rouge so I could examine it further? Sincerely, Louis Bouchard*"

My heart rose and sank at the same time. He must have been really interested, but I wouldn't be able to travel to Louisiana any time soon. I sighed loudly and tried to compose an answer. It was such a shame to write back, "*Thanks, but no thanks.*"

"What's up?" Eli stretched, rubbed his eyes, and downed the rest of his energy drink.

"Remember the cufflinks and note I told you about?"

He nodded.

"I asked an expert to verify if the signature was authentic. He wants to see the original, which is good, but he wants me to travel to meet him, which is bad."

"I'd offer to take it for you, but that won't work either."

I'd spent too much money on the project to drop it. "*Dear Professor,*" I typed. "*Any chance you will be traveling to a conference closer to my location? Pittsburgh?*" It wouldn't hurt to ask. I clicked the button to send it before I convinced myself I was silly for asking.

Habit took me to the front door of the library instead of the back. Eli was off parking his rental car as it would take a few days to get Dolores back. As I climbed the thirteen steps, counting each, the familiar ritual soothed my nerves. Luckily, the alarm code for the back door was the same as for the front, because I would have looked silly climbing back down and strolling to the back door.

The unique scent of the library—old paper mixed with the delicate leftover fragrance of dozens of perfumes—tickled my nose when I opened the doors and sniffed in deeply. As much as any place on earth, this was home. I offered up a prayer that I'd be privileged to stay working there for at least a while longer.

By the time Eli came in carrying two cups of coffee, I'd turned on the lights and started firing up the computers. Because official opening time wasn't for half an hour, I locked the door behind him. We had the place to ourselves until the rest of the staff showed. Which wouldn't be long, so my fantasy about making love to Eli between the stacks wasn't going to happen. All he got was a quick smooch before I left him to go unlock the back door.

My fears of being fired proved groundless, thank heavens. In fact, everyone seemed concerned that I needed more time off to recover from unseen injuries, and I had to convince them I was fine. To my relief, the cover story about an "accident" was accepted as the truth.

I tucked my cell phone into my pants pocket, the ringer set to vibrate. If Jake or Agent Felton or anyone from the Sheriff's department called I'd know without breaking the no cell-phone-on-the-job policy. I'd claim an emergency if anyone caught me sneaking peeks at it throughout the day.

No calls came in, at least not until my lunch break. That was when the security company from Pittsburgh was scheduled to show up. I'd arranged for Luke or Joe to let them in, so all I expected was a report on what they found—or didn't find. When the phone finally vibrated, I was knee deep in reviewing a proposal for replacing some of our older shelves that were warping from the weight of books. It was dry reading, and I didn't pay attention when I answered the call.

"Oak Grove Public Library. Hello."

"Can you come home?" Joe asked. "Those security folks are asking for a ladder. I gave them one, but thought you should know."

A ladder? What the hell? I couldn't leave, not after missing the previous day, but had a stand-in. "I'm sending Eli."

He didn't take much convincing. In fact, he didn't take any convincing at all. I returned to Janine's office and tried, without luck, to resume studying the proposal. I wondered why we didn't have a local company manufacture the shelves, instead of buying them from overseas. The bidding process needed to be reviewed. My to-do list was getting longer and I was getting little accomplished. Not the way to impress the Board of Directors.

Any thought of impressing the Board flew from my head when Eli returned with company. Joe, Luke, and Garcy, the tech from Pittsburgh, were with him. It had to be bad news.

They crowded into the office and Garcy placed a small box on the desk. "Good thing you called," she said. "You would never have found it on your own."

Found what? "What is it?" I asked on cue.

She opened the box. It contained a shiny black rectangular object. "A listening device," she said.

"Where did they put it that we didn't find it?" I glanced at Eli. The deep line that creased his forehead showed he already knew the answer.

"Attached to the window frame."

"We looked there."

Garcy smirked. "Not outside, you didn't."

Outside? When was it planted outside? It had to be sometime when Joe, Luke and I were all gone. Even then a neighbor would have seen the suspicious activity and alerted Luke or Joe.

"But how?"

"Super-strong sticky on the back." I reached to pick it up and Garcy stopped me. "You don't want to get the adhesive on your fingers. I used an abrasive hand cleaner to get it off. And don't worry, I've disabled it."

"I don't understand."

"Not surprising. I don't either. My best guess is that whomever planted this used a pressurized air gun to shoot it towards the house. That could have been done at night and nobody would hear anything more than a pop. Nothing like a gunshot that would draw attention. I need to talk to the experts and see if anyone is familiar with the technology."

"If they haven't?"

The glint in her eye suggested the concept would be reality soon enough. "We'll figure something out."

"How long do you think it's been there?" Eli asked.

"Based on its condition? Not long. There's little in the way of tarnishing, and that tells me it hasn't been exposed to any extreme weather."

I searched my memories, trying to place who'd been to my apartment recently. A representative from every law-enforcement agency in the area, I realized. Had one of them planted it? Wouldn't one of them leave it inside my apartment? Who else might have done it?

"Who?" I asked.

Garcy shook her head. "No idea. There's no visible manufacturer marking. Because the bug was outside, I doubt it picked up much. I'd say the only conversations it relayed were those you had in your kitchen. I'll run tests on it back at the shop and check."

A flash of disappointment crossed Eli's face when she closed the box and stuck it in her pocket. Had he wanted to dissect the device? I felt relief. The kitchen was cramped enough that I don't make a habit of holding important conversations there. I didn't mind too much if whoever planted the thing was treated to hours of me washing dishes and singing off-key. They deserved the torture.

"Unless you have any more questions, I'm headed back. The team is dying to see this."

"I'd like to schedule a re-check for next week."

"Your landlords already set that up." She nodded their direction. "I want to sweep their part of the house too."

That made sense. "Thanks," I said sticking out my hand. "You're the best."

Garcy grinned and shook my hand. "Hate to say it, but days like this are what make me stay with an otherwise boring job. I suggest you get that fancy car you drive checked out too."

"Already taken care of," Eli said. "I called this morning and told her mechanic what to look for while he's checking for damage."

I'd make sure I thanked him well later. When we were alone.

Chapter 33

Jake showed up around suppertime. A TTB agent dropped him off. I didn't want to go out, so Eli and I had ordered Italian and there was plenty to share. And since Jake was homeless, I didn't want to chase him away although I'd been looking forward to a quiet evening snuggling up to Eli on the loveseat.

He offered to do the minimal dishes so I let him help me. There wasn't room for all three of us in the kitchen, so Eli took care of business while I washed and Jake dried. But after that, while we were sipping wine—me—or drinking beer—them, I pounced.

"What happened, Jake?"

He picked up his beer and avoided meeting my eyes. "I appreciate what you guys did for me but I can't talk about it. The TTB guys don't want any leaks."

I wouldn't let him off that easy. "How about the moonshine? When did you figure that out?"

Beside me, Eli shifted. He pretended to watch

TV, but I sensed the moment he tensed and paid attention.

Jake took a big swallow of his beer and didn't answer. I swirled the wine in my glass and waited until the silence grew uncomfortable. I figured the hours he'd spent being grilled by various law enforcement types would have loosened his tongue.

"That night I picked up the envelopes," he said after yet another gulp of beer. "I suspected then. That was money in the envelopes, and payment for something—alcohol or drugs were my guess and I didn't catch any sign of drugs. But the day I chased you from the house out in the boonies, they'd been passing around a jar of moonshine. You did a good job that day, Angel. You made me proud. Once you got to paved roads, every move was perfect. Where did you end up hiding?"

"The Outlet Mall. Ducked in between two buildings. I'd been there before and remembered the spot."

"You have learned well, grasshopper."

"You didn't tell me about that," Eli said, accusation heavy in his voice. "What else haven't you told me?"

I'd told him the bare minimum of the story. "I was scouting for another house to remodel. If I'm going to be jobless, I need a project to keep me occupied."

"Jobless?" Jake picked up on that right away.

Shit. All the little things I hadn't told either of them were adding up to one big ball of trouble.

Now both of the Hennessey men were upset with me. I should have known better.

❀ ❀ ❀

"I didn't want you to worry about me," I explained for the umpteenth time. Jake was ensconced in the suite at The Towers on Eli's dime and he and I were alone. "You were deep in contract negotiations, and if I told you, you would have come here and ruin everything for yourself. Besides, I informed the cops about it." Well, some of it, anyway.

Eli tightened his arm around me, drawing my back closer to his bare chest. The bed was a queen, but we needed only half of it. "You should have trusted me to make that decision for myself."

In my head, I knew that. My heart was a different matter. "It's hard. Not when we're together, but when we're apart. I've depended on no one except myself for a long time, and habits are difficult to break."

His deep sigh ruffled my hair. "You aren't the only guilty one."

I flipped so we were face to face. "What haven't you told me, Eli?"

He pressed his lips to my forehead. "I worried about you. Especially after Jake left and I had no one to keep an eye on you to make sure you stayed safe. So I hired a PI firm out of Pittsburgh to check on you now and then."

I rolled away. "What? Who?"

"Different guys. They kept replacing them as you gave each one the slip." He had the nerve to chuckle as he reached to pull me back, but I avoided his grasp.

"Black cars?"

His eyes widened. "I don't know. Why?"

"I've been followed by black cars ever since the murder. One had stolen tags." Was Eli responsible for the stress I'd been under?

"I used a reputable firm. That car couldn't have been one of theirs. Who else would follow you, Buttercup?"

I was angry and confused and touched by the concern in his voice all at the same time. "What do you think I've been trying to figure out? As far as I can tell, your PIs are responsible for several near-accidents. Then they planted a bug and you acted all innocent. Did you think I was cheating on you? I don't appreciate what you did, Elijah." I was only guilty of lies by omission. Having me followed was nearly unforgivable.

"I dropped the contract two weeks ago. And they were under strict orders to not place any listening devices. The bug isn't theirs. They were only protection, not surveillance. Like what you did for Jake."

His protestations didn't deter me. I stood and slipped on my robe. "You need to leave."

He was out of bed and standing in front of me before I reached the door. He put one hand on my cheek and stroked it. "You don't mean that, do you, Harmony?"

A single tear rolled down my cheek. He gently wiped it away with one finger. I grabbed his hand and kissed his palm.

"Right now, yes. In fifteen minutes I might change my mind."

He wrapped his arms around me. "Then I'll wait fifteen minutes. And if I need to, I'll wait fifteen more. And fifteen more. What I did was wrong, and I'm sorry. I considered telling you, but I remembered how much you like your privacy, and I chickened out. How can I make it better?"

I let my body melt into his. "What are we doing? This isn't healthy, me hiding things from you, you hiding things from me." Tears trickled from my eyes. I was saying my goodbyes, even if I wasn't ready to acknowledge it yet.

He tugged me closer. "It's hard when we aren't together. We just need to work on it more."

Easy to say, tough to do. "When we're together, it's magic." I pulled away to look him in the eye. "Why isn't it like that all the time? We're adults, what's wrong with us?"

"There's nothing wrong with us. We're just two people struggling to be together no matter what life throws our way. A long distance relationship is tough."

I didn't expect it to be this hard. But when he leaned in and pressed his lips to mine, it no longer mattered. Not for the moment, anyway.

❋ ❋ ❋

"Hayword has been released from the hospital

and is out on bail," Deputy Nelson, looking as crisp as ever, told me as he stood in front of the desk. He'd refused my offer of a chair. "Thought you should be aware in case he shows up."

Zechariah Hayword was the real name of the bald man, the guy I shot. One part of me felt good that he'd recovered, but the other part of me wished he'd been thrown behind bars for a few days.

"What about Harmony?" Eli asked. He'd dropped whatever he'd been working on and followed Deputy Nelson into Janine's office.

The deputy grimaced. "It's an election year."

I nodded. Signs were popping up everywhere. Someone even stuck one in the corner of Joe and Luke's yard without asking permission. It ended up in the trash.

"What's that got to do with anything?" Eli placed his hand on my shoulder and gave it a gentle squeeze.

"The DA is playing tough. Muttering about vigilantes and people taking the law into their own hands. But the Feds are leaning on him as well as other law-enforcement officials." Nelson cocked his head towards me. "You've got friends in high places who are making it known they won't be happy if you get charged, Miss Duprie. He has three years to decide, but I predict it won't be long until he breaks under the pressure and drops the case. It would be political suicide if he pursued it."

In the meantime, I had to worry about the possibility of someone seeking revenge and not having any protection except for my bare hands. Which do no good in a gunfight.

"I appreciate the update, Deputy. Let me know if I can help," I said.

"It's out of the Department's hands. The TTB is supposed to share any information they come across relating to the murder or Miss LeRoix's beating, but as far the moonshine ring goes, we're done."

I felt bad for him. If he got credit for solving the case it would be a huge boost for his career.

Eli accompanied the deputy when he left while I pretended to return to work. Not that I could concentrate on any one task for more than a few minutes. It seemed like a good time to take a walk through the library and make sure everything was running smoothly. I'd have to deal with the stares and questions eventually.

To my shock, the staff made a point of asking only about work-related issues. When did we expect the next shipment of books? Patrons had been asking for the newest releases. Who would be the contact for the new batch of high school volunteers? Most of last year's group were off to college. Any word on Janine's mother?

By the time I finished circulating through the library, a large grin plastered itself across my face, and felt as if it would stick there permanently. It was exactly the way I'd imagined the job for oh-so-many years. The dark cloud looming over my head was chased away by the golden rays of happiness thrown by everyone around me. I didn't want to think about having to give up the job when Janine got back so, I didn't.

Eli had returned to his table and was engrossed in his laptop when I sailed down the stairs from the third floor, the children's floor. I hesitated, then returned to the office. No matter how much we pretended otherwise, things still weren't right between us and I didn't want to ruin my good mood. Faith in humanity restored, I returned to the waiting stacks of paperwork.

The rumbling of my stomach broke my concentration. It was long past lunchtime and I needed a break. I hated to leave my cocoon but could I convince Eli to pick up lunch and spend time with me?

I stopped in my tracks as I cleared the front desk. Someone sat across from Eli and the two of them were deep in conversation. Even from the back he radiated his command presence. Chief Sorenson.

The situation screamed of danger and I considered returning to my office and hiding out. I didn't want to know what they were discussing. But Eli looked up and saw me, and there was no escaping.

With my heart in the pit of my stomach, I sauntered over to the table. "Good afternoon, Chief. What brings you here?" It was no time for small-talk and niceties.

"Have a seat. We're discussing protection for

you, Miss Duprie." Chief Sorenson twisted in his chair to face me.

I had Eli. What other protection did I need? I'd had this fight with Eli before and lost, so I did as the chief asked—ordered.

"We can't offer you anything officially. Oak Grove doesn't have the resources to handle this, and no other agency deems it necessary to provide you security."

It meant only one thing. My heart shattered into a zillion tiny pieces.

"A number of my officers approached me, and I gave permission for them to guard you when they are off-duty. I also approved parking an empty squad outside your house at nights. It's waiting for repairs, so it's out of commission anyway."

I couldn't stay quiet any longer. "When do you leave, Eli?"

He reached over and put his hand on top of mine. "The company jet is on its way to Pittsburgh."

The zillion pieces of my heart turned into dust in the wind.

I forced words out of my parched throat. "It must be important."

He nodded, but didn't share any details. More secrets.

What I wanted to say couldn't be said in front of Chief Sorenson. "Travel safe," I said instead.

Eli stared at me as if trying to interpret my hidden meaning. Even I wasn't sure what it was.

"Detective Thomason is putting together a

schedule of volunteers," the chief said, breaking the awkward silence. "He'll be in touch." He pushed back his chair and stood. "Contact either of us if you have any problems."

Both Eli and I got up as well. "Thank you, Chief," I said. "Hopefully, I won't be in touch."

I no longer wanted to be at the library. When Eli left with Chief Sorenson, all the sunshine rushed out of my day. He hadn't even said goodbye. I wanted to hop in Dolores and drive as fast and as far as possible. But she was still at the mechanic's, and I didn't know if I was free to leave the area. To put on a brave face for the rest of the day would take every ounce of determination I could summon. Holed away in Janine's office, I didn't have to pretend.

I wouldn't allow myself to cry, either. That would be saved for when I got home.

Fifteen minutes alone gave me enough time to regain my composure. Fifteen minutes of staring out the window and watching dark clouds roll by. Fifteen minutes of wondering what I'd done wrong.

But I had a library to run. I hadn't finished reviewing the proposal for replacing shelves although I'd made up my mind not to sign off on it. I needed to come up with a list of reasons to justify my decision to the board.

Although the pad of paper was filled with scribbles, I was only up to reason two when the door of my office flew open. "I'm going to be late,"

Eli said. Worry lines etched his face. "But I couldn't leave yet." He shut the door with a loud bang.

Had he come to say goodbye forever? Was this the end of us? I clutched the proposal as if it were a lifeline.

Eli stomped his way over to me and tore the papers out of my hands, tossing them onto my desk. "I don't want anything in the way."

The next thing I knew, he pulled me out of my chair and bent me backwards—like in that famous photo—and his lips crashed into mine.

"I can't do it," he said when we stopped to catch our breath, "walk away and not explain. This deal has been in the works for months and it looks like I'm finally going to get it. Too many of my employees spent too much time on it for me to let it slip through my fingers."

"Eli…" My words were smothered by another kiss.

"You are everything that I never realized I needed," he said. "So tell me what I'm supposed to do. How can I leave you and how can I not go?"

In that moment, the answer became clear. I didn't like it. But I was on a first name basis with most of his employees and they needed him too. I wouldn't be responsible for any of them losing their job.

"Go, Eli." I brushed my hand over his cheek. "Go make the deal. I'll be here when you can come back."

He took my face between both of his hands and studied it. "You know I love you, right?"

"And I love you." I kissed him, a mere peck in his cheek. "Now get out of here. You have work to do. And so do I."

He left, but not until we shared another scorching kiss. One that left me in a puddle in my chair watching his back as he left.

Chapter 34

If I didn't hurry, I'd miss it. The last bus that went through my neighborhood, that was. With Eli gone and Dolores still in the shop, I'd be relying on public transportation. It wasn't the first time.

Although I stayed late, with nothing better to do than work, I wasn't going to be the last one at the library. Lock-up duties belonged to Eleanor. I reviewed the contents of my freezer to figure out what to warm up for supper as I walked down the thirteen steps, and didn't pay attention to my surroundings.

"Going somewhere?" a deep voice boomed. Shock almost had me tumbling down the last two stairs. I gathered myself and prepared to flee but finally processed that I recognized that voice. Freddie unfolded himself from the bench he'd been sitting on and met me at the bottom of the stairs.

"Figured you needed a ride home," he said, rattling his key chain. "The Mustang awaits."

Freddie's fully restored 1960's cherry-red

Mustang wasn't Dolores, but it wasn't bad. Better than a bus ride any day. "Are you my babysitter for the night?" I asked jokingly.

"The first shift. I've got a schedule for the next few days so you'll know who's on duty. You've met most of them."

I'd run into most of the guys and gals on the force one time or another. Some under good circumstances, others—well, I'd rather not remember those. Freddie held the door of the Mustang open and waited to close it until after I fastened my seatbelt. I waited until he got in the car and pulled away from the curb before asking the question bugging me.

"Why are you doing this?"

"Do you mean why do we feel it's necessary?" Freddie shifted gears and the Mustang responded with a growl.

"Well, that too. No one's been arrested, so if there is a moonshine ring, they aren't a threat." That was my theory, anyway. "But what I really mean is why people are willing to take a huge chunk of time out of their lives to hang around my place and make sure no one bothers me."

He pulled into the parking lot of Mama D's. "I ordered takeout. If you don't mind, I'll invite Sarah over so you have company." He swung his door open. "Stay in the car and keep the doors locked. I'll be back in a minute."

Alone in the car lit only by the pale rays of the overhead lights of the restaurant, I fiddled with my phone and wondered why I hadn't heard from Eli.

Surely he'd made it to Orlando. Come to think about it, he hadn't told me where he was going. I'd assumed it was back to the office. Should I call him? Text him? Or would that be the move of an overly possessive girlfriend?

The scraping of metal against metal had me reaching for my purse and Betsy. Who wasn't in my purse. But it was only Freddie, back already.

"It smells glorious," I said as he swung several paper bags into the back. The scent of tomato, cheese, sausage and freshly made garlic bread mixed together and made my stomach rumble. "What did you order?"

Freddie settled himself into the driver's seat and closed the car door. "Only half as much as what we ended up with," he said with a broad grin. "I ordered spaghetti. When Mama D. found out it was for you, she threw in lasagna and fettucine alfredo. She's worried that you aren't eating right now that you're at the library all day, so she wanted you to have leftovers."

Not *that* much had changed in my schedule and it was sweet of her to worry, but why?

"What changed, Freddie?" I asked as he pulled onto the main drag. The glare of oncoming headlights from a passing car made me blink.

He quirked his mouth and glanced into the rearview mirror. "I can't speak for Mama D. In the case of my fellow officers, the Chief may have let it slip how much work you do for him. Even before that, several volunteered just because they like you. You have more friends than you realize, Harmony."

My face warmed with the kind words, even if I wasn't convinced they were true. I'd felt like an outcast for the last few years. How much pressure had the Chief put on his officers? Still, I wouldn't argue the point. I leaned back into the seat, prepared to enjoy the ride. When he switched lanes, I didn't wonder why.

"Hold on." Freddie swung the Mustang into a hard right turn before I had time to react. I bumped my shoulder against the window.

"What the hell?"

His lips formed a tight line as he checked his mirrors. "We're being followed."

I turned as far as the seatbelt allowed. It wasn't far enough.

"Black or dark blue car," Freddie answered my unasked question.

"Eli promised to call off his PI's!"

"Local guys?"

I shook my head. "A firm out of Pittsburgh. He claimed it was for protection, not surveillance." I no longer believed it.

Freddie sped up. "Whoever that is back there isn't even trying to hide."

"What do you want me to do?"

"Call 9-1-1. Put the phone on speaker so I can talk to dispatch. I may need backup."

Easy enough. My phone was still in my lap. I punched the numbers.

"9-1-1. What's your emergency?"

"Allison. It's Freddie Thomason."

"How can I help you, Detective?"

"10-33. I'm activating Protocol One."

The dispatcher hissed. "Stay on the line." A moment of dead air followed the order. Without warning, Freddie executed another sharp turn. I clung to the dashboard with my free hand.

"Protocol One activated."

I'd never heard of that procedure. What did it mean? Freddie was too busy swerving and controlling the Mustang to bother with such a trivial question.

"Carroll and Trenton are available. What's your location?"

"Headed north on the four hundred block of Oak."

"Civilian involved?"

"Duprie. Harmony."

"I'm elevating to a level two."

Freddie sighed. "10-4."

Not being in the driver's seat made me nervous. Freddie was doing everything right, but we weren't losing the tail. "Have you been able to identify the driver?" I asked quietly.

"No." He made an abrupt right. I managed not to hit my shoulder, but if I got away without bruises from the seatbelt I'd be lucky.

"Backup in position," Allison reported. "And civilian traffic diverted. You have a go."

I'd wondered why the street was so empty.

"10-4. Hold on, Harmony. Things just got interesting." Freddie stomped on the gas. The acceleration threw me into the seat back. I curled my fingers around the phone and tightened my grip.

Nearby, sirens wailed. As the Mustang flew by an intersection, a squad car turned on its lights and slipped in between us and our tail. At the next intersection, a second squad joined the parade behind our tail, sandwiching the black car.

At the next intersection, a third car joined us. This one pulled alongside the offender. Now there was nowhere for the sedan to go to get away.

In unison, the three police vehicles slowed and stopped. Freddie kept going. Watching the lights disappear in the mirror, I felt cheated. "That was pretty slick," I said, hiding my disappointment.

"We're clear, dispatch," Freddie said loudly. "10-10." He patted my knee. "You can hang up now."

"I guess we get to eat in your office."

"What makes you say that?"

"Aren't you going to have a stack of paperwork?"

"I will, but I'm off-duty and it will wait."

That meant we'd get to eat off real plates instead of paper ones. And use real silverware instead of plastic forks. But Freddie made a left turn where he should have taken a right to go to my place.

"Where are we going?"

"You have the key to Janine's, right?"

I was responsible for watering her plants so yes, I did. "Why?"

"I want you to spend the night there. I'll get Sarah to pick up a change of clothes for you."

"Is that necessary? The guy who was following us is in custody."

"We don't know if he has accomplices."

True. But I really wanted to go home, slip into

something comfortable, and relax. "For all we know, he was after you, not me."

"And that's why I'm not going home either. After you get settled in, I'll take off and stay with a friend. Not Sarah, if that's what you're thinking."

My mind *had* wandered that direction.

"Even asking her to pack your bag is involving her more than I want to. But I know how particular you are about people touching your things and I figured you'd go nuts if a male rookie was sent to paw through your underwear."

They'd end up in the garbage as soon as I could buy new ones.

"We'll make the arrangements when we get to Janine's."

"After we eat." The excitement hadn't dulled my appetite. If anything, I was hungrier than before.

❋ ❋ ❋

"So what's with the Protocol One stuff?" I asked before stuffing another forkful of the best lasagna in the world into my mouth.

Freddie picked up another breadstick before answering. "It started as a joke," he explained as he coated the bread with marinara sauce. He grinned. "Based on your adventures last fall. There was a lot of back and forth on how to handle it if the situation ever happened again. Suggestions ranged from moats filled with alligators to guided missiles. One day the Chief overheard the discussion and set us to work developing a real procedure in case it ever happened again. Not necessarily to you, of course, but to anyone in our little town. You know, in case we ever get a celebrity passing through."

I wasn't sure whether to be flattered or embarrassed. "What about level two?"

"Oh, that." He took a bite of the breadstick and I followed his example with mine. He covered his mouth with his hand. "That means the Chief was notified. I'm surprised I haven't heard from him yet." He glanced at his phone as if the conversation would magically force it to ring.

"Either he trusts you implicitly or he's too busy to pick up the phone."

Freddie shook his head. "He doesn't trust anyone that much."

Sad but true. I'd worked with Chief Sorenson enough to see that for myself.

While we were washing the dishes, Freddie's phone rang. As he wandered off to talk to whomever was calling, I peeked at mine. No missed calls, no messages. Where was Eli?

Freddie's call took forever and he strolled back into the kitchen as I put the last plate away. "Shift change," he announced. "Reynolds will patrol outside tonight. He's got your bag. I'll introduce you before I head out."

"Any word on who the suspect is?"

"You're not going to like it."

There were numerous things in my life lately I didn't like, but I took what got thrown at me. "Tell me anyway."

Freddie sighed. "Carl Buford."

❀ ❀ ❀

The story came out in bits and pieces over the next few days. By then I'd ignored Freddie's advice and gone home. Even with Dolores out of the shop, there were no more black cars following me, and as long as Carl stayed in custody I felt safe. The off-duty officers, Freddie included, still patrolled outside, and I saw a lot more of Jake. At least when he wasn't doing door duty at the local clubs. He'd started hanging out at the library again and trailing me home to make sure I got there without a problem. He'd gotten his Charger out of storage the same day Carl was arrested.

"I still can't believe it," I told Eli. He finally called me—they'd taken a several-days break in negotiations so the other company could reevaluate the proposal one more time.

He chuckled. "His soulmate, eh?"

"Can you believe that nonsense? He's been spying on me since the night I asked him to translate the note."

"And he never asked you out?"

"No. But those missed calls and hang-ups I'd been getting have ended, so I'm betting they came from him. He told the cops he was waiting for the right moment to sweep me off my feet. Then he saw me with you the night we rescued Jake and decided to make his move."

"I shouldn't have left."

"And deny Freddie his moment of glory?" I chuckled. It had taken effort to find any humor in the situation. "He's in line for another promotion after successfully pulling off that maneuver. Besides, seeing me with Freddie is what set Carl off. He thought I was cheating on you which somehow meant I was cheating on him. Don't ask me how that process works. Between that and being suspended from his job and blaming it on me, he didn't know whether he loved me or hated me."

"Talk about messed up. So what was he doing with the moonshiners?"

"Selling to high school kids. Or giving it to them for free to gain popularity. Whichever suited him at the time."

"Be careful, Buttercup. If he's blaming you for his problems, he could come back after you."

"Not a chance," I was thrilled to report. "The judge decided he was a flight risk and a potential danger to the community and denied him bail on a laundry list of charges, including corrupting our local youth. He's been shipped to another facility to await his hearing."

"That's good." He yawned. At least, that's what it sounded like over the phone. "Sorry, Buttercup," he said. "I haven't slept well the last few nights."

Me either, for some odd reason. It might have had something to do with missing him. And stalkers, of course. "Go to bed, Sweetie. We'll talk again tomorrow." I hoped. "Love you."

I went to bed with his answering "Love you, too." still playing in my head. It didn't take long for me to fall asleep.

Chapter 35

"It'll be a quick trip to Pittsburgh and back. How much trouble can I get into?" It was my chance to get the note evaluated and translated. Professor Bouchard was presenting at a conference in Pittsburgh, and was able to work me into his schedule for a short meeting. Since the opening was Saturday afternoon, I'd need to take only half a day off from the library.

I didn't even have to worry about the not-leaving-town issue. The DA, in his wisdom, spent *hours* studying the facts of the case and determined I'd acted in self-defense. No charges were brought against me. Dan said the pressure on the DA was intense—our local judges had shared their feelings—and it would have been a political death sentence if the decision went any other way. In other words, the DA caved. I even got Betsy back.

"At least take Jake along," Freddie wasn't happy with the plan, but was powerless to stop me.

"What's he going to do while the professor and I

discuss an old piece of paper? Sit in the lobby and twiddle his thumbs?" Watch us talk was all he could do. Either that or go wander the stores downtown. Being a convicted felon, he couldn't carry a gun, so he wouldn't be much of a bodyguard. Not that I needed one.

Freddie sighed. "You know there's power in numbers. You're less likely to be attacked if you aren't by yourself."

That was the truth. "Okay, I'll ask. But I not making any guarantees."

❄ ❄ ❄

That's how Jake and I ended up sitting in a hotel bar in Pittsburgh. It was a glorious early fall day, with only a few puffy white clouds dotting a brilliant blue sky and the drive down had been flawless. As I sipped my soda, I studied the other patrons of the bar. Bouchard was supposed to text me when his panel ended, but I didn't want to miss him.

Most of the customers appeared to be road-weary travelers, taking a rare afternoon off to cheer on their favorite team. A few looked like escapees from the scholarly conference. None of them appeared to be a threat, so I tried to relax while we waited.

"There's your guy," Jake said at precisely fifteen minutes after the hour. "Right on time."

I swiveled to see. I'd found his picture on-line and knew who to look for but hadn't shared the information with Jake. He was right, but how did

Jake pick the professor out of the group that arrived at the same time? I didn't have time to ask, because the hostess pointed our direction and I rose to greet him.

"Ah! Miss Duprie! A pleasure to finally meet you." He took my offered hand and shook it vigorously. "Forgive me, I looked you up online. You are much prettier in person."

I hoped he hadn't found my mug shot. "That's very kind of you, Professor. This is my friend Jake Hennessey."

The handshake between the two men was brief, and Professor Bouchard barely glanced at Jake. When I sat, the professor slid into the booth next to me. He ignored Jake's glare and asked "Do you have the note with you? I'm most anxious to see it."

I shot Jake a look, pleading with him to not get upset. He got the message and slid onto the bench on the other side.

Before we left Oak Grove, I'd put the note in a clear plastic sleeve along with a piece of cardboard so it wouldn't get any more wrinkled on the trip. I'd laid it on the table when we arrived, so all I needed to do was slide it over to Professor Bouchard.

While he carefully pulled the note from the sleeve, I studied him. In person, he looked exactly like the pictures I'd found of him on line. Pictures that made him look like a French nobleman of the 1700's with shoulder-length hair, a mustache, and goatee. A man dedicated to his work.

"I'd need to have the paper tested, of course," he said after examining the note for too long with a magnifying class he'd pulled out of his suit coat pocket, "to make sure it's not a well-done forgery."

I held my breath and rubbed the largest chunk on my turquoise necklace. Did that mean it was the real thing? He pulled a piece of paper out of his other pocket and laid it next to mine. With the magnifying glass held close to his eye, he switched from looking at one piece of paper to the other several times.

It seemed like forever until he set the magnifying glass on the table. Then the waitress came over to get his order. I wanted to scream while he made up his mind. He eventually ordered a sidecar.

"Have you ever heard of it? A classic French drink," he explained, "from the end of World War I. I'll be tickled if the bartender knows how to make it."

I got the impression that the professor was easily distracted. Another day I'd be thrilled to learn something new. All I wanted at that moment was to find out one thing.

"Although some stories say it was actually invented by an American," he continued. Jake and I exchanged glances of frustration. I needed to head the professor off at the pass.

"About the note, Professor," I said.

"Ah, yes." He picked it up and ran his fingers across the surface. "Thank you for bringing it. Please be aware that my answer is dependent upon chemical tests of the paper and ink."

"Won't that destroy the note?"

The waitress returned with his drink. He took a

sip and smiled at her. "Almost perfect! My compliments to the bartender."

"Add it to my tab," I said when he reached for his wallet. He started to protest, but I put my hand on his arm. "It's my pleasure."

He nodded and picked up his drink. My tab included all of two sodas at the moment, but he didn't need to know that. The waitress excused herself and left to get another table's order.

"To answer your question," he said, "they can take such small amounts it doesn't ruin the integrity of the paper. I'm not sure it would be worth the effort in this case."

So, it was a fake. I couldn't keep my disappointment from showing. "Thank you for your time, Professor," I said.

"No, let me explain. The majority of the note is not Louis Philippe's handwriting. It was likely written by a secretary. But the signature? I believe it to be authentic. Notice the difference in the way the P's are written?"

I could barely make out the first one was a P at all. "Then why isn't it worth testing?"

"The cost of determining authenticity far outweighs the value of the note. The note by itself is only worth about one hundred dollars. I'd advise you to save your money, Miss Duprie. You've spent too much of it already on my fees. It's too bad you don't have the gift this note accompanied. That would raise the value considerably."

I hadn't told Jake about the cufflinks, fearing they'd be too much of a temptation for him. I tried to sound crestfallen. "Thank you. It will make a nice keepsake." I put it back into the plastic sleeve. "But what does it say?"

"Oh, that." the professor slipped the magnifying glass into his pocket and pulled out a third piece of paper. "I wrote it down for you."

His writing was almost as bad as the original note, but at least it wasn't faded so I could read it. The top section was the original French.

Présenté à Antoine Erdman, Baron de Bode
En guise de remerciement pour votre service inestimable à la France
Louise Phillippe
02 Février 1846

Followed by the English.

Presented to Antoine Erdman, Baron de Bode
In way of thanks for your invaluable service to France
Louise Phillippe
02 February 1846

"Well, that was interesting." I threaded Dolores through unexpectedly heavy traffic. The Steelers game must have ended sooner than I'd anticipated. "A waste of money, perhaps, but interesting."

"What's the rest of the story, Angel?" Jake asked.

I tried to play innocent. "What story?"

"Why you were so hell-bent on getting the note translated? That was more than curiosity. The way your eyes lit up when the professor mentioned the gift that went with the note told me you were hiding something. Something important."

How would I work my way out of this predicament? I hated lying to Jake. Concentrating on the traffic gave me a temporary excuse to avoid answering him. In my rearview mirror, I spotted a black sedan switching lanes to pull in behind Dolores. No big deal, the traffic seemed to flow faster in my lane than the one on the left. But an annoying prickle at the back of my neck was enough for me to grab an opportunity and move to my right without signaling first. I didn't leave room for a second car to get in behind me. Or did I? The other driver forced an opening, nearly causing an accident behind us.

"Angel?"

"We've got trouble. Black sedan, late-year model." If Eli had sent his PI firm after me again, I'd seriously have to reconsider our relationship.

He twisted in his seat. "Two men. Both wearing caps and sunglasses."

"So far they haven't done anything I can use as a reason to call the cops."

"There's an exit a mile ahead."

"Any bets they expect us to take it?"

Jake's smile didn't reflect happiness. Satisfaction,

maybe. Or diabolical intentions. "So we'll do no such thing."

If I got lucky, traffic might break to the left around the same point where I'd move onto the exit ramp. If I didn't get lucky, I'd need to invent Plan B in a hurry.

With less than a quarter mile to the exit, I flipped on my turn signal. With five hundred feet to go, I drifted to the right but stayed in my lane. At two hundred feet, I spotted my opening in front a double-trailered semi.

Jake grabbed the dashboard. I cranked the steering wheel to the left and stepped on the gas. Dolores flowed into the barely-there-break between cars. The honking of horns didn't deter me as I took a chance and moved over one more lane.

"Damnit," Jake muttered.

"They didn't take the exit, did they?" I asked, easing off the pedal.

"No."

I'd hoped, but really hadn't expected them to fall for the diversionary tactic. "Where are they now?"

"Not sure. The semi is blocking my view."

"So they can't see us either." That gave me a small window of opportunity. "How's the traffic behind it?"

"All piled up."

So much for my idea of dropping to the rear of the truck and getting behind our followers. "Got any ideas?"

He shook his head. "Unless this traffic clears,

we're stuck. I don't think there are any left-hand exits on this stretch of road."

Great. "How familiar are you with the back roads of Pittsburgh?"

"I'm not."

The situation had the makings of a very bad deal. I couldn't think of a single thing to use to our advantage.

While we talked, we'd inched up so we were no longer aside the semi. A quick glance to my right didn't reveal any sign of the black car. Had they given up so soon? It didn't seem likely.

Jake read my mind. "My bet is that they're still behind the truck. Probably hoping to lure you into thinking you're safe."

"They might be after you," I pointed out. "You have been mixing with some unsavory characters."

"I know." His voice held a tone I'd never heard from him before. Despair.

I couldn't give him a hug while I was driving, so I settled for patting his knee. It was neither the time nor place to analyze his mental state.

A sudden flare of taillights in front gave me the opportunity I'd been waiting for. I braked and slowed, and watched the line of vehicles beside me, including the semi, slide past. Still, I was too busy paying attention to the traffic to check for the black car.

"When I say the word, change lanes." Jake picked up my hand and put it back on the steering wheel at the three o'clock position. I gripped it, but not too tightly. "And GO."

I barely glanced over my shoulder or in my mirrors before easing Dolores to the right and stepping on the gas to match the new flow of traffic. "Surprise, surprise," I said. There, in front of us, was a black car. *The* black car.

Chapter 36

Now it was a whole different game, and I owned a big advantage. "Can you get the plate?" I asked Jake.

He leaned forward and squinted. "Can you get a little closer?"

As long as no one stepped on the brakes at the wrong moment, it was doable. "Make it quick." I eased forward, closing the gap between us. At fifty-five miles an hour, even the slightest error would be disastrous.

"Got it. Did you see it?"

"Only a few letters. MO something."

Jake quirked one side of his mouth. "M-Zero-Zero-N-S-H-N."

"Moonshine? Are you kidding me?" How stupid did the owner of the car have to be to personalize his plate that way? And how did it ever slip past the DMV? "You don't recognize the vehicle?"

"No. But I was only introduced to a few minor

players of the organization, never to the guy at the top."

"If those are the big shots, they obviously got the word about Dolores." I stepped on my brakes as they did the same. Trying to get me to back off or trying to cause a wreck? It didn't matter because it didn't work.

"There aren't too many red Jaguars on the road today."

Or ever. "Grab my phone out of my purse."

"You want a picture of the car?"

"Not a bad idea. Then call Freddie. It's time to call in a favor and see if he'll run the plate."

Of course, I owed Freddie more favors than he owed me but it wasn't like I could run an internet search for information on the car's owner. I was too busy keeping up with it as the driver dove in and out of lanes of traffic, trying to lose us. The two cars were evenly matched and I wondered out loud what kind of car it was.

"BMW," Jake said, his hand covering the phone. "Freddie wants you to back off and come home."

Of course he did. "He knows me better than that."

Jake grinned. "I'm putting you on speaker. There's no need for me to act as a relay service."

I wanted to avoid having Freddie yell at me, but I was in no position to fight. "Hope I didn't ruin your Saturday evening, Freddie," I said loudly.

"Drop off and come home, Harmony," he growled.

"This could be what's needed to break this case wide open."

"Or what gets you killed along with any innocent bystanders that get caught in the crossfire."

I couldn't argue with that. At least, I shouldn't have argued. I did anyway. "I'll only follow as long as it takes the authorities to catch up to us."

"It's not safe, Harmony. You aren't a trained professional."

"If these guys have anything to do with selling moonshine to our kids, that's a risk I'll take."

"The Chief might fire me for this."

"Either that or you'll be even more of a hero than you are now."

The dead air that followed made me wonder if the connection had dropped. I needed to concentrate on my driving anyway. The heavy traffic had started to clear out and the BMW was picking up speed. The darker it got, the harder it became to keep track of where it was.

"Do you think he'll call back?" I asked Jake.

"The call is still active."

"I'm still here. Do you know a Brent Heathman?" Freddie asked.

"I know a Brent. He was involved in the incident at the Dog House. I never got his last name."

"No way that's a coincidence," Jake whispered.

I nodded in agreement.

"Hold on, I'm checking," Freddie said.

I switched lanes, putting a car between the BMW

and me. Its distinctive taillights were my guiding beacons.

"Same guy," Freddie reported. "I don't like it, Harmony."

I didn't either. But I'd committed to my course of action and was sticking to it. "Can you call the local cops, Freddie?"

"What jurisdiction are you in?"

I suspected we'd left the borders of Pittsburgh some time ago. "Any idea, Jake?"

"No. I haven't been watching the road signs."

"I have a contact with the PA Highway Patrol," Freddie said. "They should be able to help. Stay on the line, I'll try to patch them through."

Whatever he tried, it didn't work. Jake punched the home button of the phone. "We lost him. I'll call him back."

The car in front of us made a sudden move to the right and shot off at an exit. So much for my cover. I'd hoped to stay invisible.

"Hang back," Jake advised, my phone to his ear. "All I'm getting is a busy signal."

"Freddie's probably talking to his contact. Hopefully he'll call us back."

"How much do you know about this Brent character?"

"Nothing. I didn't do any research on him."

The black car switched lanes again and cut off an economy car. Tires squealed in protest as the driver of the little car had to brake to avoid being run off the road. I held my lane for the moment. No need to mirror the BMW's rash driving. With no one in front of or beside me I could still track its path.

"Deputy Nelson never mentioned Brent being a person of interest in the murder," I said, picking up where I'd left off, "So I didn't even think about it. Weird part is, he didn't fit in with the other two guys. That should have been a clue right there." Or the fact I'd heard him talking about deliveries should have alerted me that something was going on. Of course, that was before I knew about the moonshine. "We don't even know if Brent is in the Beemer or someone borrowed it."

"I guess the cops can straighten all that out." Jake glared at my phone as if that would force it to ring.

The gap between us and the BMW got bigger. Too big for my comfort, so I pushed on the gas pedal. Dolores caught up with them in no time flat, but we were doing well over the speed limit. That should have attracted a cop, but no blue lights were evident no matter where I looked.

Finally, Freddie got back to us.

"I can't figure out the conference call setup on this cell phone," he grumbled. "So tell me where you are. I've got PA HP on my landline. I'll relay the information."

"Are we still in Pennsylvania?" I asked.

"For now. We're on 279 south of where it joins with I-79," Jake told him.

Freddie relayed the information to his connection. After a series of "uh-uh's" and "okay's," he got back on the line with us.

"They've got someone about five minutes out. If I can't convince you to take the next exit, can I at least get you to hang back as far as possible?"

"Already doing that," I said. "I hoped to convince them I'd given up, but so far it hasn't worked."

Freddie snorted. "It's impossible to make your car invisible."

It was almost possible in the dark, but each overhead light revealed our presence once again. They did the same thing for the BMW. The black car wouldn't be slipping away on an exit without us spotting it.

"You think they're waiting for us to get bored or run out of gas?" I asked.

"Or they're leading us into a trap," Jake suggested. "They've had plenty of time to call in reinforcements. If they're trying to get away from us, they aren't trying very hard."

It was too obvious now that he pointed it out.

"Drop off, Harmony." Freddie had heard Jake's comment too. "That's a direct order."

I could have told him he didn't have any authority over me, but I didn't want to hurt his feelings. "How far out is the trooper?" Maybe I could distract Freddie.

"Two or three minutes."

Still too far away. Too much room for Brent to get away. The intersection with I-76 would be coming up in a few miles giving him a chance to lose both the highway patrolman and me. "I'm watching for an exit," I said as we flashed by one.

Brent might keep heading north, but I doubted he'd want to get on the toll road and head west.

To our left, beyond a barrier, another stream of cars indicated the merge of I-279 and 79. The extra lanes would give the BMW more room for escape. That also meant that I-76 wasn't far away. Brent— or whoever was driving his car—braked and skidded from the left lane to the one on the right. If I'd reacted any slower, I would have missed the opportunity to follow. Dolores, however, proved once again she was worth every penny I'd paid for her. When Brent made his move onto an exit, I was right behind him.

The abandoned gas station at the bottom of the ramp was the perfect setup for an ambush. I breathed a sigh of relief when Brent drove past it. "The good news is that we're off the interstate," I reported to Freddie. "The bad news is that we're still following the BMW. The worse news is that I didn't catch the exit number. It's the first exit on 79."

Freddie didn't respond immediately, but I heard him talking to someone else in the background. Then he was back on our call. "HP is about a minute away." Not close enough. I needed to back off because we were headed into a residential area. The risk of causing a wreck grew higher as we intruded deeper into the cluster of houses.

"I can't do this anymore." I hit my brakes. The taillights of the BMW quickly disappeared around a curve. "Freddie, I'm done. It was a good game, but I don't want to hit a pedestrian."

"I'll pass the word along. Come home, Harmony."

As soon as I found a safe place to turn around, I would. "Good night, Freddie." I nodded to Jake who ended the call.

But I wasn't ready to go home. The adrenalin pumping through my veins screamed at me to resume the chase. I needed to distract myself before getting back on the road.

"How about we get a snack?" I asked Jake, spotting a convenience store sign a block away. "A corn dog sounds good."

"Sure."

I slowed down even farther and flipped on my turn signal. The more I thought about it the less appealing a corn dog sounded, but I needed something to settle my stomach—and my nerves. A caffeine-free soda might be a better choice.

There was only one car in the parking lot when we pulled in. A pretty blue, newer car, but no match for Dolores. Everything from the store sign to the pavement looked fresh, matching the appearance of the neighborhood and I wondered how long the location had been open.

No clerk stood behind the counter when we opened the door. That should have been my first clue. I rationalized that he was in the back taking care of stock. The absence of any customers should have been my second. But I headed straight for the drink machine, leaving Jake sauntering towards the hot dog cookers.

The angry voices coming from the back office should have been my third clue. Instead, I cocked my head and tried to listen to the conversation. The walls and closed doors muffled the sound enough to make most of the words undecipherable. The refrigerated sodas on the back wall gave me the excuse I needed to inch my way towards the hallway leading to the restrooms and storeroom. No employee might be out front, but that didn't mean they weren't watching me on a remote camera display.

With a hot dog in one hand and a bag of chips in the other, Jake sidled over to stand next to me. "What's up?" he whispered, bending over and pretending to check out the offerings on the bottom rack.

"I'm not sure. Something feels off." I took the retro glass bottle of soda he handed to me. It fit nicely in my hand and made a marvelous impromptu weapon.

"Agreed." His bag of chips ended up mixed in with a display of chocolate candies, and a bottle of orange pop took its place.

"You think it's a robbery?"

"A clerk wouldn't have access to open a safe this time of day. And no one's trying to break into the cash register."

Good points. I needed a new theory. "Can you make out what they're yelling about?"

Jake shook his head.

"Should we leave?" I was tired and with the adrenalin rush worn off, despite my curiosity, the last thing I wanted to do was get involved in yet another 'incident.'

"We can stop farther down the road." Jake's words of agreement didn't match his lack of movement. He stayed planted as close to the hallway as possible, his knees bent, ready to burst into action.

I wandered away, pretending an interest in the assorted candy bars offered. The clerk still wasn't at his post, and I considered dumping the soda on the counter and leaving. Jake would follow, right?

Chapter 37

Curiosity overcame my puny effort at not getting involved when the yelling turned ugly. Swear words splintered the silence of the store. Words I hadn't heard since I'd told Annabelle I no longer needed her services. Come to think of it…

I sidled closer to the hallway, then slid halfway down it. The door to the office stood open a crack, but not wide enough to see inside. At least I could listen to the conversation. To play it safe, I plastered myself on the far side of the door, so if it opened any farther I wouldn't be spotted.

"No!" It was a man's voice, but one I didn't recognize. "I didn't sign up for this."

"We'll make it worth your while." The second man's voice sounded familiar, but I wasn't sure.

"You'll fuckin' do what we tell you to." And there she was. Annabelle.

I warred with running back and reporting to Jake or sticking around to hear more. I stayed where I was.

"It's only this one time," the second man's voice said. And then it clicked. Brent.

Brent? And Annabelle? Together? No coherent thought formed in my brain.

I needed to tell Jake. But they were still talking, so I stayed glued to the wall like the proverbial fly.

"No guns," the first man insisted. By process of elimination I determined he was the store clerk. "Selling 'shine is one thing. Guns? Oh, hell no."

The jarring clang of metal against metal made me shrink even closer to the wall. I prayed I wouldn't have to rush in and rescue the clerk if things got worse. My puny skills would be no match against the combination of Brent and Annabelle. Especially if they had guns.

That's when the pieces fell into place. The nuisance noise complaints on my charts, the supposed gunshots being explained away as cars backfiring. Brent and Annabelle were selling guns. Moonshine was the cover.

That was way more than I was equipped to handle. I needed to contact someone in law enforcement, but did the store clerk need saving? And how could I make that happen?

I looked up to see Jake sticking his head around the corner. I lifted a finger to my lips and raised my hand in a 'stop' gesture. He nodded and stayed where he was.

"You either play along, or you can damn well say goodbye to the extra friggin' money," Annabelle said. "You don't get to fuckin' pick and choose. Without the cash, you'll have a fuckin' hard time paying for that new car of yours."

My influence on Annabelle's vocabulary had clearly not lasted.

A chime rang, indicating the arrival of a customer, and a man rushed out of the office. He didn't even glance my direction in his hurry to get to the sales counter. He left the door to the office wide open leaving me stuck in the hallway. I expected Annabelle and Brent to follow him, but they didn't appear. Instead, they started arguing with each other.

"I told you to let me handle it!" Brent shouted.

"You aren't doing so good being in charge." I imagined the sneer on Annabelle's face. "You're losing people left and right. And if one of them caves and spills information to the Feds, you're done."

"You aren't doing any better."

"If you'd give me a chance, I might."

They sounded like kids squabbling, not the big shots of a crime syndicate.

"You didn't do us any damn favors when you offed Tadd."

"And you flirt with any other guy, he'll get the same treatment. I don't want to have to teach you another lesson."

"God damn it, I told you it was part of my cover."

Not siblings. Lovers. Or what passes for love in an abusive relationship. Jake had to be warned, and I needed to call the police. And get out of there before I became their next victim.

My options seemed limited. I could sneak out the back door if the place had one. That would mean abandoning Jake. If I dropped to the floor and belly crawled to the front of the store, Brent and Annabelle might not see me. Or they might. Rushing past the opening appeared to be the safest bet.

I didn't have the chance to pick any option as Brent and Annabelle came out of the office, holding hands, apparently over their lover's spat. At the same time, Jake stuck his head around the corner, checking on me again. His mouth hung open for a second, but only a second.

While I couldn't be sure if Brent knew who Jake was, Annabelle sure did. And the hand not holding Brent's gripped a gun.

Jake had been shot for me once before. It was not going to happen again.

I launched myself down the hallway. I'd be able to only take on one person, and my target was obvious. With a satisfying smack, I rammed into Annabelle's back. The gun hit the tile floor with a loud clunk. She fell to her knees. Not good enough.

Jake should be able to handle Brent. I concentrated on Annabelle. An awkward and ill-timed kick landed between her shoulders. Although her hands hit the ground, she still wasn't where I wanted her.

In the moment I got distracted checking for Jake, she recovered and rose to a standing position. She threw a hasty punch. It landed solidly on my shoulder. I staggered backward.

I'd been hit before. In practice. With gloves.

The minor pain didn't upset me. In my head, my teacher's voice mocked me, telling me I deserved it for allowing myself not to pay attention. Lesson learned.

My returning punch met her chin, surprised at how much it hurt. Me, that is. My knuckles were going to bruise. At least it hurt her worse. I hoped. She stumbled backward.

Her eyes looked wild, like a trapped animal's. I expected her to spout a mouthful of vulgarities at any second. She leapt at me instead. With no room to maneuver, I barely avoided her. Bags of jerky scattered on the floor when I knocked over the display rack.

I answered with a kick that landed on her thigh. The dress flats I wore took away from the severity of the strike. One shoe fell off. I abandoned the other.

She rushed me, arms flailing. If she wanted to intimidate me, it didn't work. As soon as she got within reach, I grabbed one arm and whirled, twisting her arm behind her back. "Give up," I hissed.

Her response was an attempted head butt. It didn't work. I pulled her arm higher as punishment.

One of the men slammed into me from behind. I lost my grip on Annabelle and we tumbled to the floor, me on top. She twisted and grabbed my hair and pulled.

I didn't want to play anymore. I grabbed the collar of her pale-green polo shirt and yanked her head off the floor, then slammed it downwards. The thud sickened and satisfied me at the same time. I hated myself as I lifted her head to do it again.

She grabbed my hands, digging her fingernails into them, trying to make me to let go of her. I pushed her head back into the floor and pounded her nose with the top of my head, forcing her to loosen her grip and let go.

Her nose spurted blood, and she raised her hands to wipe it away. She stared at her hands and then at me and started crying. First a soft whimper, then flat-out bawling. I glared at her in disgust. If I'd known a little blood was all it took to subdue her, my tactics would have changed much sooner in the fight.

When I raised a hand as if to hit her again, she curled into a ball and hid her face between her knees. I couldn't do it and rose, turning to check on Jake.

Punches were being thrown fast and furious

between him and Brent. Both were winded, but they appeared to be on equal footing. I needed to change that.

A bottle of orange soda rolled around on the floor. I snatched it up as I struggled to my feet. Any weapon was better than none.

I circled the pair, waiting for an opening. Visions of broken glass sparkling in the air and orange soda dripping down Brent's head enticed me. The two parted for a moment, and Brent reached for his waistband. When his hand rose again, it held a revolver.

Instinct kicked in. The bottle of soda sailed through the air. It arched and landed perfectly on the top of Brent's head. To my dismay, it didn't break.

It startled Brent for a second. Long enough for Jake to body slam him to the floor. The gun landed beside him as the door chime rang again. I expected Jake to swoop it up but instead he kicked it down the aisle.

"I'd pick it up," he said with a crooked grin as he raised his hands. A bruise marred his left cheek. "But I don't want the nice trooper coming in the door to mistake me for a bad guy."

❋ ❋ ❋

"I still can't believe I was considered a suspect and Brent wasn't," I complained again to Deputy Nelson.

"He had an alibi and you didn't."

Yeah, but Brent's alibi had been provided by Paul Zavari. After Brent had taken Tadd home, he'd shown up at Paul's apartment with a bottle of moonshine. Once Paul fell asleep, Brent had snuck out and paid a visit to Tadd. At least, that's the story Annabelle spewed and the Sheriff's Department was trying to prove. Since Brent returned before Paul woke up, he assumed Brent had been asleep on his couch the whole night.

I hadn't even bothered to call Dan when the deputy had breezed into Janine's—my—office at the library. Representatives of five different law enforcement agencies had already grilled me for hours. Two sheriff's departments, the TTB, the Highway Patrol and the ATF. Felton and Garcia dropped off the case, avoiding a territorial squabble at the federal level when the Bureau of Alcohol, Tobacco, Firearms and Explosives—the ATF— claimed jurisdiction

The visit was more of a social call, anyway, so I didn't need Dan. Deputy Nelson decided it was only fair I be kept up-to-date on news about the case. At least, any news that the public would get. I'd just get it first. The newest bit of information was that Brent and Annabelle were denied bail once again, so I didn't need to worry about them showing up at my doorstep. For the moment, life was good.

Well, better at least. There'd been an offer on the house from the law firm in Pittsburgh, for the full asking price. I didn't have a good reason to turn them down, so Sarah was putting together the needed paperwork. At the closing, I'd meet the actual buyers.

I'd given the information about the cufflinks and note to Gary at the pawn shop. He tracked down the family that had rented the storage locker and set up a meeting with them to return the treasure. They would decide whether they wanted to spend the money to determine the value of the note and cufflinks and if they belonged together. I wouldn't be able to be there because I still had the job at the library. For the moment, anyway. Which was mostly good.

"What are the chances that Annabelle will claim battered wife's syndrome to avoid prosecution?" As far as I knew, she and Brent weren't married but their relationship went back to her high school years. I checked, and found Brent in the class a year ahead of her.

I didn't know how long they'd planned the scheme, but I had to give Annabelle credit. Working as a PI was the perfect cover. She could hang around sleazy bars and no one would question her presence.

"Slim. Brent carries as many scars as she does and claims she's responsible for them. Neither has hospital records to prove their story." The deputy stood and adjusted his duty belt. "By the way, the Sheriff wanted me to ask you to reconsider his offer."

The Sheriff had asked me to assist him in the same way I was helping Chief Sorenson—analyzing data and creating reports for him to present to the

County Commissioners. He'd been impressed by the charts I'd created during the investigation. "Give the Sheriff my regards," I said. "But my answer remains the same. I don't have time to tackle that for him while I'm working here. We can talk again when Janine gets back."

He nodded. "I'll pass the word along. But I think you've missed your calling. You should have been a cop."

I'd had my fill of excitement. I wanted to settle back into a routine, even if it was a new one. "Thanks but no thanks. I don't envy you dealing with bad guys every day. I prefer the library's patrons. Their biggest problem is replacing a lost book. I like my quiet little life."

Deputy Nelson shook his head and chuckled as he headed for the door. "There's a red Jaguar sitting out back that tells me different. Have a good day, Miss Duprie."

He had to remind me. It was a gorgeous fall day and Dolores was primed for a long drive. But I was stuck behind the desk preparing payroll. Or maybe stuck was the wrong word. I wanted to be there, doing exactly what I'd dreamed of for so long. Yes, things in my life were looking up.

If only Eli was there to share it with.

❋ ❋ ❋

"Do I really have to be here?" I asked Sarah, strumming my fingers on the tabletop, "When I bought the house, it was just me and the bank representative. I've got things at the library that need my attention."

We were waiting in a small conference room at the real estate office. The buyers and a representative from the law firm were taking a final walk-through the house to make sure it was everything Sarah had told them it would be. I was already bored. Although the room was appropriately decorated, the pictures of flowers gracing the walls would only entertain me for so long.

"But you dealt directly with the bank. You didn't even have to take out a loan." Sarah glanced at her phone. "They should be here any minute."

I pushed away from the table and strolled over to the nearby water cooler. "Maybe I'll feel better once I meet the people. It seems strange to turn the house over to someone I haven't met. What if they don't take care if it? Don't you have their names?" The stack of paper in front of her must contain a clue to their identities.

Sarah sighed. "I told them it wouldn't work, that you ask too many questions. I didn't even get the name of the buyer until last night. But I can't tell you who it is. They made me promise." She turned away from me, but not before I spotted a silly grin on her face.

` I eyed the paperwork. Sarah was closer, but if I pushed by her and grabbed it, she'd be too surprised to stop me.

A knock on the door startled me out of my contemplation. The firm's secretary stuck her head into the room. "They're here," she said.

Good. Time to get down to business.

Two men filed in. Their dark pinstriped suits marked them as lawyers. The lady I recognized as the firm's notary came in after them. Where were the buyers?

I waited for introductions. Or business cards. They never came.

A murmur of voices came from outside the room. Why were the buyers playing shy?

"What's the hold up?" I asked Sarah. Evidently, the lawyers wondered too because they glanced toward the doorway. One pulled a cell phone from his pocket.

"Would everyone leave the room for a moment?" he asked. "Except for Miss Duprie."

Oh, shit. Did I need to call Dan?

Sarah gave me an encouraging pat on the shoulder as she followed the two men out of the room.

I refilled my glass of water. And waited. I wiggled my shoulder, still bruised and sore from the fight. No matter how hard I tried, I couldn't hear the whispered conversation going on outside the conference room. So I waited some more. There didn't seem to be another option. But who or what was I waiting for?

I didn't like it, having no control over a situation that held so much importance to my life. But no amount of waiting could have prepared me for the moment when *he* walked into the room. It took me too long to figure out why *he* was there. "You?" I sputtered, unable to form the words needed to ask so many other questions.

"Yes, me. I wanted it to be a surprise. Then I realized it wasn't fair to you." He took a step closer. "I should have discussed it with you first. I know how you feel about the house. What I don't know is what you think about selling the house to me. If you want, I'll withdraw the offer."

I couldn't think of anyone better to live in the house than him. I closed the distance between us and took his hands. They felt cold and sweaty, but mine did too. I gulped. "You'd really do that for me?"

He nodded. "I would and I will."

I don't know who moved first. It didn't matter. We tangled together in each other's arms, separated only by the thinnest of space so we could gaze at each other's faces. We would have stayed that way forever if Sarah hadn't interrupted.

"Why don't the two of you get a room?"

"We will," Eli said, without taking his eyes off me, "as soon as I buy a house."

The End (for now)

If you enjoyed *The Oak Grove Mysteries*,
you might want to check out
Wolves' Pawn,
by P.J. MacLayne.

Dot McKenzie is a lone wolf-shifter on the run, using everything available to her to stay one step ahead of her pursuers. When she is offered a chance for friendship and safety with the Fairwood pack, she accepts.

Gavin Fairwood, reluctant heir to the Fairwood pack leadership, is content to let life happen while he waits. But old longings surface when he appoints himself Dot's protector…and becomes more than a friend.

But her presence puts the pack and her new friends at risk, and Dot must go into hiding again. When old enemies threaten the destruction of the Fairwood pack, it will take the combined efforts of Dot and Gavin to save it.

Can anything save their love and Dot's life when she becomes a pawn in a pack leader's deadly game?

Coming soon:
Wolves' Gambit
The Free Wolves Book 3